THE TRACKER'S REVENGE

INGRID SEYMOUR

PenDreams • BIRMINGHAM

Published by PenDreams
Cover design by "Covers by Juan"

ISBN-13: 979-8512563632

CHAPTER 1

The door to the agency burst open, and Damien staggered into the room, swaying, his eyes rolling back and forth, disoriented. He collapsed to the floor, face first.

A great weight settled on my chest. Pain. Regret.

Rosalina and I rolled him onto his back and stared into his ashen, pain-twisted face.

Please, God, no.

A large hole was carved in his chest, the edges glowing with crackling magic—bones and sinew visible.

Damien. Damien!

Dread suffused my regret, coating it in a heavy layer.

"You'll be all right." Rosalina's voice trembled with emotion. "Someone will be here soon to help you."

I stared uselessly, hating myself. I had no healing abilities to help him, to save his life. Death hung over him, slowly lowering its shroud.

"Who did this?" I asked.

"M-midnight Witch," Damien managed.

He didn't know her, but she must have been powerful to do this to him.

"Can you heal yourself?"

His voice trembled. "Too… weak."

Seconds ticked by like hours, like years. Damien's breaths grew more ragged. No one was coming. No one to help as his life slipped away. It hurt so bad to be unable to do anything, to watch him wither.

He glanced pointedly toward his hand. It lay open and limp on the floor.

"What is it?" I asked.

He whispered a few words under his breath. A spell? Maybe he had enough strength to heal himself, after all. When he was done, he exhaled in relief.

"T-the cure," he murmured.

I frowned and glanced toward his hand again. Two small vials that hadn't been there before now rested on his palm. They shimmered with a clear liquid. They were accompanied by the coin-shaped carving he'd used to gain passage to Elf-hame.

"Make sure… my daughter gets it. Please. She must drink it all."

I shook my head. "You'll give it to her yourself." My voice wavered with emotion, my hope slipping away.

"Promise." He moved his hand a fraction to recall my attention to the vials.

I carefully took them and the token from his palm and stored them securely in the breast pocket of my jacket. "I promise."

His entire body seemed to exhale with relief.

"The token is for you."

I would've argued about him giving me something so valuable, but I didn't have the heart, so I just nodded.

He turned to Rosalina.

"I wish… things would've turned out differently."

Rosalina pressed a hand to his cheek and smiled tenderly, then leaned forward and pressed a kiss to his pale lips. His eyes closed, and he expired.

"Me, too." Rosalina rested her forehead on his shoulders and cried.

ꙮ

I sat up panting, images of Damien's tortured body flashing before my eyes.

For a moment, I panicked. I was in a strange room, surrounded by bare walls. I hugged the covers around my body, my heart hammering out of control. It was a few beats before I remembered I was in Eric Cross's house. After Damien's murder yesterday, Eric insisted that Rosalina and I stay here, for our safety, since the place was protected by the best Stale and Skew security money could buy. Jake was also adamant about it. They wouldn't take *no* for an answer.

Rosalina was staying in the room next door. Eric's house was big with enough room to accommodate twenty or thirty more people. It was no hardship for him to let us stay.

I breathed in and out, wishing the remnants of my nightmare to dissipate. Once my heart had quieted down, I slipped out of bed and walked to the dresser in the corner, the only other piece of furniture besides the bed. I opened the top drawer to ensure the vials Damien had entrusted to me only yesterday were still there. They contained the cure for his daughter, Liliana, and my client's soulmate, Josh. The vials rested securely inside a small padded box, their clear liquid shimmering inside. I snapped the case shut, and carried it with me to the adjacent bathroom. I locked the door behind me and checked the time on my phone, which I'd left by the sink, charging. It wasn't even 6 AM.

I groaned. I didn't like getting up early. Even after all the 4-AM sessions with Eric, I still wasn't used to it, and I doubted I would ever be. I'd rather leave the wee hours of the morning to farmers and chickens.

The scalding hot shower in the luxurious bathroom did wonders for my body, if not for my mind. I felt as if instead of six hours of sleep, I'd spent the night swimming the length of the Mississippi River and had been put away wet. But the water helped my muscles relax, unknot.

With my mind feeling numb and blank, I got dressed in a pair of tight jeans, black boots, a T-shirt, and a field jacket with many pockets. Lastly, I hung the token Damien had given me around my neck. I'd attached it to a chain to make sure it was always with me. On my way out of the bathroom, I gently placed the box with the cure inside the pocket near my heart and carelessly stuffed my phone in another.

I left the room, closing the door behind me without making a sound. When I passed in front of Rosalina's door, I stopped and listened. No sounds. She was probably still asleep, and I was glad for it. Damien's death had hit her hard. They had liked each other despite their differences, and something had been brewing between them, something that might have gone somewhere nice and happy. But it had all been cut short by some fucking, cowardly Midnight Witch who attacked him without warning.

No one had seen anything, and it was no surprise. She had surely used magic to obscure the attack from any witnesses. Damien had barely made it to us, pushing himself through the pain and agony of his injuries to deliver the rhabo cure into our hands. Two vials that would save two people. Had it been worth his life?

I shook my head, pushing away the question, fearing I would never stop reliving those terrible moments, wondering if I'd ever stop feeling so impotent.

Pulling away from the door, I swallowed thickly and made my

way down the long hall. In a large sitting area that could very well belong in a European palace, I stopped and wondered at Eric's peculiar home. The front entrance and training room, which I was familiar with, looked nothing like this. The front was decorated in a cold, sparse, modern style, while other rooms were warm and inviting, filled with comfortable furniture, wood accents, and intricate rugs. I meandered through the space, dragging a finger over the back of a cream-colored sofa and making my way through a large door into another hall.

The house seemed like a labyrinth, and I wandered about carelessly, paying little attention to the hangings on the walls, and the many pieces of expensive furniture that occupied the rooms I passed.

The smell of coffee had me turning toward another corridor. I followed my keen nose past a small reading room and found the kitchen.

Eric was there, dressed in sweatpants and a sleeveless T-shirt soaked in sweat. From the looks of it, he had been up early, training, as was his habit. He didn't turn to face me, though I knew well he must've heard me coming. His senses were keener than mine, though mine were still changing, getting more refined as I grew used to being a werewolf.

"You missed another training session," Eric said, sounding angry.

The last thing on my mind was training. I had no desire, no energy left in me. I was drained, physically and emotionally. He had to know that, but maybe having lost his heart made it impossible for him to grasp the concept of grief. Damien had been his friend for who knew how long, and yet, his death didn't seem to have disrupted his routine in the least. Maybe he was a robot.

I found myself getting angry. Words rose to my lips to tell him what I thought of his cold discipline, or whatever he called it. But when he turned to face me, I forced myself to swallow my biting response.

He looked terrible. His blue eyes were bloodshot, the whites crisscrossed with tiny veins. Huge circles surrounded them, and his features were drawn and drooping as if he'd aged a couple of years overnight. His nose was red as if he'd been crying, but I knew that couldn't be it. I didn't think Eric was capable of tears.

Thrusting a cup of coffee forward in a quick toast, he nodded, then sat at the breakfast nook. "Help yourself."

I poured hot coffee from a simple pot—nothing like the fancy espresso contraption Damien had kept in his kitchen—and sat across from Eric. We sipped the bitter brew in silence, words seeming empty and dying on my tongue before I ushered them out.

"Do I really need more training?" Finally, I asked, rubbing my stiff neck.

"*Pshaw,* we haven't even scratched the surface."

"Maybe I can get by."

He made a face of disgust. "Oh, so we've grown overconfident."

"Whatever! I really don't want to talk about it right now."

I waited for him to bark in anger, but he just ran a hand over his dark brown hair, and changed the subject. "It will be a busy day today."

Unfortunately, he was right. I wasn't looking forward to today, and I would have rather avoided it altogether, but there was no getting around it.

This was a time to grieve, not to drive around town on errands. But there would be no grieving in the traditional sense, anyway.

There would be no service for Damien, no funeral. It had been the mage's wishes, Eric informed us. The mage had been so old, he'd had no family, except for his daughter, who turned out to be estranged from him. I'd found this out yesterday when, grasping at straws, I'd pleaded with Eric that we should call her, tell her Damien was dead, ask her what we should do about a funeral, but

Eric insisted, "She won't care, Toni."

"But—"

"She hated Damien. They hadn't talked in years. He was hoping the cure would patch things up between them."

"Oh no." That bit of news had broken my heart. Damien had worked so hard to create that cure for her. And, in the end, he'd died making sure it was safe and extricating a promise from me to make sure I delivered it to her. Life wasn't fair. Not one bit. It made me angry at Liliana, made me want to deny her salvation. But I'd given Damien my word, and even if I hadn't, I would never betray a man's dying wish.

Going to see her wouldn't be fun, but at least I was looking forward to the first half of the day. I couldn't wait to deliver Damien's elixir to Aaron Blackridge's boyfriend. He would be so happy, and I wouldn't have to feel guilty about ruining his life anymore. I'd paired him up with a terminally ill vampire—not exactly the kind of thing my customers signed up for.

And maybe, just maybe, after that deed, our agency's reputation wouldn't be ruined. I didn't know if Aaron had told people about what had happened, or how many of his friends had simply noticed, but I was still afraid of how that might hurt our business. If rumors spread, it could be disastrous. Rosalina and I might never get a customer again, at least not the high-profile ones we'd hoped for.

With a deep breath, I ushered those thoughts out of my mind. There was no point worrying about it. Only time would tell, and all we could do was hope for the best.

Finishing my coffee, I walked to the sink, washed the cup, and placed it on the stainless steel drying rack. "I need to swing by my place."

"What for?" Eric shouldered his way to the sink and washed his cup.

"Cupid, I have to feed him."

"Cupid? Who the hell is that? Your dog? Don't you have a neighbor that can do that? We don't have time for that."

"No, not a dog. My betta fish. And no, I don't know any of my neighbors yet. I just moved in."

Eric narrowed his blue eyes at me. "A betta fish? That's your pet?"

I nodded, holding my chin high. I wasn't going to let him talk smack about Cupid. He was a good pet. He never complained and had the prettiest, most-wavy, colorful fins. "What? You have something against fish?"

"Not as long as they're fried."

"You don't fry betta fish, you monster!"

His expression tightened. Oops, it seemed our banter had gone too far. I shouldn't have called him the "M" word.

Many considered Eric Cross a monster, many who feared him and never forgot the rumors that he'd massacred an entire pack to avenge his wife's and daughter's deaths. I still didn't know if the rumors were true. He never talked about his past, wasn't into sharing his feelings and opening up. On the contrary, whenever anyone asked things he didn't want to answer, he closed up tighter than a vacuum-sealed mason jar. Lately, he'd seemed to loosen up a bit, bestowing rare smiles on us and even one or two full-bellied laughs, but Damien's death seemed to have destroyed whatever lightheartedness he'd regained. Using the word *monster*, even jokingly, was a dumb move.

His face pinched, he leaned forward and snapped his teeth as if chomping on a small fried betta. "I guess not. They would hardly make a worthy snack. In either case, we don't need to take unnecessary risks such as *feeding your fish*. You've already insisted on delivering the cure today, even when I think we should wait until after we meet with the Pack Rule. Bernadetta and her people are watching us. I'm sure of it. She and Stephen want their hybrid army, and they won't hesitate to kill us to get the dagger back."

"We *have* to deliver the cure. One more day could mean the difference between life and death for Josh and Liliana."

"Which is why I agreed to go, but feeding your fish is out of the question."

"He'll die."

"He won't die," he said in a tired tone. "Bettas can go for up to fourteen days without food."

"You just made that up."

"I did not."

"Yes, you did. That's too specific. Besides, how would you know?"

He sighed. "I've dealt with betta fish before. My daughter had one." His gaze fell to the floor, becoming blank as he got lost in the memory.

I blinked, taken aback by the hurt that flashed across his features. I tried to think of something to say but I was struck mute.

"Once, she forgot to feed him for over a week, forgot he even existed," he said with a chuckle. "She'd been too excited over Christmas break, and it slipped her mind. We were at the table, eating dinner when she jumped up and screamed as if she'd seen a ghost."

A fond smile gently stretched his lips, and I held my breath, afraid to make a sound that would stop him from telling me the story.

"She ran to the sunroom where she kept him, so he could get natural light, and he was fine. Swimming a bit groggily, but alive. She fed him right away but then started worrying he would die anyway. So we did some research and found out that they can go quite some time without food. About fourteen days, give or take." His eyes snapped to mine. "Happy?"

I barely managed a nod. This was the first time Eric had told me anything about his family, and he'd done it to ease my worries over my fish, which he had. Not just that, he'd also done something else, something that felt monumental. He'd let me in, let me step into a circle that came closer to his center, to where he stood isolated from anything and anyone.

Perhaps, I'd been wrong and Damien's death hadn't caused him to withdraw. Instead, it'd left him more lonely than ever and willing to let someone else in.

"Now, I'm going to get ready for our first meeting today," he said. "I'll be glad when we get rid of that stupid dagger. Let the Pack Rule deal with Bernadetta Fiore and Stephen Erickson. I want nothing to do with any of this anymore. It cost Damien his life. I don't want it to cost you yours."

Eric turned on his heel and left the kitchen. His words echoed inside my head, making me feel strangely touched. He was supposed to be ruthless, but he'd been nothing but good to me. And now, he seemed bent on protecting me. I couldn't have anyone better on my side.

CHAPTER 2

I gaped at Rosalina as she stuffed two handguns at either side of her ribs, secured by a leather holster that wrapped around her back and shoulders. After strapping them in place, she picked up a leather jacket from the bed and slipped it on.

When she noticed my dumbfounded expression, she cocked her eyebrow. "What?"

"Um, dunno, I think I'm a bit scared."

"Good," she said, pushing past me and leaving the room Eric had assigned her. It was the same size and shape as mine but decorated, not bare. The walls were painted in subtle pastel shades of yellow and lavender, and paintings of pretty flowers hung perfectly spaced on the walls. If I hadn't known better, I might've guessed the room had belonged to his daughter, but I'd learned from Damien that Eric had sold the house he'd shared with his family shortly after their death.

Perhaps Eric had thought the room would fit Rosalina's personality better since she was always so done up in her makeup and feminine outfits. But at the moment, it didn't match her one bit. She looked badass, and I wasn't entirely sure how to feel about it. She was even taking sword lessons from some guy Jake had referred her to.

I followed her down the hall. She walked with confident steps, her flat-heeled boots tapping on the hardwood floors. Normally, she wore cute heels to work—she had a big collection of them—but this morning she meant a different type of business.

Catching up to her, I gave her a smile, which she barely returned. I worried that Damien's death would harden her—same as her weapon training seemed to have done. Damn Jake for teaching her! This was not the Rosalina I'd met, and I hated to think that these changes were my fault, that my messed-up life was messing *hers* up. It wasn't fair. She didn't need this, no one did.

"Um, maybe tomorrow we can get back to business," I said. "Maybe Aaron will send some of his friends our way after Josh feels better."

"Maybe," was all she said in response.

I was about to say more when Eric joined us in the hall. "There you are. C'mon, the car's ready."

"Hurry, Triple T," Rosalina said as I lagged behind.

Eric frowned over his shoulder. "Triple T? What does that stand for? No, don't tell me." He raised a finger and thought for a moment. "Oh, I got it. Toni the Tracker."

Rosalina shook her head. "No, it's Toni the Tiger, but that's a good one. I should've thought of that."

Eric snorted, then waved us down a set of steps that led to the lower level. We passed the training room and entered a large garage where a black Mercedes Benz with tinted windows sat waiting. It was an E-Class sedan with a slick, aerodynamic body that suggested zero to sixty in a sneeze.

He got behind the wheel. Rosalina climbed in the back seat, so I walked around and took my place next to a very serious-looking werewolf. He cranked the engine, and the radio came to life, transmitting a commercial.

Some Skews are giving away their immortality
It's an epidemic and it's spreading
It's not a parasite, not a virus
It's rhabo, and it kills vampires
Say no to drugs

Eric tapped the *off* button with a disgusted grunt.

We sat in silence for a long moment. I wondered how much the effects the city's drug problem weighed on him. He and Damien were responsible for its creation, after all.

"Eric You shouldn't feel g—" I started, but he cut me off.

"We're late." He picked up his phone.

O-kay, no words of comfort needed.

I started humming a tune, pretending I hadn't spoken.

What a mess! For many days, I'd been holding my breath, waiting for a full-on war to break out. Last we'd heard, Bernadetta Fiore had met with her generals to plan an attack on Ulfen. Publicly, she blamed him for rhabo, though we now knew she was behind it all. Except she'd been oddly quiet. It scared the crap out of me and made me wonder what horrors she was planning.

Eric glanced into his cell where several video feeds of the exterior of the house played in an array of tiny screens. He watched for a few beats and didn't press the garage door opener until he was sure no one lurked outside.

As soon as there was enough room between the still-opening garage door and the floor, Eric stepped on the gas and tore out of the house like his tail was on fire. My head slammed back on the headrest. I blinked at him in surprise.

Paranoid much?

I tended to be more easy-going, always hoping for the best, but he really was cramping my style. My whole body tensed up, and my eyes didn't stop darting in every direction as we made our way to Aaron's house. I was especially tense when we stopped at red lights, and Eric gripped the steering wheel with white-knuckled strength, his head swiveling, his gaze bouncing from one side mirror to the other. For her part, Rosalina had a hand under her jacket, ready to pull out one of her weapons if necessary.

I wriggled in my seat and scratched my forearm, itching to shift, burning to equip myself with sharp claws and fangs in case the impending attack they were expecting came true.

To distract myself, I glanced out the window and tried to admire the pretty spring morning with its clear blue sky and radiant sunshine. But that only made it worse because, catching a movement in the side mirror, I spotted a large SUV trailing behind us. I kept my eyes on it for several minutes and was about to say something when the SUV took a turn and disappeared.

Man, these two are going to give me an ulcer.

Gratefully, we made it to Aaron Blackridge's house without a hitch. His mansion was located in the Huntleigh area. It was a sprawling home that spoke of his success as a sought-after DJ.

Eric stopped by the wrought iron gate and pressed the "call" button on the keypad. A voice crackled through the air and after Eric explained our business, the gate slid open to let us through. As we moved down the long driveway, I admired the beautiful landscaping. Perfectly trimmed bushes and lots of colorful flowers. I lowered the window to let in their fresh scent. Eric gave me a disapproving sideways glance but said nothing. The tension inside the car had eased a little. Rosalina's hand had even come out from its hiding place, and her red-tipped fingers now rested on her thigh instead.

Eric drove around a large fountain that spewed water from the elaborate sculpture of a topless Siren. Jetting streams shot from her outstretched palms, creating dazzling rainbows. He stopped the car in front of a set of marble steps that led to a massive entrance. One half of the twenty-foot tall door opened before we even got out of the car, and Aaron strode out to meet us, hurrying down the steps, an earnest expression shaping his features. He was wearing a pair of baggy shorts, a sleeveless T-shirt, and a pair of slide-ons. He wore no jewelry, which made him look plain and not like the stylish DJ I was used to.

I quickly got out of the car and greeted him with a smile.

"Toni," he said, extending a hand in my direction, "so glad you're here."

He shook my hand a bit frantically, then his dark gaze darted to Rosalina and, lastly, to Eric, who he regarded suspiciously. His nostrils flared as he caught Eric's werewolf scent.

"You remember Rosalina," I said, quickly making introductions. "And I'm not sure if you know Eric Cross. He's a good friend of mine."

Aaron took a step backward and watched Eric wearily. This was just what I'd been afraid of, just the reason I didn't want Eric to accompany us. As much as I liked him and considered him a friend, the agency's already precarious reputation didn't need to mingle with his. Regardless of our relationship, it wasn't good business. But he had insisted we needed his protection.

Aaron seemed to weigh the situation for a moment, probably recalling every dirty rumor he'd heard about Eric Lone. I gnawed on my lower lip, my stomach making flips and threatening to send my morning coffee back into the light of day. A million computations passed behind Aaron's brown gaze, but in the end—whatever numbers he crunched—came up positive because he nodded in Eric's direction.

"Any friend of Toni's is my friend." He put a hand out, and they exchanged a sturdy handshake. There was no indication of a moratorium taking place between them, like when Jake and Eric had met. I guessed there was no need for it since Aaron wasn't an alpha and had no trouble letting Eric be the top dog.

"Please, come in." That anxious expression returned to Aaron's face as he walked up the steps and guided us into his expensive house.

As we walked in, Rosalina and I exchanged a look of surprise at the luxurious interior. The place put Eric's own house to shame. It was at least three times as big and with an interior design budget much bigger than Eric's.

Rosalina leaned close and whispered in my ear. "I feel like I'm in an episode of Cribs."

"No kidding," I whispered back.

Only Eric seemed unimpressed by the polished marble, museum-quality art on the walls, custom furnishings, and overall splendor. Unfazed, he marked every door as if making an exit plan should there be a need for one.

"This way. Josh is in the study." Aaron waved a hand and led us through an ample corridor and into a windowless room with a roaring fireplace.

The first thing that struck me was the stifling heat. It was about fifty degrees outside—a bit chilly for late spring—but in here it had to be at least a hundred degrees, much warmer than that hot yoga class Rosalina had dragged me to one day. I immediately wanted to shed my jacket, and my T-shirt, and my pants, but I kept them on. No reason to be impolite.

Aaron approached a wingback chair by the fireplace. Josh sat there, his feet propped up on an ottoman and a layer of thick blankets thrown over him, leaving only his head visible. He looked shrunken, a mere ghost of the handsome vampire I'd met only two weeks ago. Josh stirred. Suddenly, that toxic rot smell that I associated with a rhabo infection hit me like a slap to the face. I fought not to let the revulsion show in my expression and was grateful when—after quickly inspecting the room—Eric spoke from the door, forcing me to turn and hide my face until I composed myself.

"I'll stay out here. Call me if you need me," he said, then pulled the door shut.

"Hey, honey," Aaron said in a sweet, gentle voice, "someone's here to see you."

Josh blinked his eyes open with difficulty as if the simple act of lifting his eyelids were a Herculean effort. His gaze danced around the room for a moment before settling on Aaron. A slow smile stretched his cracked lips, and one of his hands stirred under the covers. Understanding what he wanted, Aaron pushed the covers aside and interlaced his fingers with his.

My heart squeezed painfully at the sight. I couldn't get used to the sight of an ill vampire. It just wasn't supposed to happen. It was unnatural. Vampires were always healthy, and they lived forever. They didn't deteriorate into empty husks. They didn't smell of death, even if they *were* dead.

Witnessing the agony in Aaron's eyes put the last painful nail in my heart. I had to swallow hard not to let my tears fall. Instead, I slipped my hand inside my jacket pocket, pulled out the tiny box, and retrieved one of the vials. Holding on to the hope that Damien's elixir would be a success, I took a step forward.

"Hi, Josh. It's Toni. Remember me?"

Josh's gaze reluctantly left Aaron's, peeling away with difficulty and taking a long moment to find me. I gave him a smile when our eyes met and moved closer still. Afraid to invade their intimacy, I held the vial in Aaron's direction.

"He has to drink this," I said, my hand shaking, good and bad thoughts battling inside my head. The negative ones tried to push to the forefront, telling me that Damien's cure would fail, and that, without him here to figure out what went wrong, Josh and Damien's daughter would die. But more optimistic thoughts fought back. Damien had been a great mage, and his potion would work just fine. He hadn't died in vain. He hadn't dragged himself to our doorstep, fighting through his terrible injuries, to deliver an empty hope.

No. The cure would work.

Gently releasing Josh's hand, Aaron rose to his feet, a grave expression shaping his features as if the battle of hoping and *not* hoping also raged inside of him.

He took the small vial from me, carefully pinching it between thumb and forefinger, then placing his other hand under it, in case it might accidentally slip. He knelt by Josh's side once more and carefully unscrewed the container's cap. A shimmery plume like a tiny galaxy of stars rose into the air.

My nose twitched as the smell of honey and burnt caramel filled the air. I was immediately transported to Damien's potions room when he was carefully brewing the liquid, watching it distill through the thin laboratory tubes, dripping into crystal beakers. A pang of regret tightened my chest. I would never see Damien again.

"Drink this, Josh. It will make you feel better," Aaron said.

I scrutinized Josh's face as Aaron lifted the vial to his lips. The vampire's expression didn't change. He was so weak that he didn't even have the energy to muster hope. Or perhaps he felt so far gone, that he didn't think anything could save him. Maybe, he only opened his mouth and drank the sweet-smelling liquid to make Aaron happy.

His eyelids fluttered, and his throat bobbed as he swallowed.

We stared, our bodies and our hope frozen.

CHAPTER 3

When every drop was gone, Aaron pulled away, stretching to his full height, placing the empty vial on the mantle, then focusing his entire attention on the man he loved. He seemed to hold his breath for a moment, his expression slowly turning into a desperate plea. His hands trembled at his sides as Josh continued to sit languidly, no sign that the elixir was having any effect on him.

I exchanged a glance with Rosalina, who stood a couple of paces behind me, nervously wringing her hands together. Collectively, we held our breaths, and after an interminable moment of absolutely no change, we all exhaled in disappointment.

Just as we gave up all hope, Josh started seizing, his arms and legs thrashing, kicking off the covers. Dark foam bubbled out of his mouth as he clenched his throat.

"Josh!" Aaron tried to grab his shoulders and hold him down, but Josh jerked so violently that he threw him off, almost sending him crashing into the fireplace.

Oh, shit!

The door behind us slammed open and Eric rushed into the room. He hurried to my side and scanned me from head to toe as if to make sure I was all right, and when Josh sprang up to a sitting position, Eric took hold of my shoulders and pulled me back.

I shook him off, entranced by the sight as Josh's feet lifted off the floor and his entire body quaked in midair until his outline grew blurry.

"What is happening?!" Aaron demanded, his dark eyes flashing in my direction with recrimination.

Helplessly, I shook my head. I didn't know what to say. Damien hadn't had time to explain anything before he exhaled his last breath on the floor of my tracking agency. I had no idea if this was supposed to happen, or if it meant it had all gone wrong.

Maybe the bitterthorn Prince Kalyll had given us in Elyndell had been bogus. Maybe something in Damien's meticulous work while creating the elixir had gone wrong. Whatever the case, when black, tarry gunk started oozing from Josh's eyes, nostrils, mouth, and ears, I gave up all hope.

My legs gave out, and I nearly fell to my knees if not for Eric who wrapped an arm around my waist and held me in place.

"What have you done?!" Aaron cried out in horror.

Dark brown fur sprouted over his arms and back. Claws and fangs unsheathed as he crouched and turned in my direction, ready to make me pay for bringing him more pain. He had always been gentle and polite. The creature that now stood in front of me was nothing like that.

"Wait!" Eric commanded in his alpha voice, a sound that reverberated in his chest like that of a hundred deep voices packed into one.

I shuddered, even though I was also an alpha.

Eric's command had an immediate effect on Aaron. He shrank

in on himself, his head lowering, his shoulders climbing toward his ears. His eyes glowed slightly and darted about, from me to Eric, from Eric to Josh, then back again. He was torn between the concern for his soulmate and his desire to make me pay for stealing whatever little time they had left together.

Tears were sliding down Rosalina's face, and I could tell by her expression exactly what she was thinking. Damien's daughter would not be saved. She would perish and die in rhabo agony, just the way Josh was dying, and Damien's last wish would not come true.

As more blackness oozed from the vampire, the room filled with the pungent stink of his disease, and now even Rosalina, with her normal human sense of smell, felt it. Her scrunched-up nose and wince left no doubt about it.

Throwing his head back, Josh cried out in pain, releasing a cloud of dark miasma into the air. It shot upward like a swarm of gnats, darkening the ceiling. The stream was as dense as smoke from a pyre. It spewed from him for several beats, thinning gradually, until only a few particles floated out past his lips, then nothing.

Josh collapsed on the floor.

In an instant, Aaron was there to brace his fall. He cradled him in his arms and drew him close, calling his name over and over. Josh fell limp against Aaron, his eyes closed, his cheeks and chin streaked with lines of what looked like black blood.

Desperately, Aaron reached for one of the blankets that had covered his soulmate and tenderly cleaned his face with it.

"Josh, Josh, say something, please," he pleaded as he removed the horrible stains of his disease.

But Josh was completely immobile, and there was nothing we could do to find out if he still lived. No breath rose up and down in his chest. No heartbeat pulsed in his neck.

Aaron cast the blanket aside. Josh's handsome face was

obscured by the dark smears left behind as he continued to lay still, quiet, void of life.

Eric made a small grunt in the back of his throat, something that sounded like *"it's a shame it didn't work."*

Rocking back and forth, Aaron glanced up at me, his anger spent. I expected to see hatred in his eyes, but all I found was resignation. Without the elixir, Josh would have died all the same. And maybe this way, at least, he had been spared some pain.

I opened my mouth to beg his forgiveness, when, suddenly, Josh sat up straight, his eyes wide and rimmed with black. He coughed and coughed, then began panting for breath, taking in huge gulps as if there wasn't enough air to fill his lungs, as if he needed it.

When the fit passed, he blinked up at Aaron who knelt next to him, looking as utterly shocked as I felt. With a sound between a laugh and a sob, Aaron seized Josh in his arms, crushed him into a fierce embrace, and cried tears of joy.

"I love you, Josh. I love you so much. Thank the witchlights you didn't leave me."

CHAPTER 4

"For a moment, I didn't think it would work," Rosalina said from the passenger seat of Eric's car. This time, I had snuck in the back, forcing her to sit in the front with Mr. Grumpy.

"You and me both," I said. "It was nerve-racking."

Eric was driving, both hands on the wheel, his eyes vigilant as we headed toward our next destination: Liliana's house. She wasn't expecting this, didn't know we had a cure for her. We'd tried to contact her, but she'd never answered. In fact, we didn't even know if the number we'd found on the Internet was correct.

"You should have never doubted," Eric said. "Damien was a damn exceptional mage."

That sobered us up, and we were quiet the rest of the way, though the tension was back, and we kept checking for pursuers that might get in the way of fulfilling Damien's last wish.

When we got to Lindenwood Park, where Liliana lived, according to an address Eric had found in an agenda Damien had kept in his desk, Eric parked in front of a bungalow-style home with a well-kept yard. We all got out of the car at the same time, bodies tense, ready for anything. But our vigilance was wasted. The street looked calm and—

A crashing sound and a scream came from the house. Before I had time to blink, Eric had used his preternatural speed and had disappeared into the house through the front door, which he found unlocked.

Rosalina and I exchanged a glance, then we ran down the walkway, Rosalina pulling a gun out of her holster and holding it next to her face, the muzzle pointing toward the sky.

We awkwardly knocked into each other as we both tried to get through the door at the same time. Rosalina took a step back and let me through first. When I walked in, a horrible scene took shape before me.

A huge creature stood in the middle of the living room, a terrible clawed hand wrapped around a woman's throat. Her face was frozen in terror, her mouth forming an "O" as if a scream had gotten stuck in her throat. She was staring at Eric, who stood crouched in front of her, his own clawed hands ready at his sides. The woman's dark eyes were pleading, begging for deliverance from the monster that held her.

My blood ran cold as I scanned the creature and recognition dawned on me like a blanket of dread. I had seen the pulsing, black veins under sparse fur, as well as the malformed, enormous claws.

Oh, fuck!

It was a hybrid.

But how?!

Bernadetta and Stephen only had part of the Unholy Vessel in their possession. They couldn't create hybrids. They needed the dagger, which Eric had hidden. Unless… unless I'd assumed wrong and that night at the coven temple hadn't been the first time they'd used the damn thing.

Shit!

Rosalina stepped around a broken coffee table and trained her gun on the hybrid, a red dot appearing between the beast's shaggy eyebrows. The hybrid growled deep in his throat, tightening his grip around the woman's throat. She whimpered, the scent of her fear mixing with that sour smell of sickness we'd left behind in Aaron's house.

She had to be Liliana, and it was our fault this creature was here. It was after us, not her. We had guided Bernadetta and Stephen's notice in this direction.

"Don't hurt her," I begged.

"I doubt that thing will listen to reason," Eric said, his voice a wild rumble. "Rosalina, take the shot," he added in a quiet, cold command.

To my surprise, Rosalina didn't hesitate. I barely had time to process Eric's words when a blast reverberated through the small living room.

Time seemed to slow. My ears rang with the shot. My breath caught in my throat as the creature stabbed his claws in the woman's chest just as the bullet blasted a hole between his eyes and sent him staggering backward, his victim falling with him, crashing atop a kitchen table in the next room. Wood splintered with a deafening crack as the creature's massive weight flattened the table to the floor.

"No!" Eric and I both shouted in unison.

We hurried into the small kitchen. Eric approached cautiously, warily watching the hybrid. When the creature didn't move, he quickly knelt by the woman, his gaze roving over her chest where the beast's hand was buried to the wrist.

"Is she…?" I couldn't finish the question and instead watched as dark, sour-smelling blood oozed out of the wound in her chest, pooling around the hybrid's hand.

Carefully, Eric pulled on the creature's arm. The clawed hand came out with a squelch. Once he'd freed her, he scooped the woman into his arms and carried her back into the living room, where he laid her gently on top of the sofa.

I followed him while Rosalina remained a few steps away from the hybrid, her gun still trained on him.

Face set in an unreadable mask, Eric peeled her eyes open and carefully looked into them. After a long moment, he closed her eyes and pulled away, stretching to his full height. He shook his head.

"H-how do you know? She's a vampire, right? She could still be alive."

"Trust me, Toni. I know the difference between a *dead* dead vampire and a not-so-dead one. The fucking beast pierced her heart."

"Then that can't be Liliana. It must be someone else," I said in denial.

"It is. I recognize her from pictures."

"God, no!" Rosalina exclaimed in a near sob. "We failed him."

Eric pulled away from the sofa, his head lowered. "It's not our fault. We tried. I swear that goddamn vamp and that traitor, Stephen, will pay for this."

I pressed a fist to my mouth, panting as if I'd run a mile.

"Those fuckers," I hissed. "I'm gonna kill them."

Like Eric, I wanted Bernadetta Fiore and Stephen Erickson to suffer. For Liliana. For the city. But especially for Damien. I didn't know how, but I would have my revenge. And as I exchanged a glance with Rosalina, I could tell she felt the same way.

Eric turned his attention back to the kitchen and the dead creature lying on top of the broken table. "I thought you said they'd only made one hybrid."

"I guess I was wrong," I said. "They must have made this one before they got to the coven temple. They were acting like they hadn't tried it yet, but it must have been for show."

"I wonder how many they made." He rubbed his forehead, wearily backing away from the hideous beast.

"At least a bullet to the head takes them down. It *did* have a wolfsbane core." Rosalina gestured toward her gun.

I nodded, feeling the same relief I knew she felt. I had killed a hybrid at the temple, but it hadn't been easy. He had broken my back and nearly eaten me alive. The only reason I was still here to tell the tale was because my tracker skills and my *werewolfness* created an interesting mixture of powers. I looked down at my hands, remembering how I'd hit a hybrid and, before that, a vampire with a sensory blast. Would I be able to do it again? Maybe Eric was right, and I needed to get back to training. He'd said we would test my limits, find out, during controlled sessions, what exactly I was capable of.

Eric looked at Rosalina's gun doubtfully.

"Something wrong?" she asked.

He shrugged one shoulder, his eyes darting between the hybrid and the weapon. "I don't know. I—"

"What's going on here?!" an agitated voice asked from behind us.

We whirled in unison to face a slender, petite woman in her mid-twenties. She was standing framed by the front door. She had jaw-length green hair with straight bangs that fell to her eyebrows, piercing green eyes, and pale skin as smooth as a baby's. She wore a pair of ripped jeans, an oversized T-shirt, and slippers. My nose twitched at the overpowering scent of her perfume. She smelled as if someone had dropped a truckload of roses on her head. Cloyingly sweet!

Eric stepped forward. "Who are you?"

"Who are *you*?" she demanded, though her voice broke at the end when her eyes drifted toward the sofa where Liliana laid, then past the living room and into the kitchen. "What happened here? Liliana," she called, raising her voice, "are you all right?"

Silence was the only response.

The woman's hand jerked towards her jeans pocket.

"I wouldn't do that if I were you," Eric warned.

She took a step back. "I'm calling the police."

I put a hand up and said in a calm voice, "That's good. We need to call the police. Let me do it." I reached for my phone, but she shook her head and kept backing away, her eyes full of distrust.

That was when I noticed someone walking up behind her, and my heart froze.

I recognized him immediately, even though I'd only met him twice. It was Bertram, Bernadetta Fiore's vampire driver. He was holding a UV umbrella and was dressed as if he were going to a board meeting.

The woman ran smack into Bertram and shrieked in surprise. She scrambled away from him, getting back into the house in her mad dash to get away from the tall, intimidating vampire. He gave her a withering glare. She shrank further, her head sinking into her shoulders as if she were a turtle. Bertram stepped in, folded his umbrella, and took stock of the scene. Teeth grinding, I waited for Bernadetta to appear, too, but she wasn't here.

A growl rumbled in my chest of its own accord. Seeing my reaction, Rosalina raised and aimed her gun at him, while Eric crouched, ready to attack.

"You know him?" he asked in a growl of his own.

"He works for Bernadetta," I said. "Just like that fucking hybrid."

Bertram frowned and opened his mouth to say something, but the petite intruder interrupted him, speaking in a shrill voice that betrayed her fear. From the looks of it, she was a Stale who'd just figured out she'd tangled with the wrong group of Skews.

"I'm just Liliana's neighbor," she blurted out. "I've nothing to do with any of this. Let me get out of here."

The burly vampire sneered down at the woman, his eyes flashing with annoyance. "I would advise you to be quiet." He made a zipping motion over his lips, towering like a giant over a pixie. When she was properly intimidated, Bertram returned his attention to us, or more accurately to me. He regarded me for a long moment, then his attention drifted to Liliana's prone body on the couch. A realization passed over his face, something that seemed to please him.

"We need to talk," he said with his slight German accent. His tone was reasonable as if one of his boss's hybrids hadn't just killed Damien's daughter.

"I have nothing to talk to you about, you fuckin' murderer."

"In case you haven't noticed, we outnumbered you," Eric spat.

My nose twitched as if somehow I would be able to smell Bertram's cronies beyond the front door, which the vampire was blocking with his refrigerator-size body. But all I could sense was the pixie's overly sweet perfume. How Eric knew that there was only Bertram was beyond me. Paired with the hybrid, he would've stood a chance against the three of us, but by himself… not so much.

"I don't want to fight," he said. "I just want to *talk*."

Eric huffed to indicate there was no chance in hell we would be sitting down to tea and pleasant conversation. He sized up the vampire for a couple of extra beats, then, like the badass that he was, he shifted into his wolf form as fluidly as water flows around a boulder, and attacked. He leaped. Liliana's friend screamed and threw herself behind a love seat. With the speed of a cheetah on steroids, Bertram pivoted out of the way, smoothly stepping into the house. Eric soared through the air, missing him completely, and landed outside. He skidded to a stop and, changing directions, leaped back.

Quickly, Bertram slammed the door shut. A *thud* sounded

outside as Eric slammed against it.

Rosalina trained her gun on Bertram's chest and squeezed the trigger five times in succession. The deafening cracks reverberated through the house. The pixie screamed. The bullets hit their target. The vampire twitched with each impact, but unlike the hybrid, he didn't go down. He was immune to wolfsbane, after all. Maybe we needed rhabo bullets. Now, that was a thought! Instead, he rushed Rosalina, snatched the weapon from her hand, and threw it across the room, where it crashed against the wall and disappeared behind the sofa.

Just as he pushed Rosalina out of the way and sent her sprawling on top of the love seat, I shifted into my wolf form, more smoothly than I ever had. Almost as fluidly as Eric, I was on all fours, my claws and fangs unsheathing, my muscles tripling in size, my clothes ripping and sliding off my back. Within the same breath, I went for Bertram's ankle, my mouth wide open, my sharp teeth ready to separate him from his right foot.

Except my legs got tangled in my clothes, and I came short, my jaw snapping inches from him, my teeth capturing only a section of his pants and tearing loudly.

Damn my stupid clothes!

This had never happened, and it would never happen to Eric, not with the shifter ring he wore. More than ever, I wanted one of my own.

Bertram wasted no time and grabbed me by the scruff of the neck, sinking his huge claws in. I fought in vain, trying to twist out of his grip as he lifted me off the floor like a defenseless puppy dog. I growled and struggled, my forelegs wheeling uselessly. He was too big and strong.

"Look," he snarled, his eyes flashing, his face a grotesque mask of violence and death, "can you…?"

More shots rang out. Bertram blinked and twitched as they struck his back. Rosalina had found her second gun and was at it again. Then there was a crash and the sound of shattering glass as Eric broke through a window and landed inside, looking so pissed I almost felt sorry for the vampire.

Just as Eric prepared to attack, a deafening roar filled the tiny house, making the portraits on the wall go askew.

Eyes widening in surprise, Bertram let go of me and turned toward the sound. As soon as my front paws hit the floor, I pivoted, also facing the sound.

Holy shit!

The hybrid was back on his feet, his huge clawed feet raking at the floor as if he were an angry bull, the wound between his eyebrows completely healed.

What the hell?

I backed away several steps, unable to believe my eyes.

The beast's face was disfigured in rage. We had pissed him off. Royally. Growling, he lashed out, going from Bertram, who happened to be the closest target. The creature was at least a head taller than the vampire and twice as thick. They clashed like two giants. The hybrid sunk his teeth into Bertram's shoulder as if he were a chew toy.

I was still petrified with shock when Eric shouted a command.

"Let's get out of here!"

I glanced back and found him throwing open the door. He was back in his human form and fully clothed thanks to his shifter ring. He urgently waved a hand. I stared at Rosalina, letting her know to go first. She started to run, then suddenly pivoted back, reached behind the love seat, and pulled the terrified pixie out of her hiding place. Pushing her along, Rosalina ran behind her.

I was about to follow when I remembered something critical. The remaining elixir vial was still in my jacket pocket. Heart hammering, I double-backed, snatched the tattered thing in my mouth, and ran out of the house, never looking back, ignoring the crashing sounds and snarls that disturbed the peace of the heavenly suburbia.

Rosalina pushed the petite woman inside the backseat of the car, while Eric jumped into the driver seat, and I leaped through the open window and into the passenger seat.

Eric started the engine, stepped on the gas, and we tore out of there like hell on wheels. Rosalina pulled out her phone and called 911, giving them Liliana's address and reporting the sighting of a dreadful creature. Nothing else.

As we made our escape, I noticed a dark SUV parked on the other side of the road, the same one I'd noticed in the rearview mirror on our way to Aaron's house.

Damn that vampire! I hope his pissed-off hybrid tears him apart.

He deserved a dose of his own medicine.

CHAPTER 5

Twenty-five minutes later, Eric drove the Mercedes into the garage of his large house. He ordered us to stay in the car as the door slid shut behind us, and he checked his phone to make sure the security system hadn't been breached and no one was inside waiting for us.

I was still in my wolf form, while Rosalina and Liliana's neighbor sat in the backseat, looking numb. The woman hadn't said anything, not even to wonder where we were going. I guessed it hadn't mattered as long as it was far, far away from the giant vampire and his deranged, equally giant pet. That or she'd completely gone mute from shock. Not that I would blame her. She lived in an idyllic, peaceful suburb, and this was probably the worst thing that had ever happened to her. The poor thing.

As soon as Eric gave us the all-is-clear, I picked up my ripped jacket.

"Let me take this," Eric said.

I nodded, allowed him to gather the jacket in his hands, then jumped out of the car through the window, and hurried into the house to find some clothes. I didn't have to go all the way upstairs. I had a duffel bag in the training room, and the sweats and a T-shirt went on easily and quickly.

Once dressed, I met Rosalina and the woman out in the hall as they made their way towards the stairs that led to the main level.

The woman was wide-eyed, allowing Rosalina to lead her into the house. She hugged her thin arms, looking as scared as a captured squirrel.

"Where's Eric?" I asked.

Rosalina shook her head. "He *whooshed* upstairs."

He could certainly *whoosh*, even faster than a vampire, something else I needed to learn from him and quickly. I'd made enemies with some very messed-up Skews, and I really did need all the skills I could get to defend myself and those I loved.

I figured Eric had disappeared to put the elixir in his ultra-secure safe—the same where he'd stashed the jade dagger that had created that hybrid. Only he knew the location of his hiding place—somewhere protected by very powerful magic, he assured me. Apparently, the same mage or witch who had crafted his shifter ring had created this safety device, whatever it was. Damien had also contributed to making the place as secure as possible.

"Good," I said more to myself than Rosalina. I didn't want anything to happen to the cure. I didn't know what I would do with it now that Liliana was dead, but I certainly wanted it as safe as possible.

As if suddenly waking up from her stupor, the woman halted in the middle of the hall and shook Rosalina's hand off her shoulder.

"What the hell is going on? Who are you, people?"

"It's okay," I said. "You're safe with us. My name is Toni Sunder, and this is Rosalina López. What's your name?" I smiled, trying to set her at ease.

"Everyone calls me Em. I don't like my name."

It was an odd answer, but she was nervous. She'd probably had the shock of her life.

"You're safe here with us, Em," I repeated. "You don't have to stay. You can go back home whenever you want, but, if I were you, I would wait a bit. Would you like some tea or coffee?"

She nodded absently. We led her upstairs to the kitchen. She glanced around at the luxury of Eric's place with a sort of curious detachment. She opted for chamomile tea, which was an excellent choice since it would calm her nerves.

Em sat at the kitchen table, and a moment later, I slid a steaming cup in front of her, then proceeded to make some strong coffee for Rosalina and me. I added extra water for Eric, in case he wanted some.

Our guest sipped her tea quietly for a few minutes before she spoke again.

"Is… is Liliana dead?"

Rosalina took the chair across from Em and answered her in a quiet tone that was almost a whisper. "She is."

A lump rose in my throat, and I busied myself with staring at the brewing coffee maker, glad for Rosalina's strength in situations like this. I was not the best at comforting people—not as good Rosalina, at any rate.

"I'm sorry," she said. "That beast killed her. We were there to… to help her, but…" She shrugged, not going into details.

"Oh, God." Em gulped.

I expected her to start sobbing, but she just pressed a hand to her mouth and swallowed thickly. "I didn't know her that well," she added, which I figured explained the lack of tears. "I moved in next door only two months ago, but I just recently started visiting her. I noticed she wasn't feeling well, so I was trying to help her." Em's green eyes flicked from Rosalina to me and then back again as if she were trying to ascertain whether or not we were aware of

Liliana's illness.

"We know," was all Rosalina said.

Em sipped her tea again, looking lost. After a while, she asked, "What was that thing? I've never seen a Skew like that."

I walked toward the table, carrying two cups of coffee. I placed one cup in front of Rosalina and took a seat.

"We don't really know," Rosalina lied.

"It was terrifying."

I nodded. "That, it was."

"You said your name is Toni Sunder, right?" Em peered at me with a frown. "I seem to remember hearing about you on the radio, am I going crazy?"

I scratched my head feeling self-conscious. "Um, it seems you heard our commercial. Rosalina and I run a mate tracker agency."

Em snapped her fingers. "That's it. Yeah, I remember thinking I could use some help in that department."

We all laughed awkwardly.

Eric stomped into the kitchen, looking pissed. He went straight for the coffee maker and poured himself a cup. I searched his gaze, and when we connected, he gave me a slight nod. Both the dagger and the elixir were safe. Or at least that was what I assumed his nod meant.

He heaved a sigh after only a small taste of his coffee and turned his attention to Em, who, under his scrutiny, seemed to shrink several inches. She stared into her cup as if she'd never seen anything cooler than pee-colored tea.

"I called you an Uber," he said dryly.

I wanted to bite his head off for being so rude, but Em jumped to her feet, appearing relieved. It seemed that despite appearances, Rosalina and I hadn't succeeded in making her comfortable.

"Thank you." She edged away from the table and awkwardly sidled toward the kitchen's exit.

I abandoned my coffee and joined her. "I'll walk you to the

front door."

She waved at Rosalina and Eric with two fingers, whirled around, and marched down the wrong hall.

"This way." I pointed her in the right direction.

She laughed nervously and joined me. Her steps were clipped, urging me along. She couldn't be rid of us fast enough. Not surprising. We had brought the chaos of this war between werewolves and vampires right to her doorstep. Bertram and the hybrid had been there for the dagger, and maybe if I hadn't taken it, Liliana would still be alive.

Em rushed out through the glass front door as it slid open. "Weird house," she commented under her breath.

I had to agree with her. The front was cold and uninviting like an office building. However, when you went deeper, you found that the frosty exterior was all for show, for keeping people away, and safeguarding what lay inside. Much like its owner.

I accompanied Em down to the sidewalk, eyes darting in every direction, looking for hostiles, but no one was around. I was grateful for the bright sunlight that shone down on us. It kept vampires from attacking in the open. Though, it did nothing for werewolves. Good thing Stephen Erickson was a coward.

He can still send a hybrid, Toni.

I shuddered at the thought, wondering how many they'd managed to make before I took the dagger. Maybe just the one? Was that too much to hope for? Perhaps not. If they'd made more, why not send them all to Liliana's house?

My train of thought was interrupted by Em.

"You have been nice to me," she said. "Maybe even saved my life, but, all the same, I'm going to the police station from here. I just thought you should know." She looked terrified for a moment as if she expected me to shift right there and then and tear her throat open.

"You do that," I said. "We have nothing to hide. We didn't kill her. Please, believe me."

She exhaled, her shoulders relaxing.

The Uber pulled up just then. I peered inside at the driver, made eye contact. Suddenly, I had a bad feeling and didn't want to let Em go, but it was stupid. She would be fine, much safer away from us. She had nothing to do with any of this. Besides, others would be here soon to escort us to the Pack Rule meeting.

Em climbed into the backseat of the car, looking relieved. She didn't glance my way as the car drove away. I noted the license plate, just in case.

Allowing myself to feel relief at her departure, I went back inside and sighed in relief as the door slid closed behind me. I made my way back to the kitchen, where I joined Eric and Rosalina at the table.

"The dagger and cure are safe," Eric said.

I nodded. "I got that much from your expression."

"How many hybrids do you think they made before you took the dagger?" Rosalina asked, clearly sharing my concern on the subject.

"I've no idea."

"This isn't good," Eric said, stating the obvious.

"My wolfsbane bullet didn't kill it." Rosalina shuddered at this.

"I honestly thought it had," Eric said. "When they were first created, there were no wolfsbane bullets or any other kind. So, of course, there are no accounts that reference any immunity to them. The records state that they were killed by decapitation, and it seems that still stands." Eric glanced up at me with a frown. "Unless, of course, you're a werewolf slash tracker with a weird combination of powers."

After witnessing the hybrid wake up from a shot right between the eyes, my powers seemed even more amazing than ever.

Eric gave me a reproachful glower. "We need to train to discover the extent of your abilities. I hope you won't continue to skirt the responsibility."

"I'm not *skirting* anything. I actually prefer pants."

He rolled his eyes.

"One thing we discovered," Rosalina said, "they don't like getting shot. It makes them angry."

"I know." I shook my head and laughed. "That thing was blind with rage. He went crazy on Bertram. That's what they get for going around creating monsters."

"Damien must be turning in his grave," Eric said.

A pang of regret tightened my chest. We had failed him so miserably.

"What do I do with the cure now?" I wondered out loud.

Eric shrugged. "Whatever you want, I suppose. Sell it to the highest bidder?"

I gifted him a nasty glare. "You've got to be kidding me. I can't do that"

"Why not?"

"It's just… *wrong*." I glanced toward Rosalina, searching for her approval.

"I'm with you," she said, throwing Eric a dirty look of her own.

"Donate it to a vampire charity then," Eric suggested in a mocking tone.

It sounded better than selling it for profit, but was it the right thing to do?

"They'll probably just turn around and *sell it to the highest bidder*," Eric scoffed.

Rosalina shook her head. "God, you're so jaded."

"No, I'm a realist."

I had to admit it was a possibility. People couldn't be trusted. I pondered, wondering what Damien would want. I honestly had no idea.

"It seems we should do something with it," Rosalina said. "It might have a limited shelf life, and then it would be useless to anyone."

"I hadn't considered that," I said.

"No, no shelf life," Eric said.

I blinked at him. "How are you so sure?"

"I was there a lot of the time when he was working on the elixir. He mentioned casting a protective spell to keep it from ever spoiling."

"Good." I nodded to myself. That surely took the pressure off of it. It felt like the contents of the vial shouldn't be wasted, and I should find someone worthy of its healing effects, someone Damien would approve of.

I shared that much with the others.

Rosalina nodded in agreement, while Eric just shrugged as if it made no difference to him.

His phone vibrated on the table. "Someone's at the door." He frowned at the screen, looking as alert as if he expected a horde of vampires to storm the house. After a few clicks on his app, he relaxed but only infinitesimally.

"Knight and Erickson are here," he announced, rising to his feet and heading out.

My heart started racing. I checked my watch. Less than two hours to the meeting with the Pack Rule. Jake Knight and Ulfen Erickson were here to accompany us and serve as added protection to ensure the dagger didn't fall into the wrong hands.

I had no desire to go with them, but they'd insisted. Both Ulfen and Eric said I had to go since I was the only person who had witnessed Bernadetta feeding her tainted blood to that poor werewolf.

Dread settled in the pit of my stomach like a bad burrito.

"It'll be all right," Rosalina said from across the table as she noticed my distress.

I nodded and tried to smile, but I wasn't so sure.

CHAPTER 6

Standing alone in Eric's study, I wrung my hands together, the dagger stuffed safely in my breast pocket where the elixir had been earlier, though it was a different jacket since the other one looked like a crocodile had gone to town on it.

I was pondering which one felt heavier, the dagger or the elixir—figuratively, not literally, of course. The former was bigger, and the jade handle was more substantial than the small vial. But the responsibility of taking the elixir to Liliana had felt weightier. I had failed my friend and was left with that bit of salvation as my responsibility. I knew I couldn't let it go to waste, but I hadn't the faintest idea who to give it to.

The dagger, on the other hand, I would be rid of it soon, and it would become someone else's concern. The werewolves had dealt with the monstrous hybrids in the past, and they would deal with them now if there were more of them. The Pack Rule would keep the dagger safe and prevent its use. Maybe it was even a good thing that Stephen had the cup, and we had the dagger. Because who was to say one of the Pack Rule members couldn't get nefarious ideas, too? A werewolf had joined Bernadetta on a quest for power and control of the city, after all.

The door behind me opened, and I glanced up. Jake came in, moving lithely, his steps barely making any sound on the many rugs that covered the floor.

I'd been standing in front of the fireplace, staring into the ashes, lost in my thoughts without realizing it. I turned my back on the mantle and the portrait of Eric's wife and daughter that hung above it.

"Hey," I said, admiring Jake's silver gaze. Its iridescent quality was still as mesmerizing as it'd always been. He'd captured me with those eyes so long ago and still held me.

God, does he have any idea what he does to me when he looks at me that way?

"Hey," he replied just as eloquently.

He was dressed in a three-piece suit that attempted to match the color of his eyes but failed. He stopped in front of me, all 6'2" of him. His broad shoulders effectively blocked my view of the rest of the room, and he became everything, like a sun blotting out the rest of the universe.

Okay, maybe not exactly like that, but it sure felt that way.

His presence could eclipse everything. I had allowed it to do just that before, and I was trying to be careful not to let it happen again. Though, it was damn hard. Especially, when he reached into my soul with those eyes. There was such tenderness in his expression, such longing.

Today, he had been away with his grandfather, Walter Knight, learning about his role during the Pack Rule meeting. As the future leader of the Knight pack, Jake would have a seat among the Pack Rule members, and apparently, Walter had wanted to school him on the proper way to behave during the proceedings.

"So, are you a Pack Rule expert now?" I asked.

He shrugged. "My grandfather doesn't think so, but I'm sure I know enough."

"That boring, huh?"

"Pretty much. He took it upon himself to teach me a history lesson on our family's involvement in the St. Louis Pack Rule and then proceeded to enlighten me on the arts of politics and diplomacy, and how I should use both to screw everyone over."

"Wow."

"Yeah, wow is right." He smiled, his eyes crinkling at the corners. "Why are you hiding here?"

After Eric announced that Jake and Ulfen had arrived, I'd come here, knowing that there would be a lot of posturing between the three alphas, and a fourth wasn't needed to make the moment more intense.

Also, I'd feared they would rehash what happened this morning, and I didn't want to talk about it anymore. Instead, I'd wanted to clear my head—not that I'd accomplished it. There were a million thoughts in my mind, reproducing like crazy viruses, which I suspected were now launching a biological assault on my body because I was starting to feel sick. There was so much going on that it was like being in a constant flight-or-fight state. My skin itched. My fingertips ached as my claws threatened to unsheathe. It was like waiting for freaking Armageddon.

Seeing Jake here didn't make things easier. His engagement with Allison Blackridge was still a thing as was the unbreakable pact he'd sworn, the one that mandated him to carry through with the wedding whether or not he wanted to, all to forge a strong alliance between the Knights and Blackridges.

He'd promised to find a way to break the unbreakable, to be with me, but I worried he might do something stupid to accomplish it. He and promises just didn't jive. And as much as I would hate to see him marry that watered-down blond, I would rather lose him.

His death just wasn't an option.

Gah! Thinking about this whole thing always made me furious. It made me wonder what I would do if I saw Allison Blackridge again. Murder didn't seem too far-fetched, and at this rate, life in prison didn't either.

"I'm not hiding," I finally said.

He made a sound in the back of his throat that let me know he smelled the lie. He stepped closer and tucked a strand of hair behind my ear, his gaze roving over my face and doing unmentionable things to my baby-making instincts.

I was dying to kiss him, to savor the curve of his lower lips so luscious and tantalizing that it must be a sin, but I knew the moment I tried to press my mouth to his, he would turn away.

"I can't," he'd said. *"I know that if I kiss you now, I won't be able to stop. I will take you and make you mine in every way I know. It wouldn't be right. Not with this engagement and pact hanging over my head."*

So instead, I rested my head on his chest, soaked in his warmth, and listened to the powerful beat of his heart.

One of his hands slid down my back, and pressing his nose to my hair, he inhaled. My skin pebbled as a shiver ran down my spine. His own scent flooded my sensitive nose, making me aware of the overpowering tang of desire wafting off him. With a sound like thunder in his chest, he pushed my hair aside and buried his nose in the crook of my neck. His lips trembled over my collarbone.

"Jake," I said in a heady breath and slid my hand over his pec.

Abruptly, he captured my hand in his and twirled me around so that my back was to him. He wrapped one arm around my waist and held me in place, his chest heaving against my back, his erection pushing against my butt. I threw my head back and moaned.

Holy shit!

"What do you do to me?" His voice was almost unintelligible in its deep rumble. He slowly let me go and stepped aside, leaving me hollowed out and unbalanced.

"I think you do it to yourself, mister." I huffed as I tried to compose myself. I rubbed my chest as if that could soothe the strange emptiness he'd left behind. Something deep inside me physically ached.

I glanced at Jake over my shoulder. He was breathing quickly and looking thoroughly bewildered. He raised a hand to his chest and pressed it below his heart.

"Well, did you learn your lesson?" I joked.

He glanced up, blinking, having a little trouble focusing on me. "My lesson?" he echoed numbly.

"Yes, to keep your distance."

He nodded, but it seemed to be a reflex more than a conscious affirmation.

I scratched my head. "That was a bit weird, wasn't it?"

His eyes finally cleared. "Not really."

I waited for him to explain—I was new at this and maybe there was some sort of werewolf mumbo jumbo that explained weird shit like this, but we were interrupted by Eric when he poked his head into the study and scowled at us.

"What are you two doing? It's time to go."

"Yeah, right." Jake met him at the door, hand still on his chest, and squeezed past, leaving the room.

"What's the matter?" Eric asked when I didn't move. "You look like you're constipated."

I relaxed my face and stuck my tongue out at him. "I would leave it to you to recognize the symptoms since you must see them in the mirror every day."

"Ha ha. C'mon, move your ass. We don't have all day."

We left the study, walking down the hall side-by-side. "Um, Jake once told me about cravedark."

He had explained that it happened when a male and a female werewolf instinctively knew they would make strong offspring. Supposedly, the attraction only lasted until the female conceived, then *puff*, it went away.

Eric's answer was a pointed glance.

I stammered. "D-do you know much about it?"

"I once met a couple afflicted by it."

Afflicted? He said it as if it was a disease. Maybe it was. Maybe Jake and I had *caught* cravedark, and that was why our proximity, or lack of it, hurt. Maybe I would just up and have a heart attack, and I would be put out of my misery—though not before I popped out his baby.

"So… it hurts?" I asked, ready for the answer.

"Hurt? What do you mean? Physically? Maybe when they're humping like rabbits in a frenzy."

"Oh."

We got to the end of the hall and took a left toward the steps that led to the bottom level. I stopped and scanned his face to judge whether or not he was pulling my leg.

"What?" he said, "You think what's between you and Knight is cravedark?" He puffed a laugh. "No way. No way in hell." He started going down the stairs, leaving me behind.

I hurried down and joined him. "How are you so sure?"

"You two are *in love*," he made it sound like this was also an affliction. "And in desperate need of a good fuck, which you would've already enjoyed if cravedark had anything to do with it."

Good, at least it isn't cravedark. Just good 'ol fashioned, rip-your-heart-out love. Fun, fun!

I mechanically went down the stairs, pondering his words. How did he know Jake and I hadn't… fucked? Was it that obvious? Maybe the lack of sex was starting to show. Was I growing horns? No, not horns. Wings were more like it. I hadn't been with anyone for almost two years. I was practically a saint.

Absently, I rubbed at my chest, at the phantom pain that still lingered.

Eric scrutinized me curiously. "Are you saying you love him so much it hurts?" He dipped his chin, his blue eyes falling to the twitching fingers over my breastbone, his steps still quick as they took the last few stairs and we hurried towards the garage.

I lowered my hand and was about to make a joke to dismiss the entire topic when I realized I couldn't just let it drop. "Something like that."

He narrowed his eyes with glinting amusement. "Everyone knows what that means."

"Huh?"

"You're mates, but that shouldn't come as news to anyone."

"What?"

"True mates. They're not that common, but we have bigger issues to worry about, don't we?"

I blinked, wondering why Jake hadn't said anything? Maybe he'd thought I knew, and I guess I did. How could there be any doubt in my heart?

But Eric was right about the *bigger issues*. Things with Jake were complicated, but nothing like what was going on in the city. Rhabo rampant in the streets, Bernadetta Fiore and Stephen Erickson aligned in a quest for power, an Unholy Vessel that made monsters, and the witchlights knew what else.

Also, there was that immediate issue of meeting with the Pack Rule. Just the thought of it made my heart *thump* faster. I honestly wished Eric would let me skip, but I had no choice. He would drag me there if I refused.

Out in the large garage, Jake was waiting along with Rosalina and Ulfen Erickson. They turned in our direction as they heard our steps. Jake glanced at me knowingly.

I approached. "Hi, mate," I said, using an Aussie accent.

He shook slightly as if a shiver had run up his back.

"Why didn't you say something?"

"I'm not the kind who likes to state the obvious." He lowered his chin and gave me a sexy wink that sent heat into my core.

God, the man could probably drive me to ecstasy with one wicked glance if he set his mind to it.

My mate. He was my mate. It shouldn't have made a difference knowing this—I loved him all the same—but it did.

He was mine and no one else's.

Eat your heart out, Allison Blackridge.

Shaking myself, I forced myself to return to the moment. I let my gaze rove around the garage.

Ulfen, like Jake, was wearing a suit and tie, but his hair and beard were untidy. He looked nothing like the collected, powerful man I'd first met when I was dating his son. Instead, he appeared exhausted and older, as if he'd worried away a few years of his life in the past week. It wasn't surprising. During a short time, he'd been in jail, discovered his son was insane and a traitor, and called a Pack Rule meeting that would likely plunge his life into further chaos. The group hadn't met in a long time. Things in St. Louis had run smoothly for decades, all the packs getting along and sharing the territory without major conflicts. Now, Ulfen and his son were seen as the catalysts for the unrest and for what seemed the end of a peaceful era.

Poor guy!

I felt sympathy toward him for, perhaps, the first time since I'd met him. It had to be hard on him to know that his own blood was responsible for the turmoil that threatened to undo the fabric of St. Louis's Skew community.

Rosalina stepped forward and took my hands in hers. "Please be careful."

I squeezed her hands back, wishing selfishly that she could come with us. But she wasn't allowed since she wasn't a werewolf. I knew it was better this way. She would be safer here in Eric's house, where she would stay until we returned. But I would still miss her support.

"I will be," I said.

She let go and disappeared back inside the house.

Ulfen inclined his head in a formal greeting. "Ms. Sunder."

"Mr. Erickson." I inclined my head back.

"Do you have the dagger?"

"I do."

"Good. I will drive the decoy." He gestured toward a car identical to Eric's Mercedes. *Sheesh,* where had they gotten it? Having money sure was nice. It took care of things that poor suckers like me could never manage.

"My men are waiting outside, and they will follow us and help in case of any eventuality."

Where "in case of any eventuality" meant "in case a derange hybrid tries to murder us."

After this brief explanation, he climbed into the decoy car and started the engine.

Jake approached Eric's car, opened the passenger side door, and ushered me in while Eric climbed behind the wheel. I squeezed Jake's hand briefly as I got in, feeling an electric jolt pass between us. He winked reassuringly, then got in the backseat. I breathed a sigh of relief, knowing he would be with me.

I always wanted him by my side.

CHAPTER 7

The garage door opened. Ulfen drove out first, followed by us. He took a right while Eric veered left. Four additional black cars waited outside. Two followed Ulfen while the others stuck to our tail. Eric kept an alert watch in the different mirrors, the same way he had when we'd gone out this morning.

We drove out of Ballwin, where Eric's house was located, and headed East on Hwy 100.

"Where's the meeting?" Jake asked from behind me.

Eric peered at him in the rearview mirror. "I'm not allowed to say."

"Same thing my grandfather told me."

"Only members are allowed to know the location. So maybe when you officially join, when you're a pack leader, they'll tell you."

"To be honest, I don't really want to know."

"I don't blame you."

Eric had once been a pack leader, but he didn't seem to think much of the position anymore, and who could blame him? If he hadn't been pack alpha, his family would still be alive.

"Shit!" Eric exclaimed, sending my heart into a frenzy. A crash followed his exclamation, and he stepped on the gas, propelling us forward at breakneck speed.

"What?!" Both Jake and I turned in our seats to glance through the back window. One of the sedans with Ulfen's men, our bodyguards, was turned around, its front facing the wrong way, its back bumper and trunk smashed in.

An SUV with its own front ruined came to a screeching halt next to it, and two men with large automatic weapons jumped out and started shooting at the sedan, riddling its side with holes.

"Fucking bastards!" Jake exclaimed.

A second SUV accelerated, trying to overtake the remaining sedan that followed us, but our bodyguards cut the wheel sharply and blocked its path. The sound of crumpling metal reached us even inside of our luxurious, noise-dampened interior, even as Eric propelled us forward.

Our bodyguards came shooting out of the sedan, loyal Erickson pack members, willing to risk their lives for their alpha's cause. I hoped they knew it was also the *right* cause. We couldn't let our enemies get hold of the dagger. If they did, it could mean the end of our city, of our way of life.

Hugging the backrest, I craned my neck to see if they would escape unscathed, but we veered from the highway, taking a sharp right, buildings and lampposts blurring past as Eric tried to push the odometer's needle into the red zone.

I held my breath, constantly looking back over my shoulder. Jake's arm rested along the top of the back seat as he, too, eyed the road behind us.

"No sign of them," he said after a few minutes of tense silence. "I think we lost them."

"I hope Ulfen is all right," I said, wondering if his group had also been attacked.

At an underground parking lot in an area of town I wasn't familiar with, Eric parked next to a large delivery van and ordered us to get out.

"What? Here?" I glanced around confused.

Eric slammed the door shut without an answer, a set of keys jingling in his hand.

Jake and I exchanged a confused glance, then followed Eric out of the Mercedes.

Eric used the new set of keys to open the double back doors of the delivery van.

"Get in," he said, pointing to the windowless, dark interior.

Jake's eyes narrowed with distrust. "What is this about?"

"It's part of keeping the Pack Rule's location a secret."

"My grandfather didn't mention any of this."

Eric shrugged as if it didn't matter. "He probably forgot. I'm sure his mental capabilities aren't what they used to be."

An unspoken question flashed in Jake's eyes as he glanced back in my direction. *Do you trust him?*

Clearly, Jake didn't.

He didn't want to get in the van, and I didn't blame him. I didn't want to get in either. But what else were we going to do? Run from Eric with the dagger in tow. No. That wasn't an option. I wanted to be rid of the thing. Besides, I *did* trust Eric.

So with a single nod at Jake, I climbed inside the van and sat on one of the benches that lined either side. Jake stood huffing outside for a few beats, shuffling from foot to foot with indecision. At last, he exhaled in resignation, climbed in, and sat across from me on the other bench.

The doors slammed shut with a clank that reverberated inside my head and plunged us into total darkness. A chill ran over my arms, reminding me of how this all had begun. Me, tracking

Stephen at Jake's request and finding him in the utter darkness of a van very much like this one.

"I hope you're right about Cross," Jake's voice echoed inside our confined space.

"If he wanted the dagger, he could have taken it already."

"Well, his plan could be to kill us, take the dagger, then tell the Pack Rule that we ran away with it."

The van's engine came to life, and an annoying *beep, beep, beep* sounded as we backed out of the parking space. Then we lurched forward, and we were on our way.

"Wow, you can certainly come up with pretty diabolical plans," I said. "I think Bernadetta should put *you* in charge instead of Stephen."

"And you can certainly be very naïve."

"I'm not naïve."

"How long have you known this man? Five days? Ten?"

I did a mental count. "Over two weeks," I said triumphantly.

"Rest my case."

"I know I can trust him, all right? I feel it in my gut."

Jake only huffed, then we sat in silence for a long moment, my ears attentive to the sounds of tires eating up miles, and my nose trying to pick up other scents besides Jake's intoxicating musk.

"Where do you think this secret lair is?" I asked, sick of the overwhelming silence.

"No idea. They call it Wolfskeep, by the way."

"Wolfskeep, cool," I echoed. "So where is it? You didn't ask your grandfather?"

"He also said it was a secret. I wish he'd mentioned this part, though." He waved a hand around the van, and I realized my sharp eyes had adapted to the darkness.

After about a twenty-minute drive, gravel crunched under the tires, and the van lurched from side to side.

"We're off-road," Jake pointed out.

Ten more minutes went by before we came to a stop. The engine shut off, and Eric came around and opened the back door, letting in the glow of warm light. I squinted, my eyes adjusting. The sight that materialized behind Eric was nothing like what I'd imagined.

Rocky walls loomed to our right, illuminated by honest-to-god torches perched in rustic metal holders. From the looks of it, we were in a cave, a large one that could accommodate a van. Eric offered me a hand and helped me step down, and I discovered that the cave could house more than just the van. Three more cars occupied the area, and there was plenty of room for twenty more. My gaze followed the curve of the wall to a jagged ceiling that got lost in deep shadows.

"What the hell is this place?" Jake asked.

"Welcome to St. Louis entrance to Wolfskeep," Eric said, a bit of deference in his tone, which made me frown. Eric didn't respect many things and showed appreciation for even less. That he held this place in some regard made me wonder.

Jake stepped away from the van, glancing all around. I followed behind me, also scanning my surroundings. The cave was massive, a dome that stretched over our heads, making me wonder if we were inside a mountain or underground. I didn't know any caves in St. Louis. Maybe we'd been magically transported elsewhere. I thought of asking, but I doubted anyone would tell. I was nothing but a packless lone wolf that would never join the exclusive circle.

To our right, a dark tunnel extended toward what I assumed was the exit. To the left, it was a dead end. I carefully examined every corner, slowly meandering around the parked cars, my nose twitching at the trapped smell of exhaust.

Where were we going to hold our meeting? Standing out here? There didn't seem to be anywhere else to go. We might as well be moles trapped in their dens.

Next, my attention moved to the members of the Pack Rule.

Ulfen Erickson and Walter Knight were already there. Ulfen was leaning against his car, examining his fingernails, while Jake's grandfather stood by Craig Blackridge. I'd never met him before, but I'd seen him on the news. He was Allison's father and Aaron's uncle, and also Jake's future father-in-law. Hurray!

He had longish blond hair and a goatee going to gray. He wore a suit, but no tie. He was about six-foot tall and seemed kind of soft around the middle.

Jake was glowering in his direction, a sharp scent wafting off of him: anger. I brushed the back of his hand with mine and gave him a nod of support. He relaxed a bit and graced me with a half-smile.

Feeling my own anger stir inside my chest, I searched for the remaining member of the Pack Rule, but he wasn't here. Maybe he wouldn't come. The knot in my chest eased a little. That was until the sound of an engine rumbled down the dark tunnel, and a couple of headlights cast their sharp beams on us.

I squinted, blocking the light with my hand until the car stopped and the engine was shut off. The car was a silver BMW, sporty and convertible. The driver-side door opened, and a tall man stretched out of the tiny vehicle and towered over it.

My stomach clenched at the sight of the man I'd only seen in pictures. In person, he was as imposing, if not more, than I'd imagined. He was well over six-foot tall with wide, squarish shoulders, and there was nothing soft about him. His dark hair shone under the torchlight, and so did his dark brown eyes. He glanced around, his strong chin held high. As he spotted Ulfen, he walked confidently in his direction, one hand casually stuffed in his pocket. He wore a black suit with a black shirt and tie, fulfilling the definition of tall, dark, and handsome.

I hated him right away.

"Hey," Jake nudged me with his shoulder, "it's all right. Don't worry about him. He doesn't know."

Easy for him to say. Travis Hillworth wasn't *his* father. But Jake was right. My mom had never told him about me. Instead, she had lied to my father and everyone else, making us believe I was Peter Sunder's daughter and not the illegitimate child of a werewolf.

With a deep breath, I turned away from the man and gathered my wits. I was here for entirely different reasons. I had no interest in this man, not someone who would cheat on his wife with another man's wife. His children, a son and a daughter, had been small when he stepped out. In my book, anyone capable of that level of deception wasn't worth my time.

I rolled my shoulders, uncomfortable with my own logic. By the same token, my mother wasn't worth my time either. Some part of me was still angry at her, but almost losing her had eased the bulk of my resentment.

After a quiet moment talking to Ulfen, Travis stepped to the center of the cave and addressed everyone. "It seems we're all here. Shall we begin?"

Without waiting for anyone to answer, he walked to the back of the cave, his long steps confident. He gave Jake and me a nod as he walked past, a brief acknowledgment that, judging by the ensuing sneer, was more than he thought we deserved.

Back at you, asshole, I thought, shooting daggers at the back of his head. He surely made the job of hating him a lot easier.

Everyone followed. Only Jake and I lingered behind, confused. There was nothing at the back of the cave but a wall of jagged rocks and a couple of torches.

Without preamble, Travis Hillworth stepped up to the wall and placed a large hand on its rough surface. One by one, Ulfen Erickson, Walter Knight, Craig Blackridge, and Eric Cross followed suit, all of them laying their palms to the same spot Travis had touched, then stepping aside to let the next person through.

When they were done, the wall dissolved right before our eyes, revealing a narrow passage, also illuminated by torches. The scent of locked, ancient things blew out, carried on a chilled wind that whistled lightly as it made its way out.

Holy crap!

I was about to step into Wolfskeep.

CHAPTER 8

My heart beat loudly as everyone just stood there, without moving. I scanned everyone's faces. They all were peering inside the cave as if waiting for something. Steps echoed down the passage. I sidled closer to Jake. Tension hummed all around him.

A shadow materialized far into the corridor, slowly growing bigger as it approached. I squinted at it, holding my breath. Who was it? Another Pack Rule member who had gotten here first? No, Eric had told me there were only the five of them, no one else. So who was this?

The shape resolved into a figure of average height, wearing a white tunic embroidered in colorful thread. It had a heavy hood lined with fur that obscured its features. A pair of fur boots completed the outfit, which was reminiscent of native Inuit attire. The person's hands were stuffed into long, wide sleeves, also lined with fur. They stopped at the mouth of the tunnel and bowed slightly.

"Welcome," a clear, feminine voice said.

Tattooed hands lowered the hood, revealing a woman with prominent cheekbones, narrow eyes, and luscious dark hair parted in the middle with two braids falling at either side of her face. A tattoo composed of three straight lines went from the bottom of her lower lip down to her chin. Another one formed a "V" in the middle of her forehead, ending between her eyebrows. She was beautiful and, indeed, appeared to be of Inuit descent.

"Please, make your vows and enter," she said in lightly accented English. She stepped aside and stretched a hand toward the depths of the passage.

Each man approached the threshold, held up their right hand, and said, "At this sacred juncture, I vow to a moratorium with all the alpha members of this and any other Pack Rule. I vow to uphold our values and make every decision for the protection of our kind."

I took a step back, making sure I was the last in line, trying to commit to memory all the words in case they were asked of me. Jake tried to be a gentleman and invited me to go before him, but I shook my head and shoved him forward. He shook his head and carefully moved up to the threshold.

Walter was already on the other side and stepped forward to say, "I vouch for him, Keeper Yura. His name is Jacob Knight. He's my grandson and the future alpha of the Knight pack. He was also a witness to the events we are here to discuss."

The woman, Yura, scanned the length of Jake's body as if she were weighing in his worth. Jake stood taller, his shoulders drawing back, his chin jutting forward. Yura inhaled, her nostrils flaring as she took in his scent as if that also were part of her judgment. After a long moment, she gave him a welcoming nod.

"Lift your right hand and repeat after me," she instructed.

Jake complied, his deep voice ringing out. "At this sacred

juncture, I vow to a moratorium with all the alpha members of this and any other Pack Rule. I vow to speak only when spoken during the proceedings, and make a vow of secrecy to never divulge to anyone what transpires here today." Then he stepped past the threshold and seemed to exhale in relief.

I hung back, casting a furtive glance over my shoulder. Had Eric left the keys in the van's ignition? Maybe I could hop in the driver's seat and tear out of here like a bat out of a cave, except Travis's car was blocking the way. *Shit!*

Yura cleared her throat. My head snapped back, and I fidgeted on the spot.

"Who vouches for her?" she asked.

"I do." Eric stepped forward. "Her name is Antonietta Sunder. She's an alpha and, like Jacob Knight, a witness to the events we're here to discuss."

"Very well." Yura beckoned with one of her tattooed hands.

If Jake and Eric hadn't been on the other side, I didn't think I could have approached to withstand the woman's scrutiny. After she was done weighing me in and taking in my scent, I expected her to instruct me on what to say, but instead, she gave me a complicit smile.

"An alpha female," she said with no small measure of satisfaction. "It's been some time since I've encountered a kindred spirit in these depths."

I blinked in surprise. She was also an alpha. Cool!

"Welcome, Antonietta Sunder." She gave a sidelong glance at the men as if to say she was glad to have another female here. I imagined that, for eons, it had been an endless parade of males walking through this hidden gate.

"Thank you, Yura, if I may call you so."

"You may." She smiled with perfect white teeth. "Now, repeat after me."

I did as instructed, my voice trembling a little as she recited the same words she'd offered Jake.

"You may enter Wolfskeep," Yura said when I was done with my vows. She inclined her head with a level of respect I didn't think I deserved from someone such as her, whoever she was.

I swallowed thickly and crossed the threshold. A strange feeling washed over me, and I felt transported, the way I did during my tracking trances. I glanced back the way I'd come. The cars still sat there, waiting for their drivers to return, and the smell of exhaust still hung in the air. Frowning, I started to turn back but stopped when, from the corner of my eye, I noticed the air wavering like water. My attention snapped back, but the illusion disappeared. I angled my head again and perceived the same effect.

"You have sharp senses, Antonietta, if I may call you that," Yura said with a gentle smile.

"Sure. Or you can call me Toni." I returned her smile. "Where are we?"

"You're not in Kansas anymore, Dorothy," Travis said with a derisive chuckle.

I threw a dirty look in his direction that made him do a double-take. I had a feeling he was used to being regarded as something special from the get-go. I thought he was special all right. As special as a lying sack of shit.

For the first time, he seemed to consider me, to perhaps wonder exactly who I was. Had my last name suggested anything to him? Had he known my father? Mom had given me few details about their relationship, and, because I didn't want to go back to hating her, I didn't press her for any more than she was willing to offer.

After assessing me for a few beats, Travis donned a bored expression and said, "I don't know about you all, but I don't have all day." He turned on his heel and headed down the long corridor.

Everyone followed him. Still unsure, I lingered behind, but now it was Yura who was walking next to me and not Jake. After a few steps, I peered over my shoulder to find that the wall behind us had reappeared, and we were trapped.

No, Toni, not trapped. I tried to think of another word to ease my tension but none came, so, hoping for a distraction from the claustrophobia threatening to overtake me, I switched my attention to the magnificent specimen of a woman at my side.

"Who… who are you?" I dared ask, expecting her to tell me it was none of my business.

To my surprise, she answered candidly. "I am Yura of Maliseet, one of the Keepers of Wolfskeep. When the Pack Rule meets, I allow them entrance."

"Maliseet?"

"Yes, in the Wabanaki Confederacy."

That still left me just as lost.

"It's an area on the border of Maine and New Brunswick."

"Ah." That made sense. I tried to remember what I'd learned about those packs in school, but it wasn't much. Mostly what I remembered had to do with the way colonists had treated them from the beginning. Stale religious zealots who thought all Skews were abominations of nature persecuted them and kept trying to eradicate them from their own lands. Even to this day, when Stales and Skews got along almost everywhere else in the world, over there, it was an open war for our kind.

I thought for a bit more about her answer, then asked, "When you say *Pack Rule,* you don't only mean *this* Pack Rule, right?"

She nodded.

"So all the Pack Rules from all over the world meet here?" I glanced around at what was still nothing but a corridor leading to who knew where.

As we went, the torches behind us went out with a *whoosh*, while others ahead of us came to life.

"Neat trick that one," I said nervously, feeling as if I were going down the gullet of some huge dragon. Maybe we were on our way down to his tummy where his digestive juices would turn us into… well, more juice. I shuddered.

"There is no reason to be afraid," Yura said in her melodic, accented voice. "You're quite safe here."

It didn't feel that way at all, but I tried to trust her.

After a ten-minute walk, we arrived at another dead end.

"Pardon me." Yura gave a light bow, walked past the others, and, with a wave of her hand, opened the passage to reveal what looked like a grand hall in some medieval castle. We all stepped through another threshold that felt similar to the last one. If before we'd left "Kansas", now it felt as if we'd left not only our state but our… time. And no doubt the passage had been nothing but an in-between.

The space where we found ourselves was large, surrounded by stone walls hung with ancient banners depicting coats of arms embroidered in fine thread. There were hundreds of them, each a different color and design, but all sporting some sort of wolf. A massive round table sat in the middle of the room. It looked heavy and ancient.

Jake joined his grandfather as he waved him toward a purple and gold banner. "This is us," he said in a reverent tone.

Jake stared up at the banner, his features solemn, awed. A pang of envy ran through my wolf, making me aware of her presence as something separate. It was a conflicting feeling that I didn't like at all. Lately, the wolf and I had been one. But here and now, half of me coveted that sense of belonging that shaped Jake's expression. It was something I would never have.

I had no pack.

I was a lone wolf.

Toni Lone, they would call me.

"What is your line?" Yura asked, stepping up beside me and gesturing toward the banners. "I can help you find it."

"Thank you, but I don't have one." My voice came out with a

lot more bite than I intended it to, and, of their own accord, my eyes flicked in Travis Hillworth's direction.

My momentary error was not wasted on Yura, who also glanced toward Travis and, after examining his face, seemed to reach the right conclusion. Had she detected some sort of resemblance? No! I refused to believe I looked anything like that butterface.

I bit my lower lip, cursing myself for being so transparent. Would she say anything? *God, I hope not.* My only goal wasn't to get rid of the dagger but also get out of here without giving anything away to that indecent man.

Tearing my gaze away from the banners, I inspected the rest of the space. I approached the table. It had enough chairs to accommodate thirty people. The face of a snarling wolf with jeweled eyes was etched in its very center, inlaid in different wood colors, and contained in a circle. Stars and moons surrounded the wolf, and runes followed along the circular pattern. It was a work of art, unlike anything I'd ever seen.

A fresh scent of pine and resin blew in from the corner, drawing me there. Wooden shutters lay open around an arched window edged with stones polished smooth by time and the contact of many hands. I rested my fingers lightly on the sill and glanced out into a navy sky bathed in moonlight and peppered with brilliant stars. I could make out the shape of large mountains in the distance, their outlines darker than the firmament above.

Where the hell were we? The other side of the world? It must have been for the moon to be out. It had been 3 PM in St. Louis, so… Unless this was only an illusion.

A chair scraped loudly, bringing my attention back to the center of the room. Travis was unbuttoning his jacket and sitting at what some might consider the head of the table since it faced the door we had walked through.

"Let's get this over with," he said, pulling on his cuffs as he made himself comfortable.

My alpha instincts bristled and so did everyone else's, judging by the way their expressions tightened. Jake rolled his shoulders as if to ease his desire to punch Travis across the jaw. I didn't want to brawl, but if he did, I would gladly join him.

I took a deep breath, feeling the weight of the dagger in my pocket. At least I could agree with him on one fact. We needed to get this over with.

CHAPTER 9

Travis looked satisfied as everyone followed him to the big table, as if this small concession meant he was the leader. I dug in my heels, bristling further. We all had vowed not to have a pissing contest, but I sure wanted to. This guy rubbed me the wrong way like sandpaper on my eyelids.

Yura cleared her throat and approached the table, too. "As usual, *I* will be the moderator. Let's get started. It's now time." As she said this, a beam of moonlight shone through a strategically located hole up on the wall and illuminated the inlaid wolf at the center of the table.

I watched in awe as the jeweled eyes shone pure sapphire, much like Eric's eyes. At this, everyone took a seat reverently, Travis and his posturing forgotten. When the angle of the moon beam shifted slightly and the wolf's eyes stopped glowing, Yura spoke again.

"It has been one hundred and twenty-three full moons since the St. Louis Pack Rule met last," she said in her melodious voice.

"Over ten years filled with accord and prosperity for the packs. But, as it has always been, accord is now being threatened, so your leadership is needed to achieve harmony once more."

Travis fidgeted in his seat, impatient with Yura's introduction. He looked like someone who had something urgent to do elsewhere, like change his diaper or apply some hemorrhoid cream.

Yura glanced around, her wise gaze alighting on Eric. "First things first… It has come to the Supreme Pack Rule's attention that the Unholy Vessel has been unearthed and that you, Alpha Eric Cross, are now in possession of part of it, is this correct?"

Eric opened his mouth to answer, but Travis spoke first.

"I'm sorry," he waved a hand in the air, "but what is *he* doing here? He's just a lone wolf with no pack. No stake in our city."

"That's ridiculous," I said. "Of course, he has a stake. He lives there. We all do."

"Regardless, this," he gestured around the room, "is called the Pack Rule, and he has none."

"He does have a pack. It's me!" I interjected without thinking.

Travis, Craig, and Walter laughed derisively. Jake and Ulfen frowned.

Embarrassed, I tried to become one with my chair, but it didn't oblige. *Shit!* Sometimes, my mouth got ahead of my brain. I glanced in Eric's direction, feeling like an idiot. I hadn't even stopped to think about his opinion on the matter. But I shouldn't have worried because the look in his eyes told me he was grateful for my support.

Slowly, he turned his attention to Travis. I expected Eric to balk at the plain hostility, but he looked as cool as an arctic wolf. "I brought this up myself," Eric answered casually, "but I was *asked* to come."

"He's still a member, Alpha Hillworth," Yura said. "Moreover, he was a witness to the events involving the Unholy Vessel. In fact, I believe he was instrumental in its retrieval. Though, I will allow *him* to explain the details of what happened."

Travis huffed. "Very well, but I do wish to initiate a motion for his removal."

Yura inclined her head. "I shall call for a vote at the end, then."

"No need." Eric waved a hand. "I quit." He smiled a smile as thin as the edge of a knife and directed it straight at Travis, whose jaw twitched, revealing his annoyance. He'd wanted to kick Eric out and hated not having the satisfaction to do it. *Petty bastard!*

"Let's proceed." Yura nodded toward Eric.

"To answer your question," he said, "yes, the Unholy Vessel has reared its ugly head again. However, I'm not in possession of it. Toni is."

Now, every pair of eyes flicked in my direction. I waited for Yura to say something, but she just waited for me to pick up where Eric had left off, so I nodded, dug into my breast pocket, pulled out the dagger, and laid it on the table. Walter, Ulfen, Craig, and Travis all leaned forward to look at it closely, their eyes shining with interest.

Travis blew air through his nose. "It doesn't look like much." He reclined back on his chair, appearing unimpressed. "Are we sure that's it?"

My wolf snarled, but I stopped any sound from getting out. Was he insinuating we'd brought a counterfeit? Instead of snarling, though, I schooled my temper and said in a cool tone, "I'm one hundred percent sure this is it. I took it right after it was used to create a hybrid."

Travis's brown eyes—so much like my own that I hated him for it—assessed me once more. He appeared to be performing a million computations to arrive at some number that would tell him exactly what to think of me. After a beat, he simply raised an eyebrow and said nothing. Maybe he'd come up with a big fat zero. The witchlights knew it was the same score I'd given him.

"Please explain to everyone how you came to be in possession of this dagger." Yura extended a hand in invitation.

I proceeded to explain things from the beginning. "It all began with Stephen Erickson's supposed kidnapping. When Ulfen couldn't find his son, he asked for my help as a tracker. Jacob Knight and I found him and thought we were saving him from harm, but it turned out he'd fake the abduction. And, in the end, we discovered that Stephen is working with Bernadetta Fiore."

I glanced apologetically at Ulfen. He tapped his fingers on the table to indicate there was no other way to go about it.

"Four days ago," I continued, "Stephen took me forcefully to a coven temple where he asked me to join him in his quest to, I don't know, conquer the city, I guess. Whatever the reason, it's insane, and it involves turning an entire pack into hybrids using that." I pointed at the dagger, my emotions rising as I told the story. "When I refused to join him, he made me watch as they used the vessel to turn a member of a small pack into one of those hybrid beasts. Bernadetta Fiore put her blood into the jade cup, then dipped the dagger in it, and fed it to that man. It was hard to watch." I swallowed thickly. "They had the entire pack there, ready to turn every member, but I was to be next. And they almost succeeded. They almost…" I trailed off and shuddered as I remembered how close I'd been to becoming a mindless monster.

Everyone waited for me to continue as silence hung heavily between us. Yura looked horrified but encouraged me to continue with a slight nod.

"My friend saved me in the last instant," I said, my throat aching. "His name was Damien Ward, and he was a Copper Mage. Now, he's dead, and all we know is that a Midnight Witch killed him. For this piece of shit!" I flicked the dagger with my hand and sent it sliding across the table. It stopped right on the nose of the inlaid wolf and spun a few times until it went still. Everyone stared at it with distaste.

"Damien wasn't the only one at the coven temple. Jake and Eric came, too." I didn't mention Rosalina because I didn't want her involved in any of this. Of course, she already was involved, but I would do as much as I could, when I could, to protect her. "We fought Bernadetta Fiore and her coven. Stephen ran like a coward and took the jade cup. Though I was able to part him from the dagger."

Ulfen's knuckles cracked as he interlaced his fingers and stared at them, a mixture of anger and shame shaping his strong features. I felt sorry for him, but I hated Stephen regardless. He was a bastard and would pay for what he'd done to Damien.

"And the hybrid they created, what happened to it?" Travis asked.

"Toni killed him," Eric answered, sparing me talking to the man.

Travis seemed to pull out his little assessing calculator once more, still tallying my worth. He looked slightly impressed, and I imagined my score going up on his card, which annoyed me. I didn't even want him glancing in my direction, much less judging me.

"Well, then it seems there's nothing more to fear from this godforsaken artifact." He made a dismissive gesture toward the dagger.

"Except for the fact that this morning, we fought another hybrid," Eric informed him.

Murmurs went around the room.

"So they made more? How many?" Craig asked, stroking his graying goatee.

Eric shook his head. "We don't know. But all the stories, all the legends about their strength, are true. The creature survived a wolfsbane shot to the head. It took him down, but the beast healed and got back up. We thought it was dead. We should've decapitated it while it lay on the floor to make sure it would stay dead. We won't make the same mistake again."

My stomach twisted at the image of that monster's neck spewing out blood.

"Let that be a warning for anyone who encounters a hybrid," Eric said.

Jake's grandfather cleared his throat and straightened in his chair. He had been listening in silence, observing everything with narrowed eyes, cold calculation shaping every slight twitch of his face.

"Stephen Erickson is a traitor," he said. "And he should be treated as such."

Ulfen balled his fists, his face going red with anger, but he said nothing in reply.

Yura nodded solemnly, her mouth turning down in a grave expression that made me wonder how traitors were meant to be treated.

Travis, Ulfen's ally, intervened. "Let's remember the new rules. A trial will be required to determine culpability."

Walter huffed and reclined back on his chair, looking as if he'd tasted something sour.

Craig, the old man's ally, spoke next. "The affair seems pretty cut-and-dry to me. Ms. Sunder's testimony leaves me no doubt."

"A trial will be required," Travis repeated, raising his voice and surprising me with his fervor. He turned to Yura. "May you please remind everyone of how things work now."

She inclined her head and obliged. "The rules are hardly new. They have been in place for fifty years."

Walter shrugged. "Our creed didn't need these changes. I never agreed. Things worked well for hundreds of years."

Travis spoke with a mocking smile. "Sorry to say this, but the old ways and the old," he waved a hand in the air as if searching for the right word, "*folk* always must give way to change and the younger generations, lest things become stagnant."

Next to him, Ulfen blinked slowly. He seemed grateful, glad to have someone at his side who would defend his son, if only because they were allies.

Walter's dark eyes shone with undisguised hatred. The tension between the two pairs of men—two sets of opposing allies—crackled in the air. Jake, sitting to the right of his grandfather, gave nothing away. His features were neutral, and his silver eyes set on a spot on the wall. By joining the Blackridge pack, he had made instant enemies of the Ericksons and Hillworths, and I wasn't sure he liked it.

"The rules," Yura continued, ignoring the exchange, "state that crimes committed against our kind, by our kind, will be judged and tried by the Supreme Pack Rule. Only if culpability is determined, the death sentence will be applied."

I blinked in surprise. Death sentence?! The Supreme Pack Rule actually killed people? And only in the last fifty years they'd made a trial a requirement?

Shit! I hope I never piss them off.

I wanted Stephen dead, and I wouldn't complain if someone gave me *carte blanche* to kill him even without proof of his guilt because I knew he deserved it, but I couldn't deny how dangerous a system without accountability must have been.

Craig steepled his fingers, his blue eyes going around the table, then stopping at Ulfen. "All I can say is that if Stephen Erickson doesn't come peacefully to face his *trial*," he said the word as if he were referring to a clown convention, "I will not risk my life to bring him in alive. The same goes for every member of my pack. I cannot, in good conscience, ask them to risk themselves."

"Aye." Walter put two fingers up in the air to indicate the same went for his pack. He glanced toward Jake, who nodded his agreement.

Jake and I owed Stephen nothing—not after the way he'd lied to us, after he kidnapped me and tried to turn me into a monster—yet, I hated to see Jake side with his grandfather and Craig. For some odd reason, it felt like a betrayal.

"That is perfectly reasonable," Yura said, "and in accordance with our rules. However, no one is to actively seek out Stephen Erickson with the goal of imparting justice. Anyone who does risks their own trial."

"Maybe we can have this *strange* werewolf track him?" Travis suggested, inclining his head in my direction.

I leaned forward in my chair menacingly. "Strange?"

He put both hands up. "I meant no offense." He smiled without it reaching his eyes, making his words a lie. "It's just I've never met a werewolf with additional Skew powers."

I opened my mouth to insult his mother, but Yura spoke first.

"She is, indeed, a rare type of werewolf, with valuable skills that don't include constantly uttering banal remarks."

Travis's eyes flashed with anger toward Yura. She held his gaze until, overpowered, he glanced away. Alpha energy emanated from her. Something more powerful than whatever Travis's *alphaness* could produce. It took a few long beats to dissipate. I understood at once why she was the Master of the meeting.

Smiling gently, she addressed me. "Could you? Use your tracking skills to find Stephen Erickson again?"

I shook my head. "No, I don't have anything that belonged to him."

"How about the dagger?" Craig said.

"No. The true owner of that dagger is long dead."

"Enough of that, what do we do with the… thing?" Walter pointed toward the small weapon, which still sat in the middle of the table. "Who shall be entrusted with keeping it safe? Clearly, Erickson and Hillworth aren't good choices."

"What are you suggesting?" Ulfen asked in a growl, speaking for the first time.

Walter smiled thinly. "This *is* ultimately *your* fault, my dear Ulfen. Your son is responsible for creating hybrids. I can't think of a more heinous crime. He's deranged, and it begs the question… why?"

Wood groaned under the pressure of Ulfen's large hands as he squeezed the edge of the table. Sharp claws sprang out, embedding themselves in the polished surface. Walter watched with amusement, an air of apathy wafting all around him like so much cologne.

I hated the old man more than ever at the moment. I doubted he would act that way if his strong, capable grandson weren't sitting next to him. Besides, Walter knew nothing of the relationship between Ulfen and Stephen, of how hard this was for Ulfen, and how desperately he'd tried to set his son on a straight path. I could understand it now. Even Ulfen's attempts to keep his son away from me had been aimed at reshaping Stephen's rotten character.

"We will refrain from taunting each other," Yura said, turning to Walter and dispensing a withering stare that carried a heavy warning in it.

I expected the old man to balk, but he shrugged, feigning nonchalance. Though, I could tell he felt the warning in his bones and not only his wrinkled hide. I got the feeling one did not mess with the Supreme Pack Rule or its leaders.

"I hope you're not suggesting that you two should be the ones entrusted with the dagger." Travis scrutinized Craig and Walter as if insinuating they weren't capable of keeping a bag of nails safe, much less an enchanted, monster-making dagger.

"I thought the Supreme Pack Rule would keep it," I said. "Isn't that why we're here? To give it to you?"

"Originally," Yura explained, "three families were involved in hunting the hybrids that were first created with the Unholy Vessel. They made sure to track and kill every single one of them, and afterward, hid the vessel and kept its secret. Those three families are represented here. The Ericksons, Knights and Crosses."

"So?" I demanded, then cringed at my tone. I'd sounded like an angry kindergartner, who didn't understand why she couldn't have more tater tots. Of all those present, I was the one who knew the least about the werewolf world and how it functioned, so I had no business opening my mouth unless I wanted them to treat me like a Stale on crack. No one listens to them.

"So, my dear—" Travis opened his mouth to explain, but I cut him off.

"I'm not your dear," I growled under my breath, throwing visual daggers in his direction.

He rolled his eyes and went on. "So… the responsibility falls back on the same families. The Supreme Pack Rule is nothing but a group similar to this. Just because they are members of a higher organization doesn't mean they're more capable or better equipped to take care of the dagger and keep it from falling into malicious hands again." He glanced pointedly at Ulfen, who suddenly had enough of Travis's posturing.

Ulfen's chair scraped the stone floor as the bear of a man stood abruptly, his entire body trembling with rage. I panicked, thinking of the moratorium we had vowed, and glanced at Yura, wondering what she would do.

What recourse would she have against someone breaking the rules? Would she kick Ulfen out? Would she open a secret door underneath him to have him plunge into a pit full of vipers? Would she pull out a magic sword that cut rabid werewolves in half?

I watched with my heart in my throat and was very surprised when Yura's attention turned to Travis rather than Ulfen.

"You dishonor Wolfskeep with your behavior, Travis Hillworth. You repeatedly point out the worthlessness of your word every time you disregard your vow to a moratorium." She turned to Ulfen then. "I admire your patience and restraint. They speak of true character." She dipped her chin respectfully.

Ouch. Talk about kicking someone's ass with diplomacy.

It was Travis's turn to fume. He went red all over, the color rising from his neck and climbing all the way up to his hairline, like mercury inside an old thermometer. I almost laughed except I figured that would count as disrespecting my vow, too, and I didn't want to attract Yura's attention and get her whiplash tongue wagging in my direction.

Ulfen composed himself by pacing the length of the room a few times. When he was in control once more, he sat back down and exhaled.

"I suggest that Eric Cross keeps the dagger," Ulfen offered, getting the meeting back on track.

Or not.

Because Walter, Craig, and Travis protested in unison.

"That is not an option."

"No way."

"He's not even part of the Pack Rule anymore."

Through all the angry objections, Eric remained calm, rubbing his chin as he'd been doing for the last ten minutes. When everyone finally went silent—though instead of screaming, they were now glaring at him—Eric crossed his arms and replied with a simple word.

"No."

All the tension left the room like teens at the end of a school day.

I waited for Eric to offer some sort of explanation, but he gave none. The last few days protecting the dagger had felt like waiting for a box of C-4 to explode right in our faces, so I couldn't blame him for refusing to take care of the thing. I also wanted it as far away from me as possible. There was no way I could go back to Rosalina with the news that the stupid thing was still part of our repertoire of problems. *No way!*

"At least there's some sense left in him," Travis said, then, realizing he was being an asshole again, blinked rapidly and shut his mouth.

"Given the circumstances and all the variables," Yura said, "it seems the only two options available for protecting the dagger are Craig Blackridge and Walter Knight."

Travis opened his mouth to protest, but Yura lifted a finger, effectively silencing him as if she possessed some sort of magic that could muffle insolent, spoiled men-children. I wondered if she would tell me her secret if I asked.

"I feel that the less people who know of its location, the better. We live in different times than when it was originally hidden. It cannot be buried or placed somewhere that appears inaccessible. These days, nothing is off-limits to anyone—not even the depths of the ocean. Therefore, I believe it should be kept under guard and protected by more modern means. Would you agree?"

I found myself nodding. I could easily imagine a group of miners or oil diggers stumbling onto the dagger in some Canadian tundra that no one ever thought would be disturbed. I could also picture them fighting over it, arguing over who should appear on the news announcing the finding, and who should receive the money once it was auctioned to the highest bidder, some starched-up old man with a huge collection of things that didn't belong to him. I could also imagine how quickly someone like Stephen Erickson or Bernadetta Fiore would come to relieve him of his new acquisition.

"I agree," Ulfen declared, surprising me and even Travis at his side. His ally frowned at Ulfen as if asking *are you stupid?* But Ulfen avoided eye contact with Travis and said nothing more.

I felt I understood his decision. I imagined he didn't want Stephen coming after him, demanding to be given the dagger and causing a confrontation that would not bode well. It had to be hard for him, to trust the object his son most desired toward those who would readily kill Stephen. But wouldn't it be infinitely harder to find himself with the choice of murdering his own son or capturing him to face a trial that would surely lead to his death?

I swallowed the lump that rose to my throat. I felt for Ulfen. I didn't want the man to suffer, but I couldn't forgive Stephen either. Emotions warred inside my chest, and I hated the way I felt, torn.

"Very well." Yura rose from her chair, reached forward, and picked up the dagger. "Craig and Walter, please, follow me." She walked out of the room without waiting for them.

Huh? Where are they going? I sent my question across the room toward Jake via a frown. He shrugged and shook his head to let me know he knew as little as I did.

Craig and Walter followed Yura out of the room. The door closed behind them and silence fell over the room. Two minutes later they were back. The dagger was not in Yura's hand anymore, and the two men walking behind her maintained serious expressions that gave nothing away.

I nodded appreciatively. One of them had the dagger, but we didn't know which one. And what if Yura had kept it? That would be clever, wouldn't it? I peered at their faces, trying to spot the smallest giveaway, but I saw nothing to indicate who was now in possession of the dangerous relic. I wondered if I would have the ability to keep such a tight poker face.

Nah, I can't even act innocent when I get into Mom's desserts before anyone else.

"I believe there is one more thing to discuss," Yura said once she was back on her chair, her tattooed hands folded neatly in front of her.

Ulfen seemed to shake himself as we moved away from the topic of the dagger and turned to other things. "Yes, we need to figure out a way to get rhabo off our streets, and we need to prepare for war."

CHAPTER 10

Well after midnight, Jake was walking beside me, quiet and pensive. His strong, tall presence made me feel confident as I climbed the steps toward my condo, located on the second floor of the building. I had refused to go back to Eric's place.

Without the dagger in our possession, I doubted our enemies would bother to come after us anymore. Everyone had made sure to publicize to their packs that the meeting was taking place. So, no doubt, the knowledge had reached Bernadetta and Stephen, and they'd already deduced that the dagger was gone and the packs were organizing against them.

Jake and I had bypassed the elevator, tired of being confined in windowless spaces. We had made it back from Wolfskeep inside of the same delivery van, and the ride had left both of us in a bad mood.

Though honestly, being trapped in the dark, enduring motion

sickness, was a treat compared to the five-hour-long discussion we'd endured after the business with the dagger had been taken care of.

It had been like pulling teeth… out of dinosaurs. It was a wonder the four alphas had agreed to anything, and it would be a wonder if they succeeded in ridding St. Louis of the awful drug and threat.

Unsurprisingly, Travis had been of the mind that we should let rhabo cleanse the city of all the vampires. Though, with Ulfen as his ally, he couldn't get any traction on the idea.

"The city has been prosperous for our packs," Ulfen had said. "Before rhabo, it ran like a well-oiled machine. The drug may very well only affect vampires, but they aren't the only ones who are dying. Scrimmages between our kind and the blood suckers pop up everywhere, and many of us are suffering. I've lost several members of my pack already as I'm sure you have. My club was attacked last week, and suffered considerable property damage."

In the end, they'd agreed that training and cooperation among the packs should be intensified. Apparently, pack members in leadership positions, mostly betas, trained together on an ongoing basis, and the packs were always ready for battle. I'd had no idea.

Damn werewolves and their secrecy!

Yura had even suggested that I join one of their training sessions in order to share what I knew about hybrids with them. She thought it would be beneficial. I really didn't want to go, especially since the place where the training was conducted belonged to Travis Hillworth, but she'd asked nicely, and I was unable to say *no*. I'd asked Jake and Eric to go with me, but they both refused—Jake because he had a pack meeting with his grandfather, and Eric because he was a cynical jerk.

"I'm not going anywhere near there, Toni," he'd said. "And you shouldn't either. They won't make you feel welcome. Quite the contrary. You don't have a pack. You don't have tradition and legacy, which is all any of them care about. Take it from someone who has none of those things anymore."

"It can't be that bad," I'd argued, feeling a need to belong with my kind despite my reticence to go.

Eric had shrugged. "It's your call."

On the way back, I'd asked Jake if his grandfather had been given the dagger, but he said Walter didn't even mention it and that he was as clueless as me. I was just glad to be rid of it, though I leaned toward hoping Walter was not the one guarding it. He was too ambitious. If he had it, all I could hope for was that he respected his kind enough not to feed them vampire-tainted blood.

When Jake and I stopped by the front door of my condo, he grabbed my wrist as I keyed the lock. He cocked his ear as if he'd heard something inside. I did the same, my heart leaping and knocking hard against my chest. I heard nothing and gave Jake a questioning look.

"What?" I mouthed.

"Just being cautious."

"Mom's protection spells are still in place." She'd come over as soon as she recovered from Blake's attack and cast some heavy-duty spells on my place. Some of her best work, she'd said. I knew no one had broken in because the doorknob was still pewter-colored. It was magicked to turn brassy if someone forced entry, a subtle change that would go unnoticed by those who didn't know how the spells worked.

Besides, my ears and sniffer weren't detecting anything unusual.

Jake nodded, his clear eyes scanning the corridor. He seemed ready for vampires, hybrids, Teenage Mutant Ninja Turtles, anything to attack.

He was still on edge and so was I. These last few days had been stressful, to say the least.

I unlocked the door and walked into my place. It was still pretty empty with barely any furniture and decorations. Jake closed the door behind him, removed his jacket, and seemed to relax, if only minimally.

He stood there, looking pensive.

I put a hand on his arm. "What is it?"

"Why did you say you're in… Eric's pack?"

I did a double-take. That was not what I'd expected. "I dunno." But that wasn't true. I did know. It was a feeling in my chest, nothing I could put into words, though it maybe meant nothing since it wasn't official or reciprocated. Eric didn't want a pack. "I just… felt he needed my support. They were being such assholes to him." I narrowed my eyes. "You're not jealous, are you?"

"No, no, nothing like that."

"Good."

"I just… always felt like you and I… you know..."

Butterflies did jumping jacks in my stomach. If we were able to be together, I'd figured I would join his pack, though he'd never brought it up like this.

"Of course you and I…" I let the words hand like he had, then added, "but that doesn't mean we can't let Eric join."

"That would never work. He's an alpha."

"I'm an alpha, too."

He looked confused as if this was too much to process and maybe it was—at least at the moment. Content with leaving it at that, I marched toward the kitchen where I kept Cupid's fishbowl. He was probably starving.

As soon as I crossed the threshold, a slightly decaying scent entered my nose. I stopped in my tracks, my eyes homing in on the murky water that now filled his little home.

"No!" I exclaimed in a strangled cry, turned on my heel, and buried my face in Jake's chest, who now stood right behind me.

"What is it?!" he asked in a panic.

"He's dead," I hiccuped, tears streaming down my eyes.

Jake rubbed my back and rested his cheek on the top of my

head. "It's not your fault."

"Of course it's my fault."

"No. As callous as it may sound, he's also to blame."

I pulled away and glared at him. Was he crazy?! How could he blame Cupid? He'd been a helpless little creature, and I'd failed to take care of him.

He laid a hand on my cheek. "He created rhabo, Toni."

Oh, God!

I scrunched up my face and cried more fiercely, balling Jake's shirt in my hands. My reaction was hysterical, I knew it, but I couldn't help it. It was all too much, and it all seemed to hit me at once as if I'd been holding up a dam, and it'd finally cracked open.

Damien was dead.

Cupid was dead.

My business was going to shit.

My city was going to shit.

And, on top of that, we had to watch our backs, worry about being murdered by Bernadetta and Stephen's minions, including an uncertain number of hybrids and a Midnight Witch.

"It'll be okay," Jake crooned, hugging me and rocking from side to side. "Shh, everything will go back to normal. We're rid of the dagger, and all the alphas are finally in agreement. We will get rhabo off the streets and fight whatever they throw at us. They won't get away with this."

Jake held me, whispering comforting words until my tears stopped. I hadn't been able to mourn Damien, and it had finally caught up with me. Stepping back, he peered into my face, his expression tender and full of love. He smoothed my hair, pushing away a few strands that had stuck to my cheek.

I wanted to kiss him, find comfort in the warmth of his lips, in the silk-soft brush of that tender caress, but I knew he wouldn't kiss me back, and that broke my heart a little more. I understood and respected his decision, but I still needed him so badly.

Sniffling, I pushed away from him, breaking free from the circle of his strong arms.

"We have to bury him," I said.

Jake's shoulders sank, and it was clear by his mortified expression that he thought the stress had finally unhinged my brain. I was too tired to clarify things, so I stepped up to Cupid's bowl and let my actions speak for themselves. From a kitchen drawer, I pulled out an aquarium net and scooped Cupid's limp little body out of the murky water.

"Oh," Jake said behind me, finally understanding.

Cupid's once beautiful blue fins and tail were colorless and slack. His beady black eyes were cloudy and void of life. From another drawer stashed with sweets, I pulled out a box of Milk Duds, dumped out the candy on the counter, and deposited Cupid inside with the utmost care.

Jake pressed a hand to my shoulder. "We'll find a good place for him."

There was no mockery in his tone, and he didn't try to tell me not to be silly or that he would get me another fish. I loved him for that, for understanding that care isn't measured by the size of the recipient or by what others may consider deserved or befitting, that love is a personal thing, calculated by the beholder and guided by no rules.

I carried the box in both hands, careful not to jostle it. Jake opened the front door and followed me outside, raising no objections to our safety or the late hour. When I got in my Camaro, he only asked, "Where to?" and drove.

Ten minutes later, we pulled up to Mom's house. All lights were off, except for a solitary porch light. I imagined her and my sister, Lucia, sleeping placidly on their beds.

This was home, the only place that had felt right for Cupid since some of our earlier pets were buried there. My condo still felt new and somehow temporary. Besides, a flower bed on the side of the building, surrounded by concrete and overlooked by a busy street, didn't seem enough for him. This was a much better place.

We found a spot in the back of the house where supple, dark soil hosted thick ferns. Jake dug a hole with his bare hand and stepped aside. I knelt on the grass, gently placed the box in, then brushed dirt over the hole to cover it. I stood, dusting my hands.

"He died because I wasn't there," I said. "Because circumstances kept me away. He was good. Quiet and aloof, but that was his nature. He shouldn't have died, shouldn't have left us. I wish he was still here."

"We will avenge him," Jake said.

At some point, I had stopped talking about Cupid and thought only of Damien, and Jake knew it. I glanced up at him. His face was bathed in moonlight, the golden-brown stubble on his jaw shining with it, his eyes intense and full of intent.

I nodded once, glad he felt as I did, even if he hadn't known Damien well. "We will," I repeated. "We will."

CHAPTER 11

The next morning at 7 AM, I pulled my Camaro into an empty parking spot and sat in front of a group of low, spread-out buildings. The name of the place was *Packmind*, and it was the facility where the beta leaders trained to keep ready for battle. There, they learned the city's alphas' common goals. After that, each beta went on to train their respective troops separately. It was how all packs kept a line of communication down to their lower members.

For a moment, my eyes roved over the place. It looked like some sort of fancy sports complex or country club. The buildings were all straight lines and glass with perfect flower beds surrounding them. Trees kept the area hidden from the road, and from the looks of it, there were plenty of outdoor training opportunities on several manicured fields and courts.

I fidgeted with the keychain still hanging from the ignition, wondering if I should go in.

Eric's words still rang in my ears. *"They won't make you feel welcome. Quite the contrary. You don't have a pack. You don't have tradition and legacy, which is all any of them care about. Take it from someone who has none of those things anymore."*

I was tempted to restart the car and tear out of there, but that wouldn't do—not when Jake was expected to become alpha, and I hoped to be by his side at some point. If I wanted to do that, I had to become a proper werewolf. I had to belong, to learn their… *our*… ways.

And not only that, this was about saving my city and ensuring the people I loved could live here safely.

Strengthening my resolve and rolling my neck to relax my nerves, I made up my mind. I was going in there.

At the glass doors, my reflection showed a sporty figure. Yoga pants, a tight tank top, and comfortable tennis shoes constituted my outfit—the same clothes I wore while training with Eric.

I took a deep breath, pulled the door handle, and walked in. A blond guard with a thick beard sat at a slick metal counter, his attention quickly snapping from an array of computer monitors to me. His nose flared as he took in my scent. Mine did the same and told me that he was a werewolf, too. He wore a uniform with black pants, a blue shirt, and a patch sewed on the right shoulder that read *Packmind - Hillworth Enterprises.*

"May I help you," he asked in an unfriendly tone.

There was a turnstile to the left of the counter, and it seemed a card was needed to gain access—something no one had bothered to tell me.

"Hi," I said, trying to sound chipper, "I'm here to… train."

Witchlights, I sounded positively clueless.

He raised a blond eyebrow, glanced at a clipboard, and pretended to read it. I knew he was pretending because the piece of paper was blank. *The jackass!*

"No one told me about any *visitors*," he pronounced the word with a tone that let me know visitors weren't welcome. The place definitely had the air of an exclusive club, where people thought their farts didn't stink, but that was only because they spent a shitload of money in potpourri and hid it everywhere.

"Travis Hillworth knows I'm supposed to visit today." I almost choked at using that buttwipe's name as a "pass go" card.

Suddenly, my skin started itching, and my back muscles tightened uncomfortably. I rolled them once, trying to relax. This situation and this guy were starting to piss me off.

"Then he should have called," the guard sneered.

I took a step closer, and this time my words came out through clenched teeth, my anger vibrating in the air. "Maybe, your computer will say something."

The guard frowned, then sniffed the air, slightly lifting his nose. The unfriendly quality of his stare gradually changed. Becoming flustered, he turned to the computer and quickly typed something.

"Um, nothing here either." He didn't sound uppity and hostile this time. Instead, he sounded apologetic, ready to do whatever it took to make sure I was admitted. "Let me make a phone call and see what I can do, ma'am."

Ma'am? Huh? What the hell? He'd sniffed me and done a one-eighty. Was it my new perfume? Rosalina had given it to me, and she had a knack for picking that sort of thing. She said a fragrance had to convey your personality. Maybe it was telling him I was a badass. But who was I kidding? That wasn't it, and I had no idea what had caused him to change his tune.

The guard explained my presence to whoever he'd reached over the phone. "Yes, sir. I'll hold." He pointed at the phone and gave me a downright charming smile. I jutted my hip out.

That's right, asshole. That's how you're supposed to treat people. With decency.

After a short wait, I heard the person over the phone say, "I have confirmed with Mr. Hillworth's assistant. He says to allow her in. Do check her ID. Her name is Antonietta Sunder."

Before the guard hung up, I'd pulled out my license and placed it on the counter right under his nose. I forced a smile and cocked my head to one side, waiting for him to verify. He gave it a quick glance and slid it back in my direction.

"Sorry for the inconvenience, I have strict instructions to only allow members in, especially these days. They say it's because of the unrest. The place has sure been busy with everyone gearing up for what's to come."

I put away my ID and allowed my frustration to wash away. Maybe the guy had only been doing his job. Maybe everyone's tempers were on edge.

"Here you go." The guard handed me a plastic card with a clip attached to it. "Just wave it at the reader in the turnstile."

"Thank you. Have a good day." I waved, my voice pleasant and not in a fake way. I couldn't expect to be treated with decency if I didn't do the same.

As I walked toward the turnstile, a guy walked into the building, striding confidently and pulling out a wallet from his back pocket. He was tall and slender, though not in a wiry way. He had shoulder-length dirty blond hair and appeared to be about my age, perhaps a little older. He wore a pair of sweats, a sleeveless shirt, and expensive tennis shoes.

"Morning, Roger." He gave the guard a military salute and gave me a quick nod of acknowledgement.

"Good morning, Mr. Hillworth."

I halted in my tracks, tensing all over. *Mr. Hillworth?* What relation was he to Travis? My heart quickened.

He stopped a few paces from the turnstile and said, "Ladies first."

"Um, thank you." I waved the card over the security device and hurried toward the elevators as the arm lifted out of the way.

He followed behind me and pressed the up arrow—the only

one available—while I read the directory attached to the wall. There were three floors, which seemed to be filled with offices and conference rooms. Before I could figure out where to go, the guy spoke.

"Where are you headed?"

"Um, the training facility," I said, glancing at him sideways, trying to find any resemblance between him and my biological father. But this guy was blond and not as tall as Travis.

"Oh, we're headed to the same place." He smiled. "It's on the third floor. The rest of the building is mostly offices and such."

"Thank you."

The elevator doors dinged and slid open. We stepped in, and he pressed the *three* button.

"I've never seen you around," he said, inhaling, taking in my scent. "My name is Marcus Hillworth."

"I'm Antonietta Sunder, but everyone calls me Toni."

"Nice to meet you."

Unable to help myself, I said, "Any relation to Travis Hillworth?"

"Yeah, he's my dad."

I almost thumped on my chest to stop myself from choking. This guy was my half-brother.

Shit! Shit shit shit.

Suddenly, the elevator turned claustrophobic, and I was on the verge of attacking the metal doors to make my way out of there. It wouldn't matter if I had to jump down the elevator shaft, but I would get out.

God, why did I come?!

Slowly, Marcus took a step away from me, nearly pressing his back to the wall. His gaze fell to the floor, and he also seemed ready to claw the doors open. This made me do a double-take.

"I take it you know my father," he said nervously.

I blinked in confusion. Marcus was acting scared of me, the

same way the guard had. Why?! What kind of vibe were they picking up from me to get so—

A thought occurred to me.

Surreptitiously, I sniffed myself, trying to pinpoint a difference in my scent. It was hard—everyone is used to their own scent—but as I made an effort, I picked up a bitter hint that made me realize I was giving off angry alpha vibes, the same kind I would sometimes pick up from Jake, though not since he'd left to go to New Orleans.

Witchlights! Eric had warned me about this. He'd said he'd never detected the scent from me and thought that I had an innate ability to control it, but obviously, I didn't. It seemed it was yet another new attribute of my developing *werewolfness,* and it had decided to make an appearance at the wrong moment.

Eric had explained that it could affect others, and it was affecting Marcus.

Does this mean I outrank him?

I struggled to get my emotions under control. I had no business walking in here, giving off the wrong vibes. Yes, I was an alpha, but that didn't mean I had real power—not when it came to packs with proper leadership, which was exactly what this place was all about.

The elevator doors dinged and slid open. Marcus stood in one corner, waiting for me to exit. I stepped out, and he followed promptly, looking glad to be out of the cramped space.

"I do know your father," I said. "But I just met him recently, and he invited me here. I'm… new to the werewolf scene here in St. Louis." I had no idea how else to explain my situation. I honestly didn't want everyone knowing that, in terms of being a werewolf, I was in diapers. "I'm a bit nervous," I added, hoping that would explain my dominant vibes.

"I see." He seemed to relax, to see that I had no intention of exerting my *alphaness* on him. "I would like to say you have no reason to be nervous, but I would be lying. It's the nature of what we are, I suppose. But I'll introduce you. C'mon, follow me."

He guided me past the elevators and down a narrow hall. Grunts, soles squeaking against the floor, thuds, frustrated growls, and even curses came through a set of double doors, letting us know that everyone was already hard at work.

As we prepared to walk in, I took a deep breath and hoped I wasn't making a mistake.

CHAPTER 12

We stepped into a large open area as wide as the building itself. It had slick hardwood floors like a high school gym and was illuminated by harsh fluorescent lights. The windows on the far end were covered by hanging blinds that swung from side to side under the blasting current of the air conditioner. Despite that, the temperature here was a few degrees warmer than in the corridor.

At first, everyone continued doing what they were doing, which amounted to one-on-one combat. About fifty people were arranged in couples. They circled each other in a crouch, displaying claws and sharp teeth as they searched for an opening to attack. My eyes snapped to one of the couples as a wiry man dressed in nothing but basketball shorts propelled himself toward his opponent, intent on murder.

Said opponent, a man twice his size, attempted to get out of the way, but was too slow and, somehow, ended up on the floor with the smaller man's legs wrapped around his neck and a pointed claw aimed at one of his eyes.

"Do you yield?" the wiry man demanded.

The large man growled and slapped his open palm against the floor, and he was released. I was so taken by the display, that I didn't notice people were starting to pause and glance in my direction. Noses twitched. Eyebrows furrowed, and, this time, I didn't have to smell myself to know I was giving off heavy alpha vibes.

Great, Toni. Just great! Way to make friends. Just show up and signal that you mean to control everyone. The only thing that needed controlling here was my messed-up *alphaness*.

I scanned the crowd and, to my dismay, discovered that Allison Blackridge was there. She looked like Fitness Barbie in a baby blue bodysuit and matching headband holding back her blond hair. She struck a pose and gave me a raised eyebrow. I dug half-moons into my palms, using the pain to refocus my indignation and anger at my own stupidity. I should've figured she would be here.

A woman dressed in black lycra pants and sports bra peeled away from the group and approached us. Her professionally highlighted blond hair swung behind her in a tight ponytail. She was about my height, 5'7", and moved with a confident air.

"You're late," she told Marcus, then eyed me distrustfully.

Marcus shrugged. "Sorry, Olivia. I tried to be here early, but Dad kept me."

Wait, what? I glanced between them and quickly saw the resemblance. I'd read online that Travis also had a daughter, and here she was.

"Friend of yours?" Olivia asked, inclining her head in my direction.

My instincts flared with hostility. I tried to fight them back, but it seemed the harder I tried, the worse they got. How the hell was I supposed to function among my kind? And why, all of a sudden, was this happening? It wasn't as if I hadn't been among werewolves before. I'd been all right at Wolfskeep. Except… my wolf was still settling, and maybe I was too used to being around other alphas.

Shit! When will all these changes be over?!

Marcus shook his head and stepped away, sidling toward his sister. "Nope, I just met her outside." He didn't look intimidated anymore, not the way he had in the elevator. On the contrary, he was standing straighter and looking rather cocky.

My gaze roved around the room, noticing how all the others were slowly inching closer. I took a trembling breath, willing myself to calm down, begging my human side to prevail over my wilder instincts.

Like a fool, I waved the access card in front of me. "The Pack Rule said I should come."

They all looked at me as if I'd sprouted an extra eye. I resisted the urge to touch my forehead to check if I'd shifted into a cyclops. I glanced toward the exit, wondering if I should run. My wolf bristled at the idea, informing me that no self-respecting alpha would do such a thing. Human Toni disagreed.

"She's not in the Erickson pack." The wiry guy who had tackled the giant to the floor stepped forward. "That I know of."

"Or the Blackridge pack," Allison said, her gaze assessing me with care.

I opened my mouth to say something, but Olivia beat me to it.

"Are you Toni Sunder?"

Hearing my name on her lips surprised me enough to give me pause.

Marcus answered for me. "Yeah, that's how she introduced herself."

Olivia's demeanor suddenly changed and she moved closer, offering her hand. "My father told me about you. My name is Olivia Hillworth. I forgot he mentioned you might come today."

Shocked into speechlessness, I shook her hand with the agility of a trained robot. A jolt of something seemed to pass through me as I touched her, my half-sister. After meeting Travis and feeling nothing but utter indifference toward him, it never occurred to me that it might be different with other members of his family. My family?

I shuddered with disgust.

No! I only had one family. And it certainly didn't include these two.

"I'm glad to have you here," Olivia said, shocking me further with her civility. "Father said you've seen the hybrids."

Murmurs ran through all those present, their faces turning curious.

"I have." I took a step back, doing my best to compose myself.

"Please," she entreated me, "you have to tell us about them." She waved a hand to usher me further into the room. "Line up everyone," she instructed.

Quickly, everyone formed rows like good little students ready for a lesson—Allison in the front, still evaluating me.

Well, this certainly took a turn.

I stood in front of the bunch, feeling self-conscious, wanting nothing more than to march out and never come back. It took a ton of willpower to get my dominant instincts under control and share what I knew about the hybrids. Everyone listened attentively, without interruption while I trudged through the details like a kid at a new school.

I wanted the floor to split open and the earth to suck me right into its smoldering core, but no such luck. At least, they didn't know me well enough to figure out what a mess I was at the moment. Meeting my half-siblings had really screwed up my cool. As first impressions went, they would probably peg me for a stuttering halfwit. But who cared? I was never coming back here.

When I finished, Olivia blinked and shook herself, looking a little pale. "Thank you. That was incredibly detailed and eye-opening."

Huh? Really?!

I had no recollection of what I'd said, but apparently, I'd done a good job explaining how scared *shitless* they should be. Maybe being nervous had actually helped.

"They sound tough," the giant of a man that had been tackled to the floor said. "What do you think would be the best way to kill them?"

A sensory overload delivered with your bare hands seemed to work the best. Though, of course, I didn't tell them about this method and the hybrid I'd killed with it.

"Well," I said instead, "bullets will take them down, but they should be of a high caliber and aimed at vital organs. After that…" I ran a finger across my throat, unwilling to say the words out loud.

No one seemed squeamish or surprised by the suggestion. A few just nodded as if we were talking about pruning roses.

The wiry guy elbowed the giant at his side. "And we should burn them afterward to make sure they're really, really dead."

"This is very useful information. Thank you," Olivia said. "We will adjust our training to take into account what you've told us. Normally, we don't use firearms—we don't need them when we're in the field—but it seems, this time around, guns *and* swords are in order."

Everyone nodded their agreement.

"My father mentioned you might train with us?" She looked me up and down, making me feel like I didn't belong, like they were above me. Travis had likely told her I was a lone wolf, a pariah without a pack. Of course, she thought I was a *nothing*. Cleverly, she disguised her silent assessment of me by saying, "it seems you're dressed for the occasion."

This time my alpha rage seemed to surge all at once, causing Olivia and Marcus to look intimidated for an instant. However, they quickly rearranged their features into something fierce and confident and, subtly, took twin stances that suggested they knew how to rely on each other.

I had people like that in my life, no doubt about it. But they couldn't help me here, not with my kind. Among these people, I was an outsider.

If I'd been thinking properly, I would've said I wasn't there to train, that I'd only come to share what I knew, but Red took over, and, with her at the wheel, there was no backing down.

"Yes. I'd love that." I rolled my shoulders, all nervousness gone.

"Are you sure that's wise? I heard you grew up somewhat… apart from pack life," Olivia jabbed, raising her voice to make sure the message traveled throughout the room.

Murmurs went back and forth as everyone made spiteful comments.

"What? Was she raised by humans?" the wiry man asked, flipping the Stale joke around since they thought that anyone who was a bit strange must've been raised by werewolves.

"As a matter of fact, I was," I said, lifting my chin and daring anyone to continue laughing.

The effect was immediate, especially among those I bothered to look straight in the eye. Their grins froze, then slowly fell away. They might feel stronger than me as a pack, but individually, my alpha superiority rattled their instincts. Almost imperceptibly, they seemed to inch toward each other, forming a tighter group.

"Untrained, huh?" Olivia's brother said. "I think my sister could take ya."

I scanned him up and down and offered him a twisted grin. "Nice of you to offer up your sister."

He bristled a little, but in the end, he simply shrugged. "I'm a gentleman. It would be impolite to fight a woman. At least until we've assessed your abilities."

Olivia gave her brother an irritated glower, then proceeded to size me up. I crossed my arms and bore her scrutiny with cool detachment. She was clearly trying to decide whether or not I was an easy opponent or someone who would end up embarrassing her in front of her flock. After a few beats, she flipped her hair in a careless gesture.

"Sure, if she wants to. I should warn you, though. I'm proficient in several martial arts. I have trained since I was five years old."

Marcus smirked. "Our father insisted on it."

"You're not the only ones," the wiry guy said, obviously feeling left out and making me realize that fighting skills in werewolf packs were more important than I'd realized.

This should have sobered me up. I had no such training, nothing beyond a little kickboxing and a few lessons with Eric. But Red was chomping at the bit, eager to test herself against this bunch, against her half-sister.

"There are a couple of rules," Olivia said, ticking them down with one hand. "No shifting and no lording."

Lording, the act of alpha shifters showing their superiority and trying to dominate others through instincts that lesser kin couldn't deny. Eric had used that name before, but I'd forgotten it.

This second rule should've been my second cue to decline such foolishness, but Red was beyond any reason, and as much as I thought I'd learned to control her, it turned out, I'd made little progress.

The next thing I knew, I was shaking my arms and circling around Olivia. She and I seemed well-matched in height and physique, much more than Lucia and Daniella were with me. My younger sister was taller, and although Daniella was my same height, she was slight, much thinner. She ate too many damn salads, I always told her. To which she argued that healers didn't need muscles. She didn't believe in exercise, not in the least.

Olivia crouched and started circling me, too. Everyone else

stepped aside, forming a ring around us. She waited, a stupid little smirk on her face. My anger spiked, but I managed to keep my alpha powers contained, if only because I really wanted to put this haughty rich girl in her place in the proper way.

She feigned an attack, stamping a foot forward. I flinched, and she laughed, sending my anger way past the red zone. I launched without thinking. With ease, as if she were handling a child, Olivia gracefully stepped out of the way, took hold of my arm, and twisted it back. My elbow screamed in pain, ready to snap. I eased the pressure by falling to my knees.

"*Phaw!*" The wiry man exclaimed. "That was anticlimactic."

He moved away and so did the others, returning to their sparring, their interest in me completely lost. Allison was the last to turn away, a half-sympathetic expression shaping her features.

Olivia let me go and took a step back, her smirk much deeper than it had been a second ago. I seethed with anger and trembled as I knelt on the polished floor.

You don't have to take this, Red growled inside my head. *You can command her. You can make her grovel at your feet.*

A tingling feeling rushed through my body, and I rose to my feet in the blink of an eye. One moment, I was kneeling on the floor, and the next I was standing, swaying a little.

Olivia and Marcus's eyes widened.

I shook my head, feeling dizzy. Since the day Red had been unleashed, I'd been able to move faster than any Stale, but this was something different. Eric had shown me he could move like this. He said it was something alphas could do—but not all of them, only the stronger ones.

I was so shocked by what I'd just done that my anger fizzled out and a smile stretched my lips. I glanced up. Olivia's face was contorted as if she'd sucked on a giant lemon.

"*Fleeting,*" Marcus said, a note of wonder in his voice.

Olivia glared at him. He closed his mouth and tried to look

unimpressed.

I cracked my neck and shook my hands, relaxing, my mind occupied by better things than anger. "I think… I think I'm in the wrong place. I won't learn what I need here."

"You've got nerve saying that after I put you on the ground in under five seconds," Olivia sneered.

"That you did, but once I master the skills that matter, no amount of *martial arts* will be able to help you."

She let out a little gasp of outrage, but I didn't linger to take satisfaction in it. I had to get back to Eric. I had to apologize and let him turn me into the alpha I needed to be.

ഌശ

Eric glared up at me from the desk in his study. "It seems I might have made a mistake giving you the security code to get in."

From Packmind, I had driven here directly, excited to tell him that I could *fleet*, but maybe I'd caught him at a bad time. It didn't matter. Once I told him what had happened he would jump for joy, or whatever Eric's equivalent was.

"I did it," I said.

He set his pen down and steepled his fingers, frowning.

"I did it. I was able to fleet."

He made a sound in the back of his throat, picked his pen back up, and returned his attention to the journal in front of him.

Huh? Had he heard me? I was about to make a smartass comment about his need for a hearing aid, but instead, I bit my lower lip and thought better of it. It wouldn't pay off to piss him off. So even though it went against my grain, I groveled.

"You were right. Going to Packmind was mostly a waste of time."

Eric's pen stopped on the paper, but he didn't look up.

At least I had his attention. I went on. "I don't know why I thought I needed to go. It was stupid. At first, I thought it would be okay. They seemed interested while I told them about the hybrids. Of course, it didn't help that I started giving alpha vibes, and I couldn't control them."

Eric still didn't say anything, but I didn't care. I was past groveling and had moved on to feeling sorry for myself.

I turned away from him and walked to one of the bookshelves, pretending to read the titles on the spines. Instead, I was remembering Olivia's face and that irritating smirk of distaste.

"I met Travis's kids," I said, the words coming out choppy. I didn't really want to talk about this with Eric, but I knew Rosalina couldn't quite understand, and Jake… well, he wasn't packless like Eric. "I wish someone had told me they were going to be there."

"I had no idea," he said. "You know I haven't cared about the goings-on of the St. Louis elite packs for a long while. You might've guessed yourself, though. The facility does belong to Travis, after all. I just figured you were some sort of glutton for punishment."

I faced him, my narrowed eyes homing in on him. "It seems that way. I'm here, ain't I?"

He chuckled, then sobered after a beat. "Perhaps, I didn't insist more on you not going there because I wanted you to see firsthand how it is with the packs. They're not gonna make way for you, Toni. Not going to welcome you with open arms. You're either pack or a rival."

A thick silence hung between us. I hated to admit he was right. The packs weren't all about pink clouds and unicorns. They seemed to be more about blond bitches and badassery.

"It gets easier. With time," he said helpfully.

Was I destined to be a lone wolf? If Jake and I never managed to be together, what would happen? I couldn't see myself loving anyone else, raising a family with someone other than him. And though I had Mom, my sisters, my brother, and Rosalina, there was still that niggling wish to belong, a void I knew nothing else could fill.

I fought the hopelessness that descended over me. There was no way of knowing what the future would hold, and Jake and I weren't giving up. If I had him, I wouldn't need anyone else. He and I would be our own pack, and when children came, then our pack would grow in the only way that mattered.

So I didn't argue with Eric. I didn't tell him again that I wanted to belong, even though I did. Desperately.

Instead, I appealed to Red's pride.

They don't want you, Red, but that doesn't matter. You don't need them. *You are better than them. We'll find our own way. We'll make our own pack.*

I felt her absorbing this, becoming determined to show them up sooner or later, and it seemed to be enough. Finally, with her understanding, I was able to nod to Eric.

"I will be here tomorrow at 4 AM. I'm ready to learn."

"No. Not here. At Damien's place."

What? I opened my mouth to ask why there, but he'd already gone back to writing, dismissing me.

This should be interesting, and I was more than ready.

CHAPTER 13

I hadn't been back to Damien's house since I'd told him and Eric about the unearthing of the Unholy Vessel. As I parked my Camaro under a fluorescent lamp post, I braced myself for any memories that might come at me when I went in.

Damien had saved my life when Blake and Jenson had ambushed Rosalina and me after they destroyed Damien's first rhabo cure. He'd healed my broken bones enough to allow me to shift and trigger my own healing abilities.

And what had I been able to do for him as he lay dying? Nothing. Absolutely nothing except hold his hand as he passed.

Stop it!

I hit my forehead with the heel of my hand. This was exactly what I was supposed to avoid. Why did we have to train here today?

Keeping alert—this area of town wasn't the best to be around at this time of day—I crossed the street and approached Damien's old, five-story mansion. The gargoyles at the top corners of the building seemed to glower as I raised my fist to knock. Before I rapped my knuckles on the wood, the door opened on its own, and an eerie voice spoke, sounding like the cross between a ghost and a monotonous AI.

"Welcome, Antonietta Sunder."

"What the hell?" I murmured as I cautiously walked in, expecting some sort of trap. This was new. The house hadn't welcomed me this way when Damien was alive.

"It's safe. C'mon in," Eric called from the top of the marble staircase to the right. He was standing on the last step, feet shoulder-width apart, fists at his hips. He wore a pair of black shorts and a red T-shirt.

I closed the door behind me and approached the staircase. "What's with the creep show? This place is spooky this early in the morning."

Eric shrugged. "Damien magicked the house to admit his friends."

I barely had time to process my surprise because Eric made a "follow me" gesture with one hand, then disappeared down a corridor without a word. I shook my head and bounded up the steps, taking two at a time until I caught up with him. I had only visited the first floor, so I glanced around curiously, taking in every detail.

Though the first floor had been modernized, the second floor seemed to have been left untouched. I felt transported to the eighteen hundreds, which was when the house had been built. The furniture, the gas sconces on the walls that flickered with what looked like magical flames, the ancient portraits, the crimson-colored worn rug, everything spoke of a different time.

"Why are we here?" I asked, running up to catch up with Eric.

"This place is… special. It will facilitate our training."

"Special?"

I waited for him to elaborate, but he just kept walking further down the long hall until he reached the last door and walked into a room, leaving me standing outside, hesitant to follow. The room was dimly lit, worse than the hall we'd just traversed.

"C'mon, you're wasting time." Eric's voice echoed from inside, sounding far away.

I inched closer to the threshold, my tennis shoes barely in, and peered into what appeared to be an empty room.

"There are mirrors everywhere," Eric said.

Huh? I was about to ask what mirrors when, in the next blink, the place turned into some sort of mirror maze at a fun house.

"What the hell?" I said under my breath.

"Quick," Eric urged. "You need to find me. You only have twenty seconds." As soon as he said this, a huge digital clock appeared on the wall, ticking down the seconds.

20, 19, 18…

I finally stepped inside, the door behind me closed on its own. Panic surged, and I almost turned around and ran out of the room, but I didn't want Eric to make fun of me.

"If you don't find me quickly," Eric's voice called out, "I'm dead."

I sputtered out a nervous laugh. "Don't be melodramatic."

His only answer was his agitated breaths. I cautiously went around one of the many body-length mirrors that stood all around the room. They weren't affixed to the wall. They were framed and freestanding and in a variety of shapes. Ovals, rectangles, oblong, and more. The one in front of me had an elaborate gilded frame with carved flowers and vines. The mirror itself was clouded, old-looking. It reflected my bleary-eyed expression that revealed a hint of panic.

Calm down, Toni, I mouthed, but my own admonishment only managed to send my heart into a quicker pitter-patter.

"Please, Toni. Hurry!" Eric's voice came from behind me in a soft whisper. I whirled around, eyes flicking from left to right, my skin itching.

15, 14, 13 …

"I don't like this, Eric," I said, my mouth moving in a dozen different places, the mirror reflecting my plea back at me.

It's just a game. Just a game. He's trying to trigger your fleeting *skill. Chill!*

"Hurry!" His voice sounded truly scared.

What if he's really in danger?

11, 10, 9 …

Either way, he wanted me to do this fast, so I had to try. I rushed around the room, looking behind all the mirrors and ignoring my own reflection as it tried to fool me. I moved deeper and deeper into the room, my eyes roving all around, trying to catch a glimpse of Eric, but all I found were more mirrors and more panicked-looking Tonis.

7, 6, 5 …

A growl of pain broke through my loud panting. I veered right, following the sound.

"Eric!" I exclaimed when I caught a glimpse of his red shirt on one of the mirrors. I lurched in that direction, then realized it was a reflection so he must be behind me. I whirled, but he wasn't there. Still nothing but a reflection.

4, 3, 2 …

At a loss, I moved closer, pressed a trembling hand to the cool surface. As soon as my fingertips came in contact with it, the reflection disappeared.

"You weren't fast enough," Eric said from behind me.

I froze for a second, then turned slowly to face him.

He stood there, his right hand wrapped around his left forearm. Blood seeped between his fingers. He was bending over and panting.

"What the…? How did you get hurt?"

"You weren't fast enough," he repeated.

I shook my head. "Are you implying that—"

"You *have* to be faster this time." He took a step back and disappeared into one of the mirrors.

I reached a hand out to stop him, but he was already gone. "No!"

The seconds reset on the clock, but only to ten!

10, 9, 8 …

"Find me. Quick!" His voice echoed throughout the room, and this time, there was more than panic in it.

I didn't waste time and started searching for him with the knowledge that I only had a few seconds before… before… I didn't know exactly what, but I had to move quickly.

7, 6, 5 …

Panic suffused me, coursing through my veins like hot venom. My limbs tingled, my vision blurred, and for a second, I thought I would start fleeting, but instead, I only staggered forward and fell to my knees.

4, 3, 2 …

Eric let out another growl of pain. I glanced up and caught his reflection in the mirror to my left. Without hesitation, I flung to the right, my arms out. They wrapped around Eric's legs. Using my weight, I tackled him to the floor.

He fell with a *thud* and a curse.

"I found you," I said.

"You cheated. You need to fleet," was his answer. Though, there was no relish in it, only relief.

He tried to extricate himself, but I held on tightly to his legs. There were two cuts in his forearm now, and blood streaked down to his hand, coating his fingers. Again, he tried to get free from my grip.

"Let go." He shuffled his legs up and down.

"No. Not letting you go." I was feeling a bit irrational, but I didn't give a damn. He wasn't about to disappear inside one of those mirrors again.

"Well, we're not going to lay here on the floor all day, are we?"

"It doesn't sound that bad to me." Better than the alternative. "This *new* training isn't cutting it. I didn't sign up to get traumatized."

"Fine," he said, then lunged to one side and reached for one of the mirrors. As soon as his fingers graced its frame, he was gone.

"No!"

I lay on the floor, hugging the air and blinking at an empty spot between my arms. Cursing, I jumped to my feet. I had half a mind to stomp out of the room and leave his ass to fend for himself. Except I couldn't. Eric didn't mess around. He was always dead serious, and I knew this was no different. I could feel it. He had upped the ante.

And the clock had reset to only five seconds now!

5, 4 …

My first instinct was to start rushing all over the room, looking for him, like I'd done before, but I wasn't a fan of *third time's the charm*, especially not in this case. I couldn't rely on luck. So instead, I closed my eyes, doing my best to recall that tingling feeling that had rushed through my body at Packmind.

Anger had triggered it. Anger at Olivia, at the way she treated me. As soon as I pictured her face inside my mind, that same anger swelled within me.

You little haughty bitch! I found myself thinking, then, the next thing I knew, restless energy burst through my limbs, making my every cell feel as if it was having its own earthquake. My legs and arms started vibrating, and when my eyes sprang open, everything around me seemed fuzzy, like I was seeing it through water. I stared at my hands, flipping them palms up. They looked normal. Next, I lifted my eyes to the clock.

It was broken.

The seconds had stopped ticking. Or had they? I stared in concentration, waiting, waiting, waiting. I scratched my head, counting under my breath. A whole minute passed by. The seconds ticked down from four to three.

Witchlights, I'm doing it. I'm fleeting!

A lethargic voice, like someone speaking from the bottom of a swimming pool, reached my ears.

Was that Eric asking me to hurry up?

Snapping out of it, I rushed around the room on tingling legs, looking into every mirror. I kept glancing toward the clock. I'd checked one half of the room, and it still read three seconds, then I spotted Eric inside a silver-framed mirror.

Fleeting there, I pressed my hand to the glass surface, then whirled around to find Eric standing behind me. He looked like a stone statue, immobile, not even blinking. I shook my head and time went back to normal. The remaining two seconds ticked by in a flash.

Concerned, I scanned Eric's arms and the rest of him. He had endured no additional cuts, and the two on his forearm were already healing. I breathed a sigh of relief.

His mouth tipped to one side with a smirk. "You did it."

Without thinking, I jabbed a hand against his chest and shoved him hard. He staggered backward, his grin disappearing.

"Asshole," I blurted out.

Anger flashed over his features, and I could feel Red gearing up for a fight. But he quickly shook himself and dismissed my assault with a wave of his hand.

"I guess I deserve that," he said. "But it worked, so you can't complain."

I took a few deep breaths, willing Red to relax, to see the benefit in his messed-up scheme.

"It was probably stupid of me to worry." I rubbed my neck. "It wasn't like you were in any real danger."

"Wasn't I?"

I flashed him a dirty look. Unwilling to press him for the truth, I glanced around the room. "What the hell is this place anyway?"

Eric let his gaze travel over the mirrors. "A place of Damien's creation. It can do anything you want it to do. This house… it's suffused with his magic, his essence." A muscle twitched in his jaw. "Go away," he said, sounding disgusted, all of a sudden.

The mirrors disappeared as soon as the words were out of his mouth. I stared in astonishment at the empty room, the walls were covered with black and white toile wallpaper. The baseboards were wide, the floors perfectly polished hardwoods, and the gas sconces imbued with magical warm light.

"Anything I want?" I murmured, striding away from the door, and running my finger along the wall.

Eric made an affirmative sound in the back of his throat.

"Damien," I said without thinking, without knowing exactly what I meant.

A figure materialized in the back of the room. I gasped at the sight of the silken cloak and top hat.

"What the fuck?!" Eric exclaimed, his voice breaking. "What did you do?!"

I shook my head. I hadn't meant to, I had just…

I outstretched a hand in Damien's direction and took a step forward. He stood tall, slender, and impeccably dressed, his blotchy pupils reflecting the light, while his copper-colored irises seemed to glow.

"Is that really you?" I whispered.

Eric growled. "Don't be stupid," he said and stormed out of the room, leaving me behind.

Nervously, I glanced back from Damien to the door, unsure of what to do. Should I go after Eric? Or should I stay here with… a ghost, or whatever this was?

"Um," I struggled with what to say, then, as I stared into

Damien's impassive face, I realized his expression hadn't changed one bit.

"You're not really here."

In answer, he disappeared, gone as quickly as he'd come. My heart clenched as I was reminded that he was really gone, and he was never coming back, no matter how much we willed him to come to us.

Hurriedly, I left the room in search of Eric. I found him sitting at the top of the marble staircase, elbows on knees, eyes staring into nothingness.

I approached, cautiously. "I'm sorry."

He only grunted in answer, but it was enough to let me know he didn't blame me. I sat by his side and heaved a sigh, the grief of Damien's loss eating at me, and stirring my anger and desire for revenge.

"He was my only friend," Eric said. "The only person left who… knew."

I didn't need him to elaborate. I understood. He meant his family. His pain, a pain that despite the years since they'd been murdered didn't seem lessened in the least.

"I know it's not much or nearly the same," I said, "but I can be your friend. I mean… I consider *you* my friend. Losing your family…" I shook my head. "I can't even imagine, but if you ever need anyone to talk to…" I trailed off again. God, I was so bad at this.

"Maybe." He glanced at me sideways and gave me a crooked grin that didn't reach his eyes. It was such an asshole thing to say, but coming from Eric, it almost made me hopeful. Maybe he would, at last, let me in.

Shaking myself, I stood up and stretched my neck from side to side. "Man, I feel like shit." I was suddenly heavy and lethargic as if my bones had been replaced with lead.

"Fleeting makes you feel like that. It takes some getting used to, but there's always a price to pay for doing it."

"Figures," I complained.

"Make sure to hydrate and take in a lot of calories today."

I started down the stairs. "I hope you weren't expecting to get much more out of me today. I have a busy day ahead. Stuff at the office. Bye!"

I continued down the stairs and as I made it to the bottom Eric asked, "How did you do it? What helped you finally fleet?"

He rarely gave me anything to work with, but he sure expected me to bare my soul to him. But if there was any hope for him, I had to show him how it was done.

"Anger," I said. "Anger toward Olivia Hillworth."

Eric raised an eyebrow.

"She completely rubbed me the wrong way," I went on. "She made me feel… like I didn't belong and never would." I hated that feeling, wished that whatever pack instinct had started to grow in me would just go away. "I don't need a pack." The words were random and out of the blue. I wanted them to be true but they stank of lies.

"I would be lying to you if I told you that the… *want* goes away. It doesn't, but it gets easier."

I nodded, wishing it could be different, wishing I could somehow extricate that part of me, cut it out with a scalpel and throw it in the trash.

"You do remind me of her," Eric whispered almost as if he didn't want me to hear him.

"Who?"

"My daughter."

I stood speechless, all words wiped clean from my brain.

He stood and walked away. "See you tomorrow at the same time," he called over his shoulder.

I blew a raspberry and left, wondering how much worse the torture would be if I didn't remind him of someone he'd loved.

CHAPTER 14

"What's that smell?" I asked, wrinkling my nose as I entered my office.

Rosalina's voice came from the lobby. "What smell?"

"Gah!" I exclaimed, realizing the stench came from my garbage can. I'd left the remnants of a previous meal in there overnight. Gingerly pinching my nose, I grabbed the can and hauled it out of the room.

Rosalina frowned at me. "I don't smell anything."

"Then you're definitely not a werewolf. I'll be right back. I need to dump this out."

Holding the can at arm's length, I walked out through the front door and veered left toward the back of the building. I passed Jake's office but saw no activity inside.

At the dumpster, I disposed of the garbage, holding my breath the entire time. The smell of those toxic juices got me gagging faster than anything. I started to head back, but a rustling sound made me whirl on my heel.

My heart went into overdrive, but it immediately settled as I noticed a smoky-colored, amber-eyed cat walking from behind the dumpster.

"Aw, how cute are you?"

The cat walked closer. Something about it told me he was male. He was big, probably over fifteen pounds of muscle, not flab like his indoor counterparts. His face was round with fluffy fur though, and his eyes were just breathtaking.

I squatted and put a hand out. He approached and carefully sniffed my fingers before letting me pet him. I rubbed his head, then under his chin, and he flopped to the ground, purring and twisting his body this way and that.

"You're a lovable fur ball, aren't you?"

He purred harder in response.

"Where is your collar?"

He licked my fingers.

"Are you a boy?" I checked to make sure. It was never good to go on assumptions. His parts were all there, safe and accounted for.

"A stray for sure. Well, keep away from animal control. They'll make sure you're singing soprano if they catch you."

I stood and walked around the corner. When I glanced back, I found him following me. I frowned, but figured once I turned the other corner, he would head back. The traffic on the main road would dissuade him. Except it didn't, and he followed me all the way to the agency's front door.

He blinked when I glanced down at him.

"You hungry?"

The cat appeared well-fed, strong, though.

"Thirsty?"

He meowed as if in answer.

Rosalina came to the door and opened it. "Why are you just

standing there? We have work to do."

I gestured toward the cat. "I've made a friend, it seems. He followed me from the dumpster."

"Oh, my gosh, he's so cute!" She got down to pet him, mumbling endearments and scratching him behind the ears.

"I think he's thirsty," I said.

"Well, let's get him some water." She held the door open, standing aside. "C'mon."

I didn't think the cat would walk in, but to my surprise, he moseyed on, his tail high up in the air. Rosalina and I exchanged an amused glance.

I filled up a plastic cup and set it in front of him. He drank his fill, then moved around the room, exploring. After a moment, he found his way into my office, hopped on a chair, and made himself comfortable, curling up tightly and closing his eyes for a nap.

I frowned. "What the heck?"

"Well, you said you wanted a cat after Cupid… you know."

I shook my head. "I can't graduate to a cat. I killed the fish."

"Oh, you didn't kill it, Triple T. Cupid was almost two years old. Betta fish don't live very long."

"You think?"

She nodded, glanced sideways at the cat, and smiled as if tempting me to a brand new toy. "I would take him, but they don't allow pets at my complex."

A pang of jealousy hit me at the thought of Rosalina taking him. It was stupid, but that made me realize I wanted him. Even Cupid with his low-profile presence had served as company, and I missed that. And my complex *did* allow pets, I'd made sure of that.

"*Soo?*" Rosalina said in a sing-song voice.

I sniffed. "Well, if he'll have me, I'll have him."

At this, the cat opened one eye then closed it again as if he were winking his agreement.

Rosalina laughed. "I guess that settles it."

So before lunch, I headed to the pet store and bought a bunch of supplies, cringing at the hit to my credit card, but feeling it was way worth it.

After getting a cat carrier, a litter box and scooper, dry food, wet food, bowls for water and kibble, a collar, and a hairbrush, I picked him up from the office, stuffed him in the carrier, and took him home.

Luckily, he didn't seem at all bothered by the experience and started exploring the apartment as soon as I let him out. I hated to leave, but I had a potion to brew back at the office, so I poured water and food for him and snuck out when he wasn't looking.

I left the condo with a smile on my face, looking forward to returning home later today.

CHAPTER 15

"Where do we stand?" The next day, I sat at my desk with Rosalina and a stack of printed pages before me.

It was Thursday. We had tall cups of coffee in front of us, and a couple of slices of cheesecake waiting in a paper bag in case we got hungry while we discussed our finances and the future of our agency.

For lunch, I'd eaten a huge steak, a loaded baked potato, and creamy mac and cheese. Eric had been right about getting enough calories. We had practiced fleeting again today, and it had left me exhausted. He also showed me how to control my alpha vibes.

Something else that had me exhausted was the lack of good sleep. Blaze—it was what I'd name my new cat because of his beautiful eyes—had woken me up a few times through the night as he tried to find a comfortable position sidled next to me. The new arrangement would certainly take some getting used to. For both of us. I was a bit worried about him, though. This morning I hadn't seen him as I rushed through a shower and dressed for work. I suspected he'd climbed behind the refrigerator, but I'd had no time to look.

After a hefty, leisurely lunch, I was feeling much better, though I suspected the cheesecake would have a short lifespan.

Across the desk, Rosalina was dressed in a silken cream blouse and black pinstripe pants. Her makeup was flawless, and there was a glow to her skin that hadn't been there in the last few days. It was as if, by putting extra time in her skincare, she could lift up her spirits. I thought of her dressed in tight leathers, toting a scoped rifle, blasting people off, and had to convince myself I wasn't thinking of two people, but only one: my best friend who turned out to be a badass in more ways than one.

She handed me the top page of her report. "This is a summary. Most of the bills are due by May the fifteenth. After we pay the rent, we will have exactly $251.35 left in our savings account."

"Shit."

"If you are able to track a mate for Mr. Taylor, we'll have enough to cover rent for May, but there won't be enough to cover all the other bills… electric, water, insurance, supplies. Not to mention our salaries."

"Double shit."

"Yep." She nodded, her perfect eyebrows furrowed. "In other words, we need new customers. Stat!"

Mr. Taylor was a divorcee in his mid-thirties who we had booked last week. He was the only customer we'd been able to snag in the chaos.

I grabbed my head, glowering at the numbers as if I could change them by mere will. I tried to wish a few zeros into existence at the end of our squalid balance, but nothing happened.

Damn! I totally have the wrong kind of magic.

"Maybe some of our radio ads will send a few customers our

way," I said hopefully.

Her mouth twisted to one side. "Sorry, I had to cancel those. We couldn't afford to pay them anymore."

I felt my energy drain all at once. When we'd started the agency, we'd envisioned people knocking our door down, desperate for a bit of love, ready to get hitched to their perfect soulmates. But it wasn't anything like that. We'd had plenty of people inquiring about our services in the beginning, but they'd all wanted to pay next to nothing for the love of their lives. *Like, what the hell?!* It wasn't as if they were shopping for a pair of socks. Why did people have to be so cheap?

After a few months in business, we'd changed our strategy and started aiming for more exclusive customers, society people with substantially more funds to spend. We'd scored Celina Morelli, hooked her up to a priest, and thought we had it made, especially after she referred DJ Slice our way.

The DJ, Aaron Blackridge, might've helped us continue the trend if not for rhabo and the terminally ill partner we delivered for him. Yes, we had saved Josh from sure death, but the damage had been done. We'd put Aaron through a heap of pain, and that was that.

Rosalina slowly lifted a finger as if carefully balancing an idea on the tip of her manicured fingernail. "I thought that… maybe… you could call Celina Morelli. First, ask how things are going with her *godly* man, then casually ask if any of her friends need to spice up their love lives?"

As she told me about the idea, she was cringing in a near mirror image of me. She knew as well as I did that it was a fat chance. Celina Morelli and Aaron Blackridge were friends. Chances were she already knew all about our screw-up, and she wouldn't knowingly put any more of her friends at risk.

"What if our reputation is damaged forever?" I asked.

"I refuse to believe that." Rosalina rose to her feet and started pacing in front of the desk. "It wasn't our fault that Josh was sick, and besides, we went above and beyond to save his life."

It was true, but that didn't diminish the awful pain we'd put our client through. Maybe with time, when all remnants of his suffering had disappeared and Aaron's happiness with Josh wasn't tainted by the awful experience, he would be willing to mention us to others, but time wasn't on our side. Not at all.

"Yes, we did go above and beyond," I said, "but…" I didn't need to finish. Rosalina understood all too well.

She collapsed back on the chair, a heavy sigh escaping her. "Oh, Triple T, what are we gonna do?"

Seeing her face etched with worry and hearing her voice tremble with doubt nearly undid me. Rosalina was my rock, my strength. She always knew what to do. I was usually the one flailing like a fish out of water, while she donned her mature expression and told me that everything would be okay. Except, she didn't think so this time. She thought we were doomed. Our dream of owning a business and being independent was dying right before our eyes.

My first instinct was to bawl in despair, to tell her I had no idea what to do but…

I couldn't fail her. She had been there for me when it mattered most, when I'd been adrift and my life had as much potential as an unfertilized egg. So instead of falling apart like a baby, I squared my shoulders and vowed to do the impossible, whatever it took, to keep our dream alive.

"I will call Celina," I said firmly. Even though it felt hopeless, and it clawed at my pride, I would do it. I would beg if necessary.

Rosalina smiled at me, though her eyes still looked heavy with sadness and a sort of defeat I never thought I'd see in her expression. "Hopefully something will come out of it."

I nodded and was about to say it would work, when a loud buzzer sounded from the lobby, making us both jump. We had just installed the thing, and it was the first time it had rung.

Since we were afraid of hostiles marching into our office, ready to decapitate us, we had thought it safer to keep the front door locked, so we'd added a bell and a sign that read "*We're open. Just ring the bell and we'll be with you.*"

Rosalina and I jumped to our feet, a hopeful air wafting between us. Maybe it was a new customer, someone ready to hire us to find their true love.

We could only hope.

CHAPTER 16

We hurried out of my office and saw a familiar figure on the other side of the glass door.

It was Em, Liliana's neighbor. I deflated. Not a new customer.

"What does she want?" Rosalina asked.

I sighed, shaking my head to indicate I had no idea. "I'll get it." Flipping the latch, I opened the door, the chime sounding above me as it opened.

"Hi," I said, putting on a smile that Em did not return at all.

She certainly looked and was posed like a hostile. *Huh?*

Something told me not to invite her in, but I didn't want to make her angrier. She looked damn scary already.

"What… brings you to our neighborhood?" I asked in a tone that was meant to sound welcoming but fell short.

She walked in, squared her shoulders, and placed her fists on her hips. "The police won't believe me."

Her cloying sweet rose scent flooded the lobby. I rubbed my sniffer and fought not to sneeze. Her green hair sat flat on her head as if she'd been wearing a baseball cap for days. Today, she wore khaki shorts that reached her knees, long socks with colorful stripes, and a Metallica T-shirt.

"Um, you mean about," I twirled my finger vaguely, "exactly what?"

"About that *thing* that wouldn't stay dead, about Liliana *being* dead, about any of it." With every word, Em's voice grew higher in pitch.

Rosalina blinked slowly, her falsies fluttering and giving her eyes an exaggerated quality of surprise. "What do you mean they don't believe you about Liliana being dead?"

"There was no body, they said. No sign that anything happened there."

"Oh, shit," I said under my breath. "H-how is that possible? The table was smashed, and there was blood all over the walls and floor and furniture. They couldn't have…"

They couldn't have erased the evidence was what I had been about to say, except I knew better. It was perfectly plausible for anyone who had a powerful mage or witch at their disposal, which Bernadetta and Stephen did. A Midnight Witch to be precise.

"You have to come with me to the police station," Em demanded. "You have to help me convince them. I don't think they really looked into it. I doubt they even sent a forensic team in there. I mean," she began pacing the short length of our sitting area, "I don't know for sure they didn't, but if they had, they would've found something, right? They have Skews that work for the police department and can uncover any sort of magical whatever, don't they?"

"Em," I walked up to her and gently laid a hand on her shoulder, "maybe you should sit down, calm down a bit. Would you like some coffee? Or tea? I can go across the street to Cup 'o

Java and get you whatever you need. Even something to eat if you're hungry."

She vigorously shook her head, making her green hair swing from side to side. "I don't need anything," she said, though she did sit down on the sofa and took several deep breaths, doing her best to calm down.

"I'm sorry." She rubbed her temples. "I know this is not your fault… I guess."

I twisted my mouth to one side, not liking her insinuation.

"I assure you," Rosalina said. "We are not responsible for Liliana's death or whatever happened afterward to the evidence."

Em scanned us from head to toe as if she could somehow deduce the truth from our postures and clothes. I smoothed my jacket, feeling grateful for our respectable office outfits.

"Then you have to help me convince those stupid cops," she said. "I couldn't sleep last night. I don't feel safe in my own house anymore. I can't allow whoever killed Liliana to get away with it."

I sat next to Em, angling my body in her direction. "Don't worry. We agree with you. Right, Rosalina?"

"Most definitely," my friend said.

"I will go with you to the police station. I know a detective there. His name is Tom Freeman. He's a good friend of mine, so just let me do the talking. He's already investigating stuff that has to do with rhabo."

"Rhabo?" Em frowned. "You mean the drug that they've been talking about on the news, the one that kills vampires."

I nodded.

"So, you're saying that's why Liliana was sick."

"Yes."

She stared at the floor, her eyes darting from side to side as she let the knowledge sink in. "I should've guessed. I'm so stupid." Her big green eyes blinked and returned to me. "You said you were there to help her. I thought there was no help once a vamp tasted the drug."

"Um, that's right," I lied. "Our intention was to make her feel more comfortable. You see, I knew her father, and he recently… passed away. He asked me to look out for Liliana, but I was too late."

Tears pricked in the back of my eyes. I glanced away, swallowing hard.

Em laid her hand on top of mine. "I'm sorry."

I gave her a sad smile and checked the time on my watch. "I have time. We can go to the police station now." I glanced at Rosalina for her say-so.

She nodded. "Sure, I'll hold down the fort." A quick shrug of her shoulders told me what she wasn't saying out loud. *It's not like there's much going on here.*

We stood and started toward the door. A towering figure appeared on the other side. I stopped and blinked up, watching as the woman's eyes roved over the sign we'd tacked to the door. It seemed she hadn't noticed me inside because she lifted a finger to press the button, but before she managed, I grabbed the handle and pulled the door open.

"Hi, welcome to Sunder Mate Tracker Agency. How may we help you?" My voice was chipper and neighborly like Mister Rogers's. This woman definitely looked like a potential customer—one of those exclusive ones we'd been trying to get.

She was easily over six-foot tall. Maybe even as tall as Jake, who was 6'2". She wore simple but expensive-looking clothes: black slacks, a high neck white T-shirt that let a dark bra peek through its sheer fabric, and a cool leather jacket that flared at the hips. She wore a pair of boots with flat heels, so her impressive height was all natural. Her shoulder-length hair was blond and super straight. Bangs hung above her deep black eyes, so perfectly straight that I'd bet they'd been cut by a laser. She wore no makeup, except for a little gloss.

She smiled pleasantly and said, "Sorry to drop by without an appointment, but I was nearby and thought, what the hell, I'll just swing by. I'm an acquaintance of Celina Morelli."

OMG! OMG! Could it be?

I did my best not to faint from excitement as she seemed to go blurry for a split second. I took a deep breath and cut a giddy look in Rosalina's direction. Her eyes, which had seemed flat and despondent just a few minutes ago, were now full of light.

Our prayers have been answered. I didn't even have to call Celina Morelli to beg for help. Maybe the stars were aligning in our benefit, at last.

"Please, come in." I opened the door wide and stepped out of the way.

The woman entered, passing next to Em and making her look diminutive. The height differential was substantial, at least a foot. In unison, Em stretched her neck and lifted her chin, and the woman hunched over, her shoulders caving inwardly. It was interesting to watch. Neither of them should be embarrassed about their height. Lovely people come in all shapes and sizes, but, either consciously or subconsciously, they both compensated for each other.

Rosalina pointed to the chair in front of her desk. "Please, take a seat. Make yourself comfortable. Would you like some water?"

The woman sat and waved a hand. "Oh, no. I'm fine, thank you."

Em glowered at me and flicked her gaze in the direction of the door as if saying *let's go*. But I couldn't leave—not when we needed to nab this client. I met Rosalina's eyes as she walked around her desk, ready to tend to our customer.

With a quick motion of my head toward the door, I said, "I need to step outside for a moment, but I'll be right back."

Rosalina gave me a pointed look that seemed to say *go but hurry up*.

I ushered Em outside, who was back to looking hostile.

"So you're dumping me?" she said as we stepped onto the sidewalk.

"No, I'm not dumping you, but this is important and—"

"Oh, and Liliana being dead, and the fact that my neighborhood is turning into murder city isn't?"

"I didn't mean that. Look, if you have time, you can wait across the street in the coffee shop and as soon as I'm done here I'll come find you and go to the police station with you. Does that sound good?"

She blew air through her nose. "How long is it going to take?"

"I don't know exactly, but normally no more than an hour."

"An hour?! I've got things to do too, you know?"

"I'm sure you do. If you can't wait, we can meet at the police station later this afternoon or tomorrow."

A crease appeared on her forehead. "No. I'll wait." She looked me up and down with narrowed eyes as if she suspected I was trying to give her the run-around.

"Good. See you in a bit." I didn't wait for an answer and simply turned on my heel and went back inside. The sweet tang of Em's perfume hit me all over again. Man, someone needed to tell her to go easy with the spritzes. It was all I could smell.

"Here is Toni," Rosalina said in a cheerful tone. "Ms. Graves was just telling me about how happy she is for Celina and Vincent."

I extended a hand in the woman's direction. "Nice to meet you. My name is Antonietta Sunder, but you can call me Toni."

"Mekare Graves," she said as she shook my hand.

"Nice to meet you, Ms. Graves."

She batted the air. "Oh, you can call me Mekare." She had a pleasant smile that made me at ease. "Yes, I was telling your partner how delighted I am to see Celina happy. She had such a rough time with men before. Same as me, I'm afraid." She sighed wistfully as if remembering regretful things from past relationships.

"We're so happy for her, too. And for Vincent, of course," I said.

"At any rate, I got a little jealous of my friend." Mekare laughed with self-deprecating humor. "And I thought to myself… Well, *there's no reason you can't find happiness, Mekare. Get your ass over to that agency before you become worm food.*"

"We're very glad you came," Rosalina said as she pulled a prepackaged folder from a cabinet and handed it to me. It included a brochure, a contract, and all the relevant information about our service. This folder in particular had a blue tab attached to it, which meant the price listed on the contract was the one we offered to our high-end customers.

I took the folder and gestured with it toward my office. "Why don't you step this way and we can talk more about it? I will be delighted to help you and get started today if you feel ready."

"I feel ready, all right." Mekare stood up without hesitation and followed me.

Once we were seated comfortably, I pulled out the glossy brochure and pushed it across the desk in Mekare's direction. "This briefly explains—"

She waved both hands at the brochure. "Oh, honey, I don't need that. Watching Celina, I know everything I need to know about what you do here, so sign me up."

I almost choked. It couldn't be that easy. A thorough sales pitch and, sometimes, backward gymnastics were necessary to get people to sign the dotted line. I'd never had someone so willing to let us help them. It was like getting ready to remove the onions from your burger and finding it didn't have any.

"Well," I said a bit nervously, my hands hovering over the contents of the folder. I blinked a few times before I thought to pull out the contract and offered it to Mekare. "Here is our contract. It lists the fee for our service. Deposit and final payment after we successfully find a mate. It also lists what can be expected in terms of time, what is needed in order to perform a tracking, as well as our cancellation policy."

Her eyes went over the contract, skimming quickly through every item. I watched in silence, twisting my hands under the desk, one of my knees bouncing up and down. If she signed, we would be able to breathe easily for another month.

After a quick moment, Mekare looked up from the contract. I stopped wringing my hands and bouncing my knee and smiled.

"Everything looks in order," she said, no mention of the amount of money required for deposit or the final cost.

Witchlights, I love rich people! Not that our services weren't worth their weight in gold.

She sighed. "I'll have to take this to my lawyer, though." She folded the piece of paper and stuffed it in her purse.

I nearly slumped over the desk and cried. Of course, she hadn't balked at the price. She had decided she didn't want to hire us after all.

"Um, is there anything you would like me to explain," I said, grasping at straws, trying to find a way to get her to sign without seeming desperate.

"Not really. Everything looks fine to me, but you know lawyers. Mine is a stickler. He won't let me sign anything without him reading it first. *You can never be too careful these days, Mekare,*" she added in a deeper voice. "That's what he always says to me."

"And he's right," I said, forcing a smile. "Well, you do what you have to do, and we'll look forward to your call." I handed over a business card.

She took it and placed it in her purse with the contract.

When we walked back into the main area, Rosalina glanced up from her desk, her brow furrowing in worry. When I talked to first-time customers, it always took longer than the few minutes Mekare and I had been in my office.

Rosalina knew right away that I'd failed to make the deal. I grimaced, fearing she would think I hadn't done enough, but I couldn't think of how I could've talked Mekare into signing without driving her away in distaste.

From the door, Mekare waved two fingers and said, "I'll be in touch." The chime rang above her as the door locked into place.

"She'll never come back, will she?" Rosalina sighed and slumped in her chair.

"I dunno. Maybe. Maybe not." I ran a hand through my hair, frustration clenching my gut and making me want to throw up.

I could almost hear our bank account draining like a leaky bucket. I knew homelessness. I knew what it was to have no money. That short time I'd been on the streets had injected fear deep in my bones. It was a wonder I didn't get eaten by a rogue vampire while sleeping in the open.

Logically, I knew that if our business failed, I would still have a roof over my head. I could move in with Mom, Dani, or Rosalina— if she would have me after failing her so utterly. She would still have her place. She had more savings than me, enough money to pay rent for a few months even if she didn't get another job right away. I would also find a job that would make me enough money to survive and pay rent to Rosalina, but what kind of life would that be?

I didn't want to live constantly scraping at the bottom to avoid sinking past the scum. When we'd started the agency, we'd had so many hopes of being solvent, at least. I would be happy if all we could do was stay afloat, even if we never made extra money for cute outfits and vacations. But not even that seemed like a possibility anymore.

"She said she just wants her lawyer to read the contract to make sure it all looks good," I explained. "She made it sound like she would come back, but you know people…"

A little light returned to Rosalina's eyes. "Well, let's hope for the best then. Send good vibes into the universe."

Stretching my hands toward the ceiling, I wiggled my fingers. "Sending good vibes into the universe," I chanted.

Rosalina mimicked me, also wiggling her fingers and humming in the back of her throat like some sort of yogi master.

We both laughed, peering into each other's eyes with understanding. She should be mad at me. It wasn't her fault we were in this situation. Yet, she had nothing but kindness to offer me.

God, how did I get so lucky to have a best friend like her?

I ended my chant and said, "Em is waiting for me at Cup 'o Java."

"Oh, I thought she'd left."

"She wouldn't. She thought I was trying to get rid of her and insisted on waiting. But it's fine. We'll go see Tom, get this over with. Besides, it won't hurt. We need all the help we can get to take down Bernadetta and Stephen. Maybe, Tom and his people will be able to figure something out."

"I hope so." She blinked slowly. "I really hope so."

I left and crossed the street, hoping that all our hopes could become a reality soon.

CHAPTER 17

Em had a small scooter—a Vespa, she'd said, which explained her hat hair since she probably wore a helmet—which she'd parked around the corner and would not accommodate the both of us, so we rode to the police station in my Camaro.

Before driving off, I called him to make sure he was in. He was and promised to wait for us to talk for a few minutes. Apparently, there had been an altercation between werewolves and vampires in The Scourge—a commercial district reserved for Skews—and he needed to head there with his partner to interview potential witnesses.

When we walked into his office, Tom looked up from his paperwork, a white, perfect smile flashing on his kind face.

"Toni, it's good to see you. Come in. Take a seat."

He rose from his chair like a perfect gentleman and stayed on his feet until we sat. He nodded at Em in greeting.

"What brings you here today? Have you uncovered more… exciting things?"

I shrugged. There were a few things I hadn't told him since our last meeting, more importantly, the events that had transpired at the coven temple, but the lines of what I should share with him and what I shouldn't were starting to blur.

We had killed several vampires, and even though *they* had practically killed an entire pack, I doubted Tom would take kindly to vigilantism. No one was supposed to take the law into their own hands. No one was supposed to leave a crime scene or use magic to scrub all the evidence away.

The Enright Massacre, the news had called it, because the temple was located on Enright Ave. The details had been scant, no mention of what the police knew or didn't know. I wondered what they had made of it. I felt bad for keeping things from Tom, but it wasn't only me I was protecting. Eric, Jake, and Rosalina had been there, too.

I shook those thoughts away and focused on what I was here for, instead.

"There is something," I said. "Um, it relates to Damien Ward."

"Oh." Tom scrubbed his goatee.

Tom and his partner had taken Rosalina's and my statement after the mage died right on the floor of our agency. That was when we'd started lying to Tom, telling him we had no idea why someone had attacked Damien and that the only reason the mage had been there was to pick up Rosalina to go out on a date.

I had a feeling Tom didn't believe us. His narrowed eyes and detailed questions seemed to be aimed at tripping us up. But, we had managed to keep our story straight, and in the end, he gave up.

"Well, um," I continued so eloquently, "he had a daughter. Her name was Liliana Ward. They were estranged, and Damien had told us she was sick. I went to visit her to tell her that Damien died. I thought she deserved to know. But when we got there, there was…

a creature there." God, I hated to lie further, but I had to.

Tom leaned forward. "A creature? What kind?" His dark gaze paused on Em for an instant.

"I don't know what kind? But it wasn't a regular Skew. I've never seen anything like it."

I could feel my stomach churning. I wriggled in my seat and thumbed the hem of my jacket. Lying to someone you love was a bitch. But what else could I do? I couldn't tell him about the Unholy Vessel, and the monsters it was capable of creating. It would lead to too many questions. Questions that involved my friends and the Pack Rule.

Tom rested his elbows on the desk. "So... you mean a new kind of Skew?"

Em's eyes went from Tom to me, but she didn't interrupt.

I opened my mouth to answer, to say *yes*, but I realized, in time, that this could be a trick question. Tom was smart. I had to tread carefully. Besides, why would he ask that? Why would he think there was a new kind of Skew running around unless he knew something?

"I'm no Skew expert," I said with a shrug. "All I know is that I've never seen anything like it."

Tom huffed and reclined back in his chair. "So then what happened? After you got there?"

"The creature was angry and had a hold of her," I continued. "We tried to calm it down, but it…" Images of Liliana's ravaged body flashed before my eyes, upsetting my stomach further.

"Take your time, kiddo," Tom said kindly.

I took a few deep breaths, willing the contents of my stomach to stay put. "Um, when the thing tried to attack, I shot the creature. Between the eyes," I lied yet again, knowing that if I said that Rosalina had done it, it would just raise more questions. Tom had no idea she'd turned into a badass markswoman.

"Between the eyes, huh? Good thing I insisted on target

practice, and you getting a gun."

"Yeah, good thing." I smiled stiffly, my face feeling as if it would crack to pieces exposing all my lies.

"I'm wondering…" Tom scratched his head. "At what point did you dial 911?"

"Right after that."

"Right after you shot the creature between the eyes?"

"Yes."

He pursed his lips. "Curious, I haven't heard anything about this."

"That's exactly why we're here," Em piped in, her voice shy. "Toni and her friends did call the police. I was there. And then I came here and filed a report, but they're doing nothing about it."

"*Toni and her friends*?" Tom asked.

There was a real problem, a complaint, in what Em had said, and Tom chose to focus on us? Really?

"Yes," Em said in an annoyed tone, also mad at the way the detective was focusing on the wrong thing.

Tom turned to me. "Which friends exactly is she talking about?"

"Um, it was just Rosalina, Eric, and I," I said with a pleasant smile stamped on my face.

"Eric? And are you referring to Eric Cross? Or Eric Lone as some call him?"

"Yeah. He was… Damien's friend. He wanted to be there to tell Liliana what happened."

Tom huffed again, but he turned to Em. "What were you doing there?"

"I am, *was*, Liliana's next-door neighbor. I went to check on her since she'd been ill because of rhabo."

I cringed. This was getting worse. Tom was going to drill me after this, and I wouldn't be surprised if he decided to throw me in jail when I didn't tell him anything. Em was supposed to let me do the talking, but the hell?

Because I couldn't tell him anything.

Gah, coming here was a bad, bad idea. I really hadn't thought this through.

"So I take it Liliana was a vampire?" Tom said.

"Yes," Em and I said in unison.

He rubbed his forehead and, for an instant, he appeared as tired as a hundred-year-old man. "This drug is out of control. So many people are dead. We're finding it all over the city, and now it's in the suburbs." He exhaled and blinked up at us as if he'd forgotten we were there. "Um… now, why do you say the police aren't doing anything about it? It seems unlikely that—"

Em interrupted, pushing to the edge of the chair, looking irate. "They said they went there, sent a patrol car or something, but they didn't see anything out of the ordinary. They entered the house and saw nothing out of place, but when we left, when we ran out of there after that creature tried to eat us then that other… guy showed up—"

Tom threw his hands up in the air. "Hold on. Hold on. The creature was still alive after being shot between the eyes and there was another guy."

"Yes, I think he might've been a vampire. He had one of those UV umbrellas they advertise on TV."

I shrank in my chair, wanting to disappear. I fingered Damien's token around my neck, wondering if I could disappear into Elfhame. Maybe I would never come back, and I would become a legend.

The werewolf that mysteriously vanished from the police station and was never heard from again. Yeah, that would work.

Tom puffed his cheeks, then blew out the air. "Why does everything have to be so damn complicated?"

"Right? It's just what I've been asking myself all along." I grinned nervously.

He shook his head, not buying my act at all. "Okay, I think I'll go get my partner, and we're going to have to go over this one more time. Interviewing those witnesses can wait. This is *far* more interesting." Tom stood and watched me from over a flaring nose, looking like an angry father who was carefully crafting a mean speech for his unruly daughter.

Shit.

He was onto me, and at this rate, he was going to expose all my lies and throw me in a cell.

CHAPTER 18

By the time we were leaving the police station, my stomach was rumbling like a derailing train. I was so ravenous that the image of a triple-stacked burger combo with a thick, chocolate shake and curly fries kept interrupting my thoughts. Best of all, I knew just the place to get my fix. I pressed a hand to my stomach and winced at its embarrassing commentary.

As we stepped outside of the station, Em gave my roaring stomach a look. I grinned apologetically, wincing a bit. I also had a hunger headache, but at least it was better than starving *in* a jail cell.

Tom and his partner, Frank Archer, had drilled us mercilessly. I stuck to my original story and managed not to contradict myself. At least I thought so. The lies kept multiplying, and I felt dirty for it. Tom didn't deserve it.

Before letting us go, he pulled me aside and gave me one of his assessing, questioning stares as if trying to draw the truth out of me by sheer will.

"What?! Why do you keep acting like this?" I'd said, fighting to keep eye contact.

"Because I know you, Toni. You're hiding something to protect your friends, I think. You're lying to me more and more every time I see you."

Gah! That made me feel shitty about that. I had to figure out a way to fix things. I was tempted to tell him everything, but I didn't know how to get out of the thick ball of yarn I'd been weaving. Besides, the Pack Rule had sworn me to secrecy. I couldn't begin to tell him anything without running into details I would have to hide anyway.

"Well, I'm not," I said and actually managed to keep a tight poker face.

"Fine, have it your way, but please, be careful. What you're toying with is extremely dangerous, and I would be remiss not to warn you. Your father asked me to look out for you, and I'm never gonna stop."

"I know, Tom, and I love you for it. Just… just find whoever murdered Damien. Find Stephen and lock him behind bars. That's all I ask."

"I'm working on it, kiddo. I have every cop in the area combing the city, asking questions. If he's still in St. Louis, we'll catch him."

Now, finally free, I turned my attention to Em and asked, "Happy now?"

She nodded. "I honestly thought that you and your friends… I dunno…" She shrugged. "But you told him everything, and I believe that he'll really look into it."

"He will," I assured her. "Tom's a man of his word. His promise is like gold."

Obviously, I hadn't told him *everything*, but Em didn't know that. She had no way of guessing how deep the rabbit hole went.

I started walking toward the parking lot. "I'll take you back to your scooter, though I have to make a quick stop for some food. I'm starving!"

"Yeah, I was afraid you might eat me."

"Mmm. An *Em* combo."

We stopped by one of my favorite hamburger joints and ordered at the drive-through. Em was hungry too, though apparently not as much as me. She only ordered a kids' meal, which she said was plenty enough for any normal person, and went on a rant about portion sizes in America.

It was easy for her to criticize my supersize appetite. She was petite and a Stale. She had no idea the amount of energy it took to do things like shift and, sometimes, keep from shifting. Red still wanted revenge for all those years she'd been caged.

I dug into my fries as soon as I got my food, but Em kept the paper bag on her lap, only sipping her water. Once we got back to The Hill, I parked around the bend from the agency, we got out of the car and met on the sidewalk.

"I guess this is goodbye," Em said.

She seemed to be waiting for me to say something like *Oh, no—not goodbye. Let's be best friends*, so it was awkward as hell. I didn't have anything against her. She was nice enough, but, for some reason, she made me uncomfortable. Maybe it was because she'd been so pushy and desperate. It had been her right, of course, but I wanted to put what had happened at Liliana's place firmly into the past as quickly as possible.

So instead, I smiled and said, "Um, I guess. Unless you're ever in need of a mate." I started walking toward the office and waved before turning my back.

A moment later I heard a small, sputtering engine come to life, and when I glanced over my shoulder, I caught a glimpse of a baby blue Vespa driving away, backfiring as if the carburetor was about to break. I breathed a sigh of relief and peeked through the agency's window. The lamp on Rosalina's desk was off, which meant she'd already gone home.

I sent her a quick text to tell her everything had gone all right with Tom, then strolled next door to see if Jake was in his place.

When I pushed the door, it swung open, and immediately, I felt the tension I carried on my shoulders dissipate. It made me realize I'd been going about my day in a state of alertness, waiting for the ball to drop. And now that the sun was going down and vampires would be free to prowl without their ridiculous UV umbrellas, I was glad not to be alone.

"Jake," I called, my eyes roving around the space. It was nice. He had fixed it up quickly. There wasn't much in the way of decor except for functional furniture—a desk, a few chairs, a set of cabinets—but the paint, new hardwood flooring, and detailed woodwork made the place feel professional and fresh. With all that had been going on, he hadn't opened for business, and sometimes I wonder if he ever would. Maybe this was like his man cave or something.

"I'm up here," he called from the loft.

I bounded up the steps, sipping my milkshake, then stuffing a handful of fries into my mouth. When I reached the top, I found Jake sitting in front of his impressive array of computers. He was typing away in front of one monitor while three others moved in a flurry of activity: images flashing, lines of text scrolling, lights blinking.

"What are you doing?" I mumbled, a lump of half-chewed fries squirreled away in my cheek.

Jake whirled his chair around, his nose twitching. "I smell food," he said, his eyes flashing with hunger.

"Oh, no!" I pointed a finger straight at his nose. "You're not taking my food this time."

He narrowed his eyes. "I suspect you have a triple-decker."

I blew air through my nose.

"Don't be so selfish." He crooked a finger and made a *come here* motion. "Give me one of those patties, a few fries, and a sip of your milkshake."

"Nah-ah, get your own damn food."

"You would make a poor pack leader," he said. "You're supposed to take one for the team."

"I wholeheartedly disagree. I'd be a great pack leader, and the team would take one for me. All the time." I sat on a chair in the corner a safe distance away from him, set my milkshake and fries on an end table, unwrapped my hamburger, and bit into it. I gave a moan of pleasure. The hamburger was delicious.

Jake judged me hard with his silver eyes, then resumed typing on his computer.

"Who would've ever thought you would turn out to be a computer wiz?" I wiped my fingers on a napkin and stared at the intricate array of CPUs, monitors, cables, and several more devices I had no name for that filled the loft.

"It comes naturally to me for some reason. These days, with everything stored on the cloud, a lot of detective work happens behind the keyboard."

"And what exactly are you *detectiving*?"

He cringed at the word but let it pass without comment. "I'm just looking for anything that may shed some light on Stephen's location, Damien's death, the rhabo trade. Anything."

I set my burger down on the end table. "Interesting. So what do you have so far?"

He pointed at a stack of papers. "A list of all the registered Midnight Mages and Midnight Witches in the city. Another list of abandoned warehouses. They're bound to need another one for storing their drug supply. Stephen's known accounts. I thought I might be able to track his financial transactions. Credit card usage. Money withdrawals. There's a lot of stuff on Bernadetta also, but none of it has led anywhere."

They all sounded like interesting and legitimate ideas. "Maybe I should take a look. See if something speaks to me."

"Be my guest." He pushed the stack of papers in my direction.

I grabbed it, set it on my lap, and started leafing through it. We sat quietly for a moment while I slurped my drink, and Jake typed on the keyboard. The pages were full of names, numbers, addresses, but nothing gave me any ideas. I felt disappointed, wishing there was a way I could use my tracking skills to find our enemies.

I shook my head and set the papers back on Jake's desk. "Nothing," I said.

He didn't say anything, which probably meant he hadn't expected me to find anything.

"I heard from Tom about an attack at The Scourge. Was that part of the Pack Rule's plan to fight the distribution of rhabo?" I casually set what was left of my fries next to Jake's keyboard.

He smiled crookedly, snatched the box, and popped a fry in his mouth. I would keep the meat, but I could do away with the carbs. Maybe they would go straight to *his* tight ass.

"It was," he mumbled as he chewed.

"That's what I thought." I walked around the room, nibbling on my burger and sipping my milkshake until I finished them and threw the wrapping and cup in the bin under Jake's long desk. I reached for the token at my neck to rub it, but it was under my shirt. "I've been thinking…"

Jake didn't glance away from the screen but acknowledged me with a drawn-out *hmm*.

"I would like to put the spare elixir that Damien gave me in a safe place."

His hands froze over the keyboard, and he finally abandoned his work, whirling in his chair to face me. "I thought it was in a safe place. You left it in Eric's house, right?"

"Yes, but I don't know... I thought, elsewhere might be safer."

"Elsewhere? And safer than with Eric? Or is it that maybe you don't trust him?"

"Oh, I trust him. It's not that. I don't know. It's just a feeling I have. That this cure is important. That it can save someone who needs to be saved."

"Where else could you hide it? What do you have in mind?"

"Elf-hame," I said hesitantly.

"Elf-hame?" Jake looked completely confused. "Who do you know there who could hide it for you?"

"There's a guy."

"A guy, huh?" His features hardened and he stood from the chair and towered over me. His raw masculinity hit me like a hammer blow. The T-shirt he wore strained over his strong pecs, and his corded, tanned arms made me dream of his embrace. He was such a specimen. I rolled my eyes to disguise the way he affected me.

"Jealous, *Jakey*?" I asked, though if anyone had a right to be jealous it was me. He was the one with a fiancé that called him cutesy names.

"I already told you not to call me that," his voice rumbled in his chest.

I threw my hands up in the air. "Fine."

Since he'd promised me to find a way to be with me, I hadn't asked him how his quest to get out of his engagement with Allison Blackridge was going. I figured if he'd come up with a way out of his unbreakable pact, he would tell me, but maybe calling him *Jakey*, like his fiancée did, was a little jab in that direction. Maybe I wanted to know if that research took second place to the one he was doing here.

"So who is he?" he pressed.

"Just some guy. He's nice, and he helped Damien and I find the Prince when we were looking for the bitterthorn. If I give it to him for safekeeping, no one would suspect he has it."

"Then you should take it to him," Jake said.

"Um, want to… go with me?"

"To Elf-hame?"

I nodded.

He frowned. "I haven't been in years. Last time was on a school field trip when I was thirteen, I think."

"We wouldn't be going to one of the tourist posts. We would be going to Elyndell."

His eyes shot wide open. "Wow, that would certainly be interesting, but how."

I pulled on the chain to retrieve Damien's token from under my shirt.

"What is that?"

"Something Damien gave me before he died. It will help us get to Elyndell."

"Well, what are we waiting for?"

CHAPTER 19

We started with a trip to Eric's house to retrieve the elixir. Eric thought it was unnecessary to take it elsewhere, that it was safe in his house, but he didn't argue. Damien had entrusted it to me, so he understood it was my decision to do with it as I pleased.

"You can flush it down the toilet, for all I care," he said as we stood in his study, and he handed me back the small vial. I placed it in my breast pocket, feeling my anxiety kick up a notch as I worried about it breaking.

I stared at him as if he were simple. "I would never do that. This can save someone's life."

"A vampire's life, you mean. The world could do without the lot of them."

"I have to agree," Jake piped in.

"Who's asking you?"

Jake shrugged. "She's an idealist." He said it as if my respect for life needed an explanation.

"God, I'm glad I didn't grow up a werewolf!"

Both men shook their heads as if to indicate I didn't know what I was talking about.

I rolled my eyes. *Whatever!* Arguing with them about this was a waste of good breath.

Jake grew serious then and addressed Eric. "Um, did you get what I asked for?"

Huh? What's he talking about? My curiosity reared its head.

"I did," Eric said. "You'll find it in the training room."

"Thank you."

I opened my mouth to ask, but Eric turned his back on us and walked to his desk. I mouthed "what?" at Jake, but he took me by the arm and guided me out of the room.

"What's going on?" I asked as he closed the door behind us.

"You'll see."

When we entered the training room, my eyes zeroed in on two tall stacks of boxes. "What is this?"

Jake rubbed his neck, his silver eyes dancing around the room. "I like it here. There's another Toni in view." He was referring to my reflection on the large mirror affixed to the wall. Why was he being so cryptic? Obviously, it wasn't something he wanted to hide from me, or he wouldn't have asked Eric about it in front of me.

I decided not to press him and made a dismissive gesture with my hand. "*Pshaw*, she doesn't hold a candle to me."

He smiled and stepped closer, stopping a mere inch from me. "No one does." He perused my face, his lips parting.

"Stop, you're going to make me blush."

"You're gorgeous when you blush."

"Is that what you tell Allison?" I asked, finding it hard to play along.

His expression darkened. "Don't do that. You know I don't

care about her that way."

"That way?" I asked. "That seems to imply you do care about her somehow."

He sucked in a breath to say something, seemed to think carefully, then finally said, "She's not a bad person, Toni. She's a pawn of the circumstances as much as I am."

Maybe she was, but I still remembered the way she had seemed to rub their engagement in my face along with Walter the day I found out about it.

"I wouldn't be so sure about that. She delighted in calling you *Jakey* in front of me."

He shook his head. "That had nothing to do with you. She was angry, blamed me for the arrangement between our packs. Her father practically forced her. She had less say than I did, and was only trying to mock me."

"Does that mean she's not angry anymore?"

She could do a lot worse than Jake. He was hot as hell, a strong alpha, and a good man. Maybe, after having some time to think about it, she was starting to like the idea of becoming his wife and was making nice with him.

"No, she isn't mad anymore."

Bingo!

"We've talked since. I told her about the promise I made to my father, explained that it was what led me to accept the pact. She understands the responsibility of keeping the Knight legacy alive, the weight of it."

The way he said it made it sound as if *I* didn't understand any of it, and maybe it was true, but his words still hurt.

"I'm glad to hear," I said in a biting tone. "If you can't find a way out of the pact, at least you won't be marrying a total nitwit."

"C'mon, Toni. It's not like that," he said in a reproachful tone.

"No? So… you told her about us?"

He rubbed his forehead. "Um, not yet. I don't know if it would be wise."

"What if she gets attached to you?" I asked, afraid of throwing that out there, but unable to hold the words back.

"That won't happen."

"How can you be so sure?"

He lowered his eyes to the floor and spoke in a low murmur. "I guess I can't be sure." After a moment, he glanced up again. "The only thing I can be sure of is what I feel for you, and the promise I made you. I will find a way, Toni."

"How long will that take?"

He pressed a fist to his mouth, looking as if he wanted to hold whatever needed to be said back. It was clear there was something he didn't want me to know.

"What?" I demanded. "What aren't you saying?"

"The wedding… my grandfather and Craig set a date."

The air froze in my lungs as I gasped. I took several steps back, shaking my head, imagining Jake dressed in a tux with Allison hanging from his arm, resplendent in a white dress. My brain got carried away, and the next thing I knew, I pictured them walking down a set of church steps, the crowd waiting below, clapping and throwing handfuls of rice. And my imaginings didn't stop there, they quickly devolved and had me waiting on top of a tree with a bucket of scorpions that I would dump on the happy couple as they walked by. Shaking my head, I snapped out of it and uttered the question that begged to be asked.

"When?"

"I have exactly two months to find a solution."

My ribs seemed to shrink around my lungs, making it hard to breathe. There was a deadline now, and it felt like it marked the end of all happiness and the beginning of a death row sentence.

"Oh, Toni." He pressed a hand to the side of my face and wiped away a tear with a brush of his thumb. I swallowed hard, shocked to find myself crying.

On instinct, I wanted to lash out, but I found that his eyes were wavering, and his lips were pressed into a thin line as he fought to contain his emotions. This had been his mistake, his fuck up, but he was paying for it, too. He hadn't done it out of malice, only out of a desire to be honorable, to fulfill a promise to his father. I couldn't keep berating him for screwing up—not when *I* had screwed up plenty of times in my life, not when he wanted to fix it.

Instead, what I needed to do was help him find a solution. Maybe I didn't know anything about unbreakable pacts and werewolf traditions, but we could find a way out of this together.

I wrapped my arms around his waist and rested my head on his shoulder.

"We'll find a way," I said. "I'll help you."

He hugged me back and made a sound in the back of his throat, something that sounded vulnerable and incredulous at the same time. "I don't deserve you. I got myself into this mess, and you shouldn't have to suffer for it."

He was so strong in my arms, and yet, the way his voice was breaking made my heart squeeze with emotion. I couldn't face this like some sort of spoiled child who threw a tantrum and pointed fingers because things hadn't gone her way. The old Toni would've done that. The old Toni let her entire life fall apart when Jake left. She had done nothing but despair. It had taken Rosalina walking into my life to put it back together, and I wasn't that person anymore.

If I'd learned anything from my best friend it was that you had to help those you cared about. Besides, it would be stupid not to do it when my own happiness depended on it. And in the end, if we couldn't find a way, at least I would have no regrets. I would know that I'd done everything in my power to stop the wedding, that I'd fought for the man I loved.

"You sure screwed up," I said, hardening my resolve, "but if I'm to keep you, I can't lie on my laurels, fanning myself. No, I will fight tooth and nail for you."

Jake pulled away from our embrace, tears pooling at the corners of his eyes. His lips trembled, and then he said, "The hell with it," and he kissed me.

Holding my face in both hands, Jake pressed his mouth to mine, making my body shudder. It was a kiss unlike any other he'd given me. There was no desire in it, no sexual current of electricity coursing through my veins. Instead, I was suffused in Jake's intense emotions of relief and tender love. It occurred to me for the first time that the weight of what he must do to break the unbreakable was more than he thought he was capable of bearing on his own, and that now that I'd offered to fight by his side, he found more hope than he'd had so far.

He pulled away, a tear sliding down his right cheek, cutting a path toward his stubbled jaw. It was my turn to wipe it away with my thumb. It was the second time I'd seen Jake cry. The first was when I shifted in front of him and showed him I was a werewolf. That he was crying, now, because he thought he might lose me, just brought me to a whole new height of adoration for him.

I exhaled, thinking *I'm fucking lost.* Really, the man could have, then and there, asked for my heart on a silver platter, and I would've carved it out of my chest and put a cherry on top.

Jake stepped away, batting a hand across his eyes. "Um, I know just how you can help me."

He walked toward the pile of boxes, took one down from the top, and opened it. "Books," he announced.

Indeed, several books that smelled like they'd come from my Nonna's attic were stuffed inside. Their leather bindings were old and dusty.

"Uh, you've decided to become a scholar instead of a private eye?" I rubbed my nose as I fought the urge to sneeze.

"No." He closed the box and put it back on top of the pile. "They're research material."

I cocked my head to one side.

"For how to break an unbreakable pact." He smiled sheepishly and gave a little shrug.

"Oh. I didn't know you'd asked Eric for help."

"He's the only one I felt I could trust."

My heart did a weird flip as I realized Eric was willing to help us.

"We can split them up," he said.

I nodded, a stupid smile spreading over my lips. It was no time to smile, but it felt good to have hope.

Jake smiled back, then heaved a sigh. "Maybe we should leave. Whoever your Fae friend is, he won't be happy if we come knocking on his door too late." He was avoiding eye contact at any cost, embarrassed about our emotional exchange.

Inwardly, I was amused. He was such a macho man that one little tear was too much to give. Yet, it had been there. I had seen it, and if I'd used it in a potion to track his mate, it would have led straight to me in a matter of seconds.

This man was mine and no one else's, and the hell if I was going to let anyone take him from me.

"All right," I said, interlacing my fingers with his. "We are off to Elf-hame. Hold on to your panties."

As I took my hand to the token at my neck, it felt like this was the beginning of more than just a trip to Elf-hame. Maybe, it was the beginning of a trip to a new life.

CHAPTER 20

Like the time I had traveled with Damien, all the color that surrounded us washed away, then were remade into a different scenery.

We rematerialized at the edge of the city, facing an ample forest of massive trees that made our realm's trees pale in comparison. What we could see of the sky above was peppered with millions of stars and a pale crescent moon. Lightning bugs flitted over flowering bushes. It was so magical, I almost ached inside.

Jake stood in a slight crouch as if he expected someone to leap at us from the woods. His nose twitched, his eyes roved around, and his hand squeezed mine tightly.

First, I thought his attitude was silly, then I remembered what Damien had said about the many creatures that lived in Elf-hame's forests. I had wanted to shift instead of riding a pony, but he warned me against it.

"That would be a bad idea. Your wolf stench would make the creatures around us feel threatened, and I can assure you it wouldn't bode well for us."

So Jake's caution wasn't silly at all. Besides, it was nighttime, and the moon cast elongated shadows all around us, making the forest downright spooky.

"We should head for the city," I said.

"Which way?" He peered at the forest with distrust.

I grabbed him by the shoulders, turned him around, and watched his face as he took in the majestic Fae capital. His mouth opened in an "O" of amazement, and I was tempted to kiss him again, to trap his full lower lip between my teeth and lightly suck on it, but instead, I faced Elyndell too and got my own fresh wave of astonishment.

By night, the Seelie Fae capital looked entirely different than it had during the day. Impossibly, it was more beautiful than I remembered.

From where we stood, Elyndell looked like a sprawling Christmas tree with the Vine Tower as its peak. Warm lights glowed inside the many buildings that seemed to grow straight out of the ground. Lanterns hung from branches, illuminating the mossy paths that meandered between the structures. A sense of wellbeing, quiet, and comfort suffused me at the sight of such an idyllic place.

"Wow," Jake exclaimed in a rush of breath, "I had no idea."

"I know, right? It's like heaven or something."

Just then, the sound of rustling bushes came from behind us, sending my heart into a dash.

"Um, maybe not exactly heaven," I said, peering wearily over my shoulder. "Unless heaven hides unknown creatures with equally unknown intentions. Let's get out of here." I grabbed Jake's hand and led him forward at a clipped pace.

"Unknown creatures of unknown intentions?" He staggered as I jerked his arm.

"Damien said to be cautious, especially at night."

It was Jake's turn to pull me along toward the city. When we reached its edge, he finally stopped. "Which way?"

"Down this path."

As we walked in front of a row of houses built straight into the trunk of a tree and waved awkwardly at all of those who glared at us from their windows, I was struck by the timid quality of Jake's movements. He had always seemed so confident back in our realm that it was odd to see this behavior. Talk about a fish out of water. Not that I didn't understand how he felt. I was in the same boat, but I never thought of him as insecure or vulnerable, and in the last hour, I'd seen both. It warmed my heart to see the different depths of who he was.

"So tell me more about this guy we're looking for?" Jake asked under his breath.

"His name is Glimlock Oakenhorn."

"Is he a nice guy? Or one of those creatures of unknown intentions?"

"Oh, no, he's very nice. If it wasn't for him, we wouldn't have this." I placed a hand over my breast pocket, where the vial of elixir rested safely.

"And he lives nearby?" I could sense in his voice that despite the beauty of the city, Jake had no desire to stay longer than necessary.

"Yeah, just up the hill." I pointed toward a flower-covered knoll, across a stone bridge ahead.

"Good. Let's hurry." He pressed forward, marching over the bridge and totally ignoring the crystalline brook below us.

We trod up the hill, the smell of honeysuckle blossoms thick in our noses. As we reached the peak, a tall shadow stepped from behind a tree and blocked our path. We came to an abrupt stop. Jake crouched, his claws unsheathing at the first sign of the threat. My own claws threatened to make an appearance, but the shape and the scent emanating from the person were terribly familiar.

"Wait!" I put a hand on Jake's shoulder.

I knew just the guy who always seemed to be shrouded in shadows and had a knack for crossing my path at unexpected moments.

"Prince Kalyll, is that you?" I asked.

There was a deep chuckle, then the Seelie Prince stepped forward, the shadows falling away like some sort of discarded cloak. His midnight blue hair shone under the dim moonlight, pointed ears peeking through the few beaded braids that hung at the sides. His face tattoos were a stark contrast against his pale skin, making him look intimidating. He wore an embroidered tunic with a sword at his hip that added to the threatening air.

"Well met, Antonietta Sunder," he said with a small bow.

Jake maintained his threatening stance, his claws showing no signs of retreating. "What the hell is he doing here?" he demanded with a rumble in his chest.

This was so *not* the time for male posturing, especially with the Prince of the realm. If we pissed him off, we could end up in some earthen dungeon to never be seen again.

I took a step forward and intervened before all the male hormones mixed into a Molotov cocktail that would singe my eyebrows.

"Jake, this is Kalyll Adanorin, Crown Prince of the Seelie Fae. Your Majesty, it is great to see you again."

I glanced pointedly at Jake's claws and nodded, encouraging him to put them away. He did, rolling his shoulders in an effort to relax. Still, what he said next was as far away from friendly as a pissed-off dragon.

"The Prince, huh? And is it his habit to appear unexpectedly in dark places?"

"Jake," I chided him under my breath.

"I make it a habit to appear anywhere I am supposed to

protect," Kalyll said in a stern voice.

Oh, shit!

This was totally going in the wrong direction, and I might soon need cover from the impending testosterone explosion. Why, oh why, were women always caught in the middle of dick-measuring contests? Would it help if we carried a ruler around to help settle matters? Of course, my thoughts then dived straight into the gutter, wondering who would win. *Damn!* I had no business thinking of the Prince's… package. I shook my head. Cheeks flaming with heat, I took it upon myself to let some estrogen do the talking.

"Oh, yes, and what a protector he is. You should see him wield his sword, Jake. It's like watching Luke Skywalker with his lightsaber." I mimicked using a sword and made buzzing sounds by blowing air through my clenched teeth.

Both Prince Kalyll and Jake looked at me as if I'd gone crazy.

"Oh, but you probably have no idea who I'm talking about." I glanced apologetically at the Prince.

"I know who Luke Skywalker is," he said, surprising me.

"You do?" Both Jake and I asked in unison.

"Yes, I've watched many popular human films."

Who would have figured? I scratched my head, thinking this rather odd and wondering exactly which movies he'd watched and why. I opened my mouth to ask something along those lines because what could be more intriguing than finding out what movies a Fae prince was interested in, but Kalyll had something else in mind, something that I should've suspected the moment he stepped into our path.

"How have you come to be in our realm without your mage friend?" he asked, his expression full of suspicion.

Crap!

I tensed.

Was I breaking the rules? Was no one else supposed to use the token? If so, why did Damien give it to me? *Oh, God!* Someone was alerted the moment it was used, but the Prince? It seemed the token was more important than I could've imagined.

For a moment, I thought of spinning some kind of lie, but in the end, I was too frazzled to come up with something convincing on the spot, so I decided that the truth was the best option.

"I'm sorry to say that my friend… is dead."

Kalyll's beautiful arched eyebrows dipped in consternation.

"The token belonged to him," I went on. "He gave it to me as a parting gift, I suppose. I guess I shouldn't have used it. I apologize if I've broken any of your laws."

The Prince shook his head. "Not at all." He pressed a fist to his heart. "My condolences about your friend. I owed him my gratitude for his help with the reapgrubs. I hate to think that I didn't repay his kindness. I do hope that," his eyes flashed to Jake, cautiously, "our exchange was fair and served to settle my debt with him as his untimely death makes it impossible for me to do more."

I was touched by the Prince's thoughtful words and didn't know what to say.

Jake, recognizing that we were dealing with a decent person, spoke with the same level of care as the Prince. "I assure you that your debt was repaid. Damien was very grateful for the bitterthorn you shared with him. It allowed him to create the elixir he required."

For his part, Kalyll seemed to do his own reassessment of Jake. Behind his cobalt-blue eyes, a thousand little judgments and conclusions seemed to hurry past. In the end, he seemed to also readjust his first impression in a positive way.

"Then his daughter was saved," Kalyll said.

At this, Jake and I hung our heads.

"Unfortunately, she wasn't," I said. "But, Damien never knew. He died before he had a chance to get the elixir to her, and when I tried to deliver it… I was too late."

"What a dreadful and unfortunate turn of events." Kalyll appeared genuinely upset.

"I know this doesn't excuse my presence here, my use of his token, the thing is—" I started, but the Prince interrupted me.

"There's no need to apologize for that. You have not broken any rules. That token is, indeed, a very important passport. There are few of them in existence, and they are only given to trusted individuals, who are then free to pass it on to whoever they wish. Someone saw it fit to pass it on to Damien, and he, in turn, decided you were trustworthy to possess it. I wholeheartedly agree with him." He smiled, his fine features brightening in a way that made him impossibly beautiful.

Next to me, Jake shuffled from foot to foot, seeming uncomfortable. I had the feeling that he felt threatened by the Prince's undeniable charm, and maybe, he was even jealous. *Go figure!* He thought I had a chance with a prince. I thought of myself as special, but not *that* special. I almost laughed.

It was stupid of Jake, anyway. By now, he should know that I belonged to him, despite all his mistakes and the heavy baggage of our relationship. No one but Jacob Knight could ever occupy my heart.

"I should be completely forthcoming," the Prince added, growing serious. "It is no accident that I am here, that I was alerted to your presence. In fact, after you and Damien left, I had one of our wizards place an alert on your token."

"Oh," was all I was able to utter.

Jake's expression hardened as if he were re-reevaluating his new impression of the Prince. "Why would you need to keep track of her?" he asked, his voice reverting to that initial rumble that put the hairs on my arms on end like eager little soldiers.

I expected Kalyll to respond similarly, but instead, he put his hands up and said, "Worry not. I mean nothing untoward. I assure you. I've been unable to leave my duties here, so I feel fortunate you decided to visit. If I may explain, but perhaps, this is not the best place, and we might go elsewhere to talk about it."

Jake and I exchanged a glance. We had come here for a different purpose, and this would certainly derail us. Or would it?

I thought of Glimlock, a good-natured Fae that no one would suspect, but was he a better candidate than the Prince of the Seelie. I highly doubted it. If Kalyll put the elixir in his Vine Tower, no one would be able to get to it—not unless they decided to wage war against the Seelie family's royal guard. And if no one would suspect Glimlock, then not even my mother, who loved me to death and thought I could command the moon and the stars with my *snowflakeness,* would begin to imagine that I could have the favor of a prince.

"Yeah," I found myself saying. "Sure, Jake and I have time, and in the end, maybe, we can tell you why we're here." I gave Jake a meaningful glance, trying to convey the idea that had just occurred to me. He gave a slight nod to indicate he understood.

"Very well," the Prince said. "Follow me then."

Unable to believe the turn of events, I walked the way we'd come in the company of the Seelie Prince.

CHAPTER 21

We followed Kalyll down the hill and across the stone bridge and headed down a wide moss-covered path. We had no idea where he was leading us, and more than once I wondered if, after all, he was luring us to some inaccessible dungeon for daring to use a transfer token that didn't belong to us. With every step, Jake seemed to also entertain the same thoughts, judging by the tension rolling off of him.

But when Kalyll invited us to enter a familiar tavern, my worries dissolved. I recognized the walls made out of thousands of tiny branches and the honeycomb windows right away. It was the same place where Damien had first taken me, and where I'd met Glimlock.

The Prince was an astute man and had surely figured that a public place would set us at ease. Though, if it was privacy he sought, we were in the wrong place.

It turned out, however, that the Prince was able to command a private room in the tavern as soon as he walked in. He guided us through a passage lined with twisted branches as thick and dense as actual walls. At the end of the short walk, he requested the attendant—a man with blue skin and leopard eyes—to bring ale for everyone, as well as their dinner fare.

We sat at a table that, like everything else in this place, grew from the ground like a tree, the wood twisting and bending into perfect chairs and flat surfaces for eating. We'd barely exchanged smiles when the attendant hurried back in with the drinks, then left with the same efficiency.

"Had you ever visited Elyndell?" Kalyll asked Jake, making pleasant conversation as we waited for the food to arrive.

"No, this is my first time. It's a beautiful place."

The prince inclined his head and smiled graciously. "Thank you. We Elyndelleans are extremely proud of our city."

"How about you?" Jake said. "You don't sound like a stranger to our realm—not if you can identify a reference to Star Wars." He chuckled, and I had to agree. It was somewhat comical to think of the Fae watching Hollywood blockbusters. They didn't own TVs or even have electricity in their realm, and in fact, repudiated our technological advances and kept access back and forth to Elf-hame as restricted and controlled as possible.

Kalyll nodded. "You are correct. I am no stranger to your realm. My tutors made sure of that. I am versed in your history and popular culture. It is my responsibility as future King to understand our neighbors."

It made sense, but I had never thought about it that way.

"Have you spent time there?" I asked.

"Certainly. I've visited regularly with my father on state matters, and, during my formative years, I spent months at a time in several of your cities."

"Really? Where?" I was curious to know which locations the

Fae considered worthy of their attention.

"Cold Spring, Crawley, Ávila, Elmadağ, places like that."

I frowned, same as Jake. I didn't recognize any of the names.

Noticing our confusion, the Prince explained further. "What all these cities have in common is their proximity to bigger places. Cold Spring is near New York City. Crawley near London. Ávila close to Madrid, and Elmadağ just outside of Ankara. You will forgive me for saying that I much preferred nature and fresh air, so those smaller locations were more suitable. Though, they still afforded me proximity to other areas of import."

Just then, the attendant walked in with a large wooden tray and set down a deliciously smelling stew accompanied by freshly baked herb bread. It was all very simple, but it seemed cooked to perfection, judging by its appearance and wonderful scents.

"Enjoy," Kalyll said, gesturing toward the food.

Jake dug in without further invitation, and I followed suit, the triple-decker burger long gone from my overactive stomach. My hunger had always been particularly disturbing, but since Damien failed to renew his spell on me, I seemed to have developed a hollow leg where everything I consumed emptied in a matter of minutes.

After a polite amount of time, Kalyll set down his spoon and said, "Even if it doesn't appear so, we may speak freely here. One of my wizards sits beyond the door at the moment, ensuring no one can hear us."

I considered that for a moment and decided I had no reason to distrust him. I doubted he wanted his affairs known by tavern dwellers.

Jake seemed to agree with me and with a shrug said, "We're all ears."

The Prince pushed his bowl of stew out of the way and turned his unsettling eyes on me. "Do you remember Gonira?"

"Do you mean the Fae female that was driving the van, the one at the repair shop that night?"

"Yes." He assented with a dip of his chin. "I am embarrassed to say that she has, once more, returned to your realm, and I fear she has rejoined those who are responsible for the conflicts ailing your city."

"Um, I hate to hear that," I said as I wondered about the Prince's need to inform me of this. There was only one possible explanation. He wanted me to track her. I held my breath, hoping I was right. Maybe he could exchange favors again. Jake's eyes flashed with the same realization. I wasn't useful to the Prince in any other way. This had to be it.

"You see," Kalyll continued, "Gonira is my cousin, and my aunt—my mother's sister—has begged me to find her. I am sure you know where I am going with this. I suspect that, given your talents, it is not a novelty for you to be approached by individuals requiring your aid. I know your agency specializes in locating mates, not spoiled brats, members of Fae royal families, but I was hoping that you might make an exception and take on this task. For a fee, of course."

With every word he said, my heart had sped up, but at those last few, it threatened to jump into my throat. A fee could easily become a favor.

"I should say that we have tried to find her on our own without success," the Prince continued. "We found her before, as you well know, but this time it's different. She is going to greater lengths to conceal her location. Magic is definitely involved, and I am not sure if your skill allows you to see beyond such tampering."

My heart sank a little, not all the way, but it wasn't floating in my throat anymore.

"Well," I said, "depending on the type of magic and the level of the witch or mage concealing your cousin's location, my skills could prove ineffectual."

If Gonira was with Stephen and close enough to his circle, the

Midnight Witch who'd killed Damien might be responsible for Gonira's disappearing act. If that was the case, I doubted my skills or anyone else's could pierce through such a power.

"I see." Kalyll nodded. "But there is a possibility you might be able to find her."

"There is."

"Will you try then?" He seemed to choke a little as if it hurt his pride to ask a human for help. "Will your agency accept the case?"

I had the urge to mess with him, to tell him I'd have to check my calendar, but I managed to act like a proper adult.

Instead, I inclined my head gracefully. "Of course, it is what I do."

The Prince seemed to exhale a sigh of relief, which made it clear he'd run out of ideas on how to find his cousin and out of excuses to give his aunt and mother. "The fee is not of import, and, as before, I will be in your debt."

"Well, perhaps not a fee, but… a favor." I exchanged a glance with Jake.

The Prince seemed to grow tense.

"Since you mentioned you'll be in Toni's debt," Jake said. "It should be no hair off your back to help her with what she needs."

Gah, that was so *not* subtle! But of course, subtle was not one of Jake's qualities. And I had to admit that his directness saved a lot of time and saved me from fretting over how to best broach hard subjects.

Kalyll's dark blue gaze cut in my direction. "Please, tell me how I might begin to repay you for your aid."

"It's not a terribly difficult favor," I said, pulling out the vial from my breast pocket and placing it on the table.

The Prince stared curiously at the insignificant thing that lay in front of him. "What is that?"

"It's the elixir Damien Ward created to cure his daughter," Jake answered.

"I fail to see how I can help with this." Kalyll looked puzzled.

"I would just like to keep it well guarded," I said. "It's a life-saving potion, the only one of its kind, and I feel it shouldn't be wasted on just anyone. Things in St. Louis are precarious right now, and this elixir might become important. I could be wrong about that, but one thing is for sure, since I couldn't give it to Damien's daughter, I want to make sure that whoever gets it deserves it. I feel that it's the least I can do after failing him." My voice broke at the end, and I had to swallow to force down the lump that rose in my throat before I could continue. "I also haven't given up hope that it can be duplicated and more than one life might be saved thanks to it." I opened my mouth to continue, trying to make the Prince understand the elixir's importance, but Kalyll raised a hand.

"Say no more." He palmed the elixir and placed it in a pocket inside his tunic. "I will keep it safe for you. I promise that no one will learn of its existence through me, and I'll deliver it safely to you and no one else whenever you want it back."

"Thank you," I managed in a soft voice that revealed how emotional this whole affair made me feel.

"Thank you," Jake echoed. "I know this is a great relief to Toni, and no small favor in her book."

"And you were quite right," the Prince added with a friendly smile, "it is *no hair off my back* to help her with it."

"Your mentors taught you well," Jake said in an amused tone. "You understand our crazy sayings. Maybe one day you can teach us some of yours."

Kalyll smiled, his expression friendly toward Jake, which surprised me. It seemed the Prince had appreciated Jake's directness. Strangely so, I had a feeling the two could become friends if given the chance.

"Toni is the best tracker I know," Jake put in. "If there's anyone who can find your cousin, it's her."

"That is also my understanding," Kalyll said.

I raised an eyebrow. It seemed he'd been doing his research, and I wasn't sure how to feel about that.

"Um, normally, there is a contract to sign, but," I extended my hand, "maybe we just shake on it?" I knew I didn't actually need a contract with the Fae. If they gave their promise, it was binding since they couldn't lie. Besides, from what I'd surmised about the Prince, he was honorable.

He wrapped his big hand around mine and gave it a firm squeeze. "I promise to abide by the terms of what we've discussed."

The Prince let go, reached into a pocket of his tunic, and came up with a metal key. The top was intricate, beautifully wrought. The stem was long, and the bit possessed several notches shaped into a flower. He handed it over. It was heavy, substantial.

"It belongs to Gonira. I believe you need something of her to track her."

I put the key away and nodded. *Yep*, he'd certainly done his homework.

ঌঔ

"This trip couldn't have gone better if I had planned it," I said to Jake as soon as we materialized back in Eric's training room an hour later.

"I think you're right. The Prince seems like a stand-up guy."

"Yeah, he does. I'm not worried about—" I was interrupted by Eric storming into the room, his expression so troubled it immediately sent my heart into a full gallop.

Jake turned and, without missing a beat, read the same urgency in our friend's face. "What's the matter?"

Eric's gaze went back and forth between us, lingering for a

moment on me, then finally settling on Jake.

"For fuck's sake, man!" Jake stepped forward, towering over Eric. "Tell us."

"I got a call from Craig Blackridge," Eric finally spoke, his timbre thick with emotion. "It's your grandfather. He's dead."

CHAPTER 22

The air was sucked out of the room, leaving me breathless, and it seemed it was the same for Jake because his shoulders dropped an inch as he exhaled. I took a step forward, pressed a hand to his back, and glanced up at him, my heart constricting to half its size.

Jake, oh, Jake.

What was he feeling?

I couldn't fathom exactly what this would do to him. I didn't know how strong the bond with his grandfather had been, but the way the color drained from his face told me maybe it was deeper than I had suspected. The news was wrecking him, shredding him to pieces.

I wanted to wrap my arms around him, but I was afraid to move, afraid to do anything that might cause him to fall apart.

He opened his mouth as if he would say something, but nothing came out. I tried to guess what he wanted to say and turned to

Eric.

"What happened?" I asked, my voice trembling. "Who did it? Why?" Not knowing exactly what Jake wanted to say, I clumsily tried to cover all possibilities.

Jake pulled away from me, taking a step toward the door. "I need to go."

No. I didn't want him to go anywhere, not like this, not in this emotional state. So I was grateful when Eric didn't move out of the way and stayed at the threshold, feet planted firmly on the floor.

"You need to stay," Eric said calmly. "I don't think it would be smart to go anywhere right now."

"I need to see him," Jake said.

"And you will, but first, you should take some time to process. Or if you must go, let Toni or I drive you."

Jake grabbed his head as if deciding who should go with him was a monumental choice. It was enough to let us know he *wasn't* fit to go anywhere alone.

"Craig is taking care of things right now," Eric added. "So if you're worried about that, don't be."

Jake appeared at a loss and just stood there holding his head. Walter was Jake's only living relative, and it was sad to think that Craig Blackridge—the Knights' new ally—was taking responsibility at a moment like this. Surely, Jake felt it should be him, but he really needed time to process first. I wondered if there was no one in their small pack who could help him. Jake had never mentioned anyone in particular, but he'd just started to get acquainted with his pack members.

"Let's go upstairs. I'll get you a stiff drink," Eric suggested.

A few moments later, sitting in front of the unlit fireplace in Eric's study, Jake sipped oakfire from a tumbler, staring blankly at the floor without saying a word.

Eric and I exchanged concerned glances. I worried about what might be going through Jake's head. But once he finished his drink and set the tumbler on the coffee table, he composed himself and turned to Eric.

"What do you know?" His voice was husky but other than that he appeared in full control of himself.

"It's not good. He…" Eric hesitated, which made my heart beat at a frantic rate. "He was the one given the dagger at Wolfskeep."

Oh, no!

That must mean Bernadetta and Stephen had come for the dagger and killed him. Guilt descended like the sky collapsing on top of me. I should have kept the dagger. If I had, Walter would still be alive.

"They will pay!" Jake said in a growl, fluidly rising to his feet as if ready to bolt in search of our enemies. "Bernadetta and Stephen will regret coming for him."

"No, Jake," Eric shook his head, lowering his eyes. "They didn't come for him. Walter went to them."

"What?!" Jake demanded.

"He was attempting to negotiate. It seemed he wanted the jade cup. He wanted to be in control of the Unholy Vessel."

Jake shook his head. "No, he wouldn't…"

But he didn't finish because, deep inside, he knew that Walter had been *that* kind of man, desperate for power, willing to go to any lengths to get what he wanted. He lowered his head, embarrassment coloring his face. His right eye twitched a couple of times before he got this new, unexpected emotion under control.

"He lost the dagger, Jake," Eric said, his words reluctant as if he wished to spare Jake the blow.

I couldn't stop the gasp that burst through my lips.

This was bad. Very bad.

Jake took a few steps back and collapsed back on the sofa. Slowly, his silver eyes lifted and met mine. There was so much confusion and pain in them.

I turned to Eric. "Would you mind giving us a moment?"

Eric said nothing. He simply stood and strode out of the room. I sat next to Jake and wrapped one of his large hands in both of mine.

"How could he?" Jake asked. "What was he thinking?"

"I'm so sorry, Jake."

"I should have listened to William."

"William?"

"My grandfather's lawyer and old-time friend. He's a member of the pack, too. He… warned me that Walter wasn't in his right mind. He said that maybe I should take him to see a doctor, a neurologist. He thought that the first signs of dementia were setting in. Of course, I talked to Walter, but I'm sure you can imagine his reaction to that conversation."

I could definitely imagine it. There was no way Walter would've admitted to any sort of mental fragility. I hadn't known him well, but I knew what type of man he had been. He would have rather worn a tutu in public than admit he was losing his mental abilities.

Jake continued, "And he seemed so strong, so capable. You saw him. I didn't think there was anything wrong with him other than his normal cantankerous, old man shit."

I had seen him and remembering him at Wolfskeep made me wonder if Walter really had been mentally unstable. He had seemed fine while ganging up on Ulfen to indirectly blame him for what Stephen had done. Or was Jake just making excuses for his grandfather?

"But I didn't know him that well, not like William does… did. We were never close, not really. It wasn't until Mom and Dad died that he showed any interest in me. He never approved of Dad's choice of mate. He always thought he should've married into some sort of alliance. I didn't learn any of that until recently, until after he manipulated me into a pact with the Blackridges. He became more… vocal once I was trapped. Don't get me wrong, I don't blame him for my mistake. I went along with it because of the promise I made to my father. Walter didn't force me."

It looked to me as if Jake was trying to excuse his grandfather's behavior, maybe to spare his memory now that he was dead, but I didn't think Walter deserved to be spared. He *had* been manipulative, and that was that.

"Why would he try to do something like that? If I'd just—"

"*Shh,* don't torture yourself about it," I said. "Only the witchlights know his real reasons at this point, and it does you no good to try to guess or blame yourself. For what it's worth, he didn't seem unstable to me. He was ambitious, Jake, and the Unholy Vessel is a source of incredible power. I'd hoped Yura hadn't chosen him, but I had also hoped he would respect his kind too much to turn them into mindless monsters."

Jake chuckled sadly. "It never even crossed my mind to doubt him. I trusted him intrinsically because he was family. I should have known." He said the last words in an angry growl that made the tumbler on the coffee table vibrate.

"Please, don't blame yourself," I repeated. "You can never fully know someone's heart. I never suspected my mother of being a world-class liar, and look at how she kept my badass wolf hidden for over twenty years."

He blew air through his nose, half amused. He squeezed my hand gently and leaned his head against mine.

After a long moment, fighting to hold the urgent question that had jumped into my mind almost as soon after Eric gave us the news, I couldn't help myself any longer and quietly gave voice to my thoughts.

"What does this mean for your pact with the Blackridges?"

"I don't really know."

"Do you think Craig will still want his daughter to marry you?" I couldn't help the hint of hope that crept into my voice. Maybe after Walter's monumental screw up, Craig would not want his pack's name associated with the Knights.

"Ah, but that's the beauty of an unbreakable pact and why Walter insisted on it."

"Yes, but, if he were to change his mind and we all pulled in the same direction, we might find a solution."

Jake responded with silence.

"Of course," I hurriedly added, "that's secondary right now."

He sat up straighter and angled his body in my direction, reaching for my other hand and squeezing it to impress his next words onto me.

"You're never secondary. Never. With Walter gone, you're all the family I have left. You are everything to me, Toni, and I won't let any of this change things. My promise stands. I am the Knight pack's alpha now, and though it's not a responsibility I ever wanted, I need to step up, but just know that this doesn't mean, in any way, that my feelings for you will change. Toni, if you will have me I…" He stopped.

I held my breath, desperately wanting to hear his next words. Except, they didn't come. He held them back and gave me only a smile. For a moment, I thought to press him, to demand what he'd been about to say, but I couldn't. Perhaps, he'd been about to ask me to marry him, then realized he had no right to do so—not when he was engaged to another, whether or not he wanted to be.

So I just said, "I know, Jake. It doesn't change my feelings either. I don't think anything could make me stop loving you. I swear I tried, but I failed miserably."

He caressed my cheek, his thumb brushing the corner of my mouth. "You don't know how glad I am about that. I know it makes me a selfish bastard, but God, Toni, all the time I was apart from you was hardly worth living. I couldn't imagine a life without you."

"You don't have to," I said. "You don't have to."

He pressed his forehead to mine, and we sat like that for a long moment, inhaling each other's scent and wishing the world could stop, so we could stay this way forever.

The world was going to shit, but at least we had each other.

CHAPTER 23

Later that night, I sat curled up in front of my coffee table, several thick books cracked open in front of me. Earlier, I had offered to go with Jake to see about his grandfather, but he'd insisted it was something he needed to do on his own. I'd sensed it was a pack thing, and he didn't want me to feel unwelcome. And since I wanted to make the situation as painless as possible for him, I'd relented. Instead, I did the next best thing and grabbed a bunch of the books Eric had gotten for him while Jake took the rest.

I'd had a terribly long-ass day, starting with work and ending with the terrible news of Walter's death. So at this point, reading was a task for the wicked—the kind that never rested.

Of course, I had food to help me fight the fatigue. An extra-large sausage, pepperoni, and mushroom pizza from *Adriana's on The Hill*—half of it anyway since I'd already devoured four large pieces.

No self-respecting woman should be able to eat one of them all by herself, but it seemed I was about to do just that. I should've been full by now, but as I read, I kept eyeing the leftover slices. If I was honest with myself, I *was* worried about gaining weight. My metabolism ran high. There was no question about that, but high enough to keep eating like this? I didn't have money to buy a new wardrobe, and at the rate I kept ripping clothes every time I shifted, I might need to start making regular trips to the thrift store.

Maybe I should sell that pair of Louis Vuitton ankle boots, I mused. They had been an extravagance anyhow, from when I'd thought the agency would take off like a rocket.

Rolling my eyes at my useless train of thought, I picked up another slice of pizza and bit into it. The books in front of me were frustrating as heck. After two hours of scanning their pages, I hadn't been able to find anything that referred to unbreakable pacts—unless I counted the admonishments never to make one, unless death was an appealing prospect to you. Needless to say, I hadn't found anything on how to break them.

I finished riffling through the pages of the second book, set it aside, and moved on to the third. Blaze appeared suddenly, jumping on the sofa, and settling behind me as if to read over my shoulder.

"Hey, buddy. Had a good day?" I'd looked for him when I first came in, but I hadn't been able to find him. I still had no idea where he hid himself to sleep. He was so sneaky, but I guess that meant he was a proper cat.

His nose twitched as I took another bite of pizza. He looked at the slice so longingly, then toward his bowl of kibble in the corner of the still-empty dining room. I had to feel sorry for him. Plucking a piece of sausage from the gooey cheese, I held it out to him in my palm. He lapped it and licked his lips with his raspy tongue, a look of utter pleasure in his amber eyes.

"Good, huh?"

He narrowed his eyes as if saying *duh* and meowed at the pizza, begging for more.

"You'll get sick. I'm not supposed to feed you *hooman* food."

He let out a little hiss that I swear sounded like *pleeeaseee.*

"Okay, so you won't get sick?"

I waited for an answer, but he proceeded to lick his butthole.

Really?! He went from being the most eloquent cat to this?

I turned back to the books and leafed through them for another twenty minutes. True to form, I polished the pizza off while Blaze slept placidly behind me. Without food to distract me, my frustration with the futility of the search got to me. With a huff, I smacked the book closed, startling Blaze awake. He meowed, putting an inflection at the end as if he were asking a question.

"Sorry, I woke you up, cutie pie. It's just, this is a waste of time. I can't find anything on unbreakable pacts. I've been through ten of these books and nothing. I don't think it's worth it going through the whole pile." I gestured toward the three tall stacks that sat in front of the fireplace.

Blaze, seeming lucid again, stood, stretched his back, arching it in a perfect semi-circle, then hopped off the couch. Waving his tail in the air, he meandered toward the stacks of books. I watched him with a frown.

He sidled next to one stack and rubbed his body against it, his tail curling over the spine of one of the books as he circled around the stack. He did the same with the other stack, then the third, and when he was done, he plopped himself in front of the books, staring at them.

"And… ?" I prompted. "Any luck?"

He ignored me, and set his head on top of his outstretched front paws, ready for another nap.

"Worthless cat!" I spat, then realized I was just taking it out on him. "Sorry, I didn't mean that, Blaze. I'm the one who's worthless. I know nothing about my kind. How can I be of any use to Jake?"

Exhausted and knowing I had to get up early tomorrow to train with Eric, I picked up the empty pizza box and took it to the kitchen. I was doing my best to fold it and stuff it in the already-full garbage can when there was a horrible crash from the living room. My heart gave a jump, and I ran in to find one of the book stacks scattered on the floor while Blaze sat on top of a particularly thick tome, happily licking one of his paws.

I walked closer and read the title on the spine. *Blood Treaties: My life in France by Alodar Rune,* and under that, in very small letters, *Pacte de Sang: Ma Vie en France.* I'd seen the book when I first picked a few from the stacks, but I didn't link the word treaty to pact, and I didn't notice the French title either.

"What the…? Are you trying to tell me something?"

He glanced up, his eyes blank, his expression so purely feline that I felt like a total idiot grasping at straws. Of course, he wasn't trying to tell me that I would find the answers I sought in this book. Of course, he wasn't any sort of Skew cat.

Still, I picked up Blaze, set him on the coffee table, then collected the heavy volume.

"I might as well take a look at this one next," I said. "It's not like it makes any difference."

I walked toward the sofa, leafing through the first few pages. I was about to sit down when my phone rang. I set the book down when I saw that it was *Rosalina.*

"Hey!" I said, frowning. It was rare for her to call this late. "Everything all right?"

"I've got good news. I checked the agency's after-hour messages and guess what?"

"What?" I asked, my heart beating quickly, responding to the excitement in her voice.

"Mekare Graves called and said her assistant is coming by tomorrow morning with a signed contract and a vial of the best heartfelt tears she's ever cried, and best of all, a check for the deposit! Fifteen thousand dollars, Toni. We live to fight another day."

"Witchlights! Really?!"

"Yep!"

My knees almost buckled in relief. "I'll get to work on her potion as soon as they deliver those tears."

"We have all the ingredients we need. I triple-checked everything this morning. I'll schedule time for the tracking trance to make sure nothing gets in the way."

"I'm so relieved." I needed to tell her about the deal I'd made with Kalyll. I would soon need to track Gonira, but this was the priority.

"Me, too. Make sure you get lots of rest now. You'll have to do two trances soon. One for Mr. Taylor and one for Ms. Graves."

I nodded as if she could see me. "Yeah, I can do that this weekend."

"Like I said, rest."

"Will do."

Well, no more time to waste on useless book searches. Succeeding in tracking a mate for these two clients was as high on the priority list as Stephen's payback. So I made sure I had an alarm set for 3:30 AM, brushed my teeth, and crawled into bed.

CHAPTER 24

The next morning, after training with Eric, my second order of business was to swing by the agency, check on Mr. Taylor's potion, *and* start Mekare's after her stuff was dropped off. Rosalina and I did a little dance, our moods only dampened by Walter Knight's funeral, which had been arranged with expediency and would take place in the late afternoon.

I'd asked Eric if he was going, but he hadn't decided.

"Normally, I wouldn't," he said, "but I like Jake."

I'd paused and stared at him. I didn't think I'd ever heard him say he liked anything, not even puppies or French fries.

"Oh, don't look at me like that." He flashed a *you'll keep your mouth shut if you know what's good for you* glare at me.

I'd done just that, pressing my lips together into a thin line, but aware that he was making some progress, moving from Cro-magnon to Neanderthal. Wow, maybe soon he would make it to full Homosapien, even one with feelings.

Now, Rosalina and I ate lunch at her desk, doom scrolling on our phones.

"There was another vampire attack on werewolves, this time in Sunset Hills. Five dead," she said, thumbing through the news, which lately was little less than a war report.

"Any mention of hybrid monsters?"

"No."

A wave of apprehension rolled over me. Bernadetta and Stephen had the dagger back, what were they waiting for? Not that I was looking forward to seeing the streets of St. Louis flooded by monsters, but the suspense was killing me.

Disgusted, Rosalina set the phone down and stuffed a piece of lettuce in her mouth. "Have you heard from Leo?" she asked, changing subjects.

I shook my head, trying not to let my concern for my brother compound with everything else going on.

"He's still off trying to become a powerful mage." That was the latest excuse he'd given us for not visiting. When he'd left, he was a White Mage, the lowest level. He'd advanced to the next level, Brass Mage, but he had a way to go to make it to Midnight Mage, which was his goal.

"I'm sure he's fine," she enthused.

"Yeah, he's just an inconsiderate jerk. He'll get an earful from Mom when he finally gets in touch. I'm sure."

"And he'll deserve it."

"Yep!"

When we were done eating, we halfheartedly headed toward the funeral home. I parked my Camaro in the first empty spot I could find. It seemed all the werewolves in St. Louis had turned up for this. I stared at the forlorn building, a knot forming in my gut.

"Are you all right?" Rosalina asked.

I shook my head.

"I'm sorry. Would another donut help?" She reached in the back of the car and retrieved the box we'd bought on the way here. She peered through the clear top. "There's one left. It's chocolate."

Rosalina had eaten one out of the dozen, and I'd polished off the rest. Normally, I only ate half a dozen, but fleeting about was doing a number on me.

"No, I'm good." The sight of that last donut was tempting, but I didn't want to risk getting my dress dirty. It was a miracle it'd come out unscathed after all the donuts I'd eaten on the way here. Of course, when you've practically become a vacuum cleaner, maybe worrying about crumbs on your clothes was unnecessary.

I chewed on my bottom lip, worrying about running into my father, my half-siblings, Jake's fiancée.

"Jake said he would understand if you didn't come," Rosalina reminded me. She had talked to him on the phone earlier to ask if there was anything he needed.

I inhaled a shuddering breath. "What kind of… friend would I be if I can't be with him at a time like this?"

She nodded. Rosalina understood things like this too well. She was the kind of person who always did the right thing. Nothing deterred her. She was brave even under the worst circumstances, and, with her example, she taught me to be the same.

I took another deep breath, trying to gather courage from the air. I found none, of course, and had to rely on my own wavering inner strength. Maybe one day, when I grew up, I would measure up to my best friend.

"Let's do it." I threw the door open and got out of the car.

"You look great." Rosalina winked as we made our way to the front door.

I smiled. "I learned from the best."

Her compliment boosted my confidence a little. I was wearing a knee-length black dress with an elegantly pleated skirt and lace short sleeves. For my makeup, I'd used a few of the techniques

Rosalina had shown me, and I managed to masterfully conceal the purple circles under my eyes—4 AM training sessions with obsessed werewolves didn't help a girl look her best. Then a bit of bronzer and highlight powder on my cheeks graduated me from zombie to attractive young woman.

Two men dressed in black suits and ties stood at either side of the door. They stared straight ahead, unblinking. They didn't glance in our direction as we entered and were the first hint of the somber air we would encounter inside.

We walked shoulder to shoulder down the carpeted hall and entered a large room arranged with rows of chairs to the left and right in front of a casket surrounded by massive floral arrangements. I was shocked by the heavy silence despite the large number of people occupying the room. Barely anyone spoke, and those who did whispered so softly that not even werewolf ears could catch what they were saying.

Several heads turned in our direction. Noses twitched taking in our scent. Distrust quickly shaped their features as they failed to recognize us. We were newcomers, a Stale and an unknown werewolf. At least, I was succeeding at controlling my alpha vibes. I'd been practicing with Eric. Displaying my dominance here wouldn't only be bad but completely inappropriate.

Their attention quickly moved away, though it came back every few beats, assessing, distrustful. Werewolves weren't quick to trust. And if this were anything but a funeral, I would expect more than glares.

"There's a couple of chairs over there," Rosalina pointed to the last row.

Perfect, I thought as we moved in that direction, walking behind the row of chairs and letting my eyes rove over the crowd, searching for Jake, but he wasn't here.

Just as we were about to reach the end of the line, two people appeared from a door we hadn't noticed and started to sit in the empty chairs. And it would've been all right by me—they hadn't seen us coming—except they turned out to be Olivia and Marcus Hillworth, and without rhyme or reason, their presence made my anger reach volcanic proportions in a split second. It was an irrational reaction, but I seemed to have no control over it.

I was about to say something that I would've probably regretted for the rest of my life when Olivia looked up and noticed us.

"Oh," she said. "I didn't notice you, Toni. My apologies. We'll find somewhere else to sit. C'mon on." She gestured to her brother and they were off.

My mouth opened and closed, but no words came out. And my anger? Well, it fizzled out like air leaking from a worn-out balloon.

"Was that your… um?" Rosalina said.

I nodded and took a seat, a jumble of confusing feelings crowding my chest. *That* hadn't been the same woman I met yesterday, and if she hadn't used my name, I would've guessed she hadn't recognized me. It seemed she did know how to be nice, if only because she was at a funeral.

After we'd been sitting in silence for a few minutes, Jake came in through a door in the front of the room, Allison at his side. He wore a black suit, tailored to perfection while Allison wore a white, form-fitting dress with a tie neck.

My stomach clenched at the sight of them together. They passed the casket without looking in its direction and stood off to the side.

Taking this as a signal, the people sitting in the front stood to shake Jake's hand and whisper their condolences. Soon, as more people stood up, a line formed, everyone waiting their turn to offer their sympathy.

Jake kept a tall, dignified posture, shaking hands and nodding politely. I watched him, every twitch of his face, every forced smile, and knew this was very hard for him. I wanted to be by his side, holding his hand in mine and offering my support. But instead, it was Allison, flashing her white teeth in an exaggerated smile as if she were a hostess at a party.

Didn't she understand that this must be awful for Jake? Not only because his only close relative was dead, but because he'd gone through something as tragic with his father, mother, and brother. Did she realize the painful memories this must be unleashing inside his heart?

When the line was reduced to a trickle—people were steadily filing out of the room into an adjacent area—Rosalina patted my hand.

"I'll go pay my respects. You don't have to go. You can stay here." Her green eyes were kind and told me it would be all right if I stayed, but I knew I had to go. For Jake.

"I'm coming."

We stood and joined the back of the line. Jake didn't notice me until I was standing right in front of him. He blinked and his silver eyes lost their dull quality.

"Toni!" He seized my offered hand as if it were a lifeline, as if I could rescue him from this.

I felt the loneliness rolling off of him in waves. He was forced to endure this, surrounded by people he hardly knew. It wasn't right. He held on to me for longer than was polite, our gazes locked, saying so much.

Jake, I'm sorry. I wish I could be by your side.

Please don't go, Toni. I need you.

Rosalina put a hand on top of ours, making us aware of the many eyes lingering on us.

"My condolences, Jacob," she said in a gentle voice, dexterously extricating my hand from his and replacing it with hers. "If there is anything I can do to help, just tell me. I am so sorry for your loss."

"Thank you, Rosalina. Very kind of you." For the first time, Jake's expression was sincere.

Next to him, Allison glared at me. She flicked her eyes toward the door through which people were exiting in a clear indication that it was time for me to leave. I swallowed the lump in my throat and left, willing myself to push away the frustration and hatred that Allison inspired in me.

For Jake. For Jake.

Once in the other room, Rosalina put a finger under my chin and guided my gaze to hers. "You did good."

I'd been staring at the floor, my ears roaring as I did my best to calm down. For the first time, I became aware of my surroundings. People were milling about, talking in normal tones, and carrying little plates with cups of coffee or hors d'oeuvres. There was a long table at the back of the room, covered in a white tablecloth, and replete with finger foods. Next to the food, there was another table set up with a metal coffee urn. There was also a glass one filled with water and slices of lemon.

There was a freaking dead person in the next room and people were standing here eating?! What the hell?!

Suddenly, I felt claustrophobic. I glanced around and headed into the first door I spotted. I ended up in a small sitting room with two armchairs, a wooden table between them, and a round rug under foot.

Calm down. Calm down, Red.

I took deep breaths, staring out a window, focusing on the trees outside. My heart slowly went from pounding against my chest to a more acceptable knocking. After a few quiet moments, I turned to leave, but the door opened, and there was Jake.

He looked relieved as if he'd been looking for me, and it'd taken him too long to find me. Without a word, he took two strides in my direction and wrapped me in his arms. He buried his face in my neck.

"I can't wait to get the hell out of here," he said.

"I know."

"Can I come to your place after this is over?"

"Of course."

He pulled away, a hand caressing the side of my face.

Suddenly, without a knock, the door opened behind us. Allison slipped inside. The door handle clicked behind her as it engaged.

"Really?!" she said in a quiet but angry tone.

"Allison," Jake began, but she cut him off.

"Spare me," she spat. "I know what's between you two, but do you have to be this obvious?" She shook her head, giving us an *are you really this stupid?* look. "You don't see me sneaking out with Maxwell, do you? We have to keep appearances."

Jake's eyebrows drew together. "Maxwell?"

Allison rolled her eyes. "You really *are* dense."

"Appearances?" I said, finally able to form words. "You mean…" I didn't know how to put into words what I was thinking.

She walked over to one of the armchairs and collapsed in it. "I guess I'm glad you *are* sneaking around, even if you have as much sense as two baked potatoes. At least it served to prove my suspicions right." Abruptly, she sat up and glanced between Jake and me, narrowing her eyes. "You two *are* in love, right? This is not just some sort of hook up?"

Jake interlaced his fingers with mine, which seemed to serve as a response because Allison let herself relax back on the chair.

"Good. Good!" she said in an exhale. "This should make things a lot easier for all of us. By the way, I'm in love with Maxwell, just so you know."

Jake nodded very slowly. "I had no idea."

"Of course, you didn't. I know what I'm doing. Your grandfather kept a constant eye on me. He certainly wasn't fooled. Every time he saw me, he made sure to remind me of my responsibilities. He would say *Jake can't wait till the wedding day,*" she huffed in a deeper voice. "I know *he* couldn't wait." She rolled her eyes. "No disrespect to the deceased, but he was just as obsessed as my father is about our pact."

"Your father forced you into the pact, didn't he?" I asked.

Allison nodded. "I had no choice. He threatened to kill Maxwell." At this, her voice trembled with fear.

I pressed a hand to my mouth, unable to comprehend how a father could do that. Quickly, my hatred toward Allison turned to pity.

She sniffled, her eyes wavering. "That's why we have to be careful. My father can't know. No one can. I've only met Maxwell a couple of times since we swore the pact."

"That's awful," I said.

She shrugged. "Yes, but not unheard of for weak females." She shook her head and focused on Jake again. "But you're an alpha. Your grandfather couldn't have forced you. So if you're in love with her," she flicked a hand in my direction, "why did you agree? Screw the legacy. Screw the promise you made to your father."

It was Jake's turn to shrug.

She sighed, understanding all too well. "That fucking legacy. It's always about that, isn't it? Maxwell is a member of a lesser pack *and* a beta. That's why Dad would never approve of him. We've been dating since high school, but my father isn't impressed by that or by the fact that he truly loves me. He's only impressed by *Jacob Knight*." She scanned Jake from head to toe, looking unimpressed herself.

This Maxwell guy had to be something else. If Jake didn't measure up to her standards, her love was certainly blind.

No one measures up to Jake!

I shook my head to dismiss the stupid thought. It belonged to Red, not the more sensible Toni who understood love was the only thing that mattered.

Witchlights! I'd been so wrong about Allison. I never imagined that she could be in our exact situation. I glanced sideways at Jake, wondering if he was thinking what *I* was thinking.

Could Allison become our ally in finding a way to break the

pact? I didn't dare ask. She might be madly in love with someone else, but was she willing to go as far as to oppose her father? The same question seemed to flash behind Jake's eyes, but he remained as reserved as me. He wanted to tread carefully on this, and I didn't blame him.

Allison's blue eyes flicked between us, shrewd and calculating. Clearly, we weren't the only ones being cautious. She opened her mouth to say something, but we never knew what because a commotion came from the next room. There were shouts, high-pitched screams, growls.

Then the gunshots began.

CHAPTER 25

Jake rushed to the door. Knowing his impulsiveness, I lunged forward and wedged myself between him and the door.

"Move out of th—" I pressed a hand to his mouth.

"*Shh.*"

Rather than just rush out there, we needed to assess the situation.

Allison seemed to agree with me because she whispered, "Be quiet. Let's see what's happening first."

Jake clenched his teeth, jaw twitching, and nodded, if reluctantly.

I turned around and slowly turned the knob. Holding my breath, I cracked the door just a fraction and peeked out. Towering over me, Jake did the same. We couldn't see much but a small section of the adjacent room. A couple of people ran and tripped over each other, but most stood still, their backs to us, their attention focused on one of the exits.

There were more shouts, followed by a spray of bullets. Shrieks of fear and low growls issued back in response.

God! Was Rosalina okay? I couldn't see her.

Witchlights protect her!

"No one move or they get shot with wolfsbane bullets," a voice that I immediately recognized rose above all others.

"Stephen," Jake whispered in my ear.

I nodded.

"Or perhaps they get to meet my little friends," Stephen added, and, in response, matching bloodcurdling roars made the walls shudder.

"And hybrids," I said.

My stomach clenched with the memories of the awful beasts, then my anger grew into a living thing, a mass that throbbed inside my chest like a second heart ready to explode.

"How many?" Allison whispered.

I shook my head. I had no idea. I shuddered to think how many more Bernadetta and Stephen had created now that they possessed the dagger again.

I was pondering what we should do next when, behind us, Allison slid the window open. "Let's get out this way," she urged. "We may be able to surprise them from the back."

I eased the door closed, and we followed her without hesitation.

Allison stuck her head out through the open window. "It's safe," she said over her shoulder, then dived out as if into a pool. As she hit the grassy lawn she rolled smoothly to her feet, flashing a pair of lace underwear in the process. Jake turned his eyes away, cheeks reddening.

I blew air through my nose and rolled my eyes. *Men!*

Gathering my dress, I went next. I stuck a leg out through the window, ducked my head, and clumsily slunk out of the room. Jake followed in a similar fashion except with grace despite his bulk. *So not fair.*

The sun had started to descend, coloring the sky in different hues.

Once we were all out, Allison waved us over as she carefully made her way to one corner of the building. There, she stopped and took a quick peek. Almost as quickly, she pulled back, wincing.

"Not good," she whispered. "There are about five armed guys blocking the door, along with five more in their wolf shapes."

"What do they want?" I asked no one in particular, unable to understand why Stephen would do something like this. Why would he disrespect an old man's funeral? The man he, himself, had murdered?

In answer, Stephen's loud voice came at us through the window we'd left behind. It was barely discernible, something I wouldn't have been able to hear without my werewolf abilities.

"Where is Jacob Knight?" he demanded.

Next to me, Jake stiffened.

"What the hell?" I mouthed.

What could Stephen want with Jake?

Another spray of bullets. More screams.

"Where is Jacob Knight?" Stephen shouted again. "Don't hide, you coward."

Jake took a step forward, but I grabbed him by the wrist. "No, don't go."

"I can't hide. He might hurt those people."

"He'll hurt *you*."

He shrugged as if that didn't matter.

A single shot rang out, followed by a heart-wrenching scream.

"NOO!"

"I will kill these people one by one until you show yourself, Jake," Stephen growled.

I let go of Jake's wrist, understanding all too well that there was no other choice. He had to go. Well, he wouldn't be going alone. He started to walk, and I followed. Noticing me, he stopped and shook his head.

"I'm with you. Always," I said.

"Aw, how admirable," Allison put in.

I ignored her, expecting Jake to argue, but he simply nodded and let me follow. As we stepped around the building, we laid eyes on the armed people and wolves that stood by the entrance. They noticed us immediately and aimed their weapons and sharp teeth in our direction. A large Escalade SUV sat atop a flowerbed, door thrown open, engine still running.

Jake put his hands up, and I did likewise.

"I'm Jacob Knight," he said, loudly enough to be heard inside, werewolf hearing or not.

"He's out here," one of the armed men called out, taking a step in front of the others, asserting himself as one of their leaders.

I directed all my anger in his direction, glowering and doing my best to communicate exactly how I felt, though without using my alpha skills to push the thought into his head.

I hope you die, and Satan himself feeds you your balls for breakfast every morning for the rest of eternity.

It seemed he got the silent message loud and clear because he looked me up and down, bared his teeth, and pointed his gun in *my* direction, while everyone else focused on Jake.

A moment later, Stephen walked out to meet us, stopping about ten feet away, an automatic gun in his grip. He seemed to be on his own with no signs of Bernadetta or her vamps.

"I was starting to think you didn't care about your guests," he said, his red hair gleaming in the sunlight.

"What are you doing here? Have you no respect for anything?!" Jake demanded.

Stephen ignored his question and slid his gaze in my direction. "Toni, I thought I might see you here."

There was a certain ring of regret in his tone. He had wanted me by his side, going along with his deranged scheme for the sake of power. And maybe he hadn't entirely given up hope yet. Clearly, he had absolutely no idea how much I'd grown to hate him and how quickly I would slit his throat given the chance.

I had no words for him. All I could offer him was death, and my fingers twitched with eagerness to impart it.

He blew air through his nose, trying to appear indifferent, but I knew him well enough. He'd seen me as some sort of prize, and he hated the fact that he'd lost me. I had no doubt that, if given the chance, he would attempt to make me his slave again. He'd had no qualms about feeding me tainted blood from the Unholy Vessel before. Whether or not I followed him willingly, it made no difference to him.

But I would die first, and I would do my best to take him down with me.

He turned to Jake and belatedly answered his question. "You know why I'm here. Give it to me."

I frowned.

Give what to him? What was Stephen talking about?

Out of the corner of my eye, I tried to judge Jake's reaction, but he showed none. My brain started whirling at twice its normal speed, trying to figure out what was going on.

"This is not the place for any of this," Jake said. "You murdered my grandfather, then you come here and do *this*? You're a fucking bastard."

Stephen let out a tired sigh. "I don't have time to mess around." He flicked two fingers over his shoulder, and two massive shapes walked out of the building. They'd been waiting in his wake, ready for his signal.

The hybrids took their positions at either side of their master. I recognized the one from Liliana's house. They were both tall and monstrous, standing on two legs, displaying their grotesque nakedness, patchy fur, and pulsing black veins that ran like cords over their bulging muscles.

I tried to look past the threshold to see if there were more of them inside, but it was impossible to tell. Were more waiting for another signal from Stephen?

"Give me the dagger or suffer the consequences," Stephen hissed between clenched teeth.

My breath hitched. The dagger?! But he'd killed Walter to steal it. Had he failed? Did Jake have it? He hadn't mentioned anything. What the hell was going on?

"It's not here, obviously," Jake said. "And hurting these people won't help you get it. I can assure you that."

I glanced questioningly in Jake's direction. Still, his expression was impassive, giving nothing away, but if I knew him well, he was bluffing. He didn't have what Stephen wanted.

My gaze went back and forth between the two hybrids. *Damn!* I was so confused. If Stephen hadn't gotten the dagger from Walter, then it meant they'd made these two monsters before the coven temple. Had they only managed to make the pair? Or an army?

I wanted to know, desperately.

Stephen's mouth twitched, anger flashing in his blue eyes. Jake's composed attitude was unsettling him. He seemed to think for a moment, then, as he made a decision, his expression grew intent.

"Of course you don't care what happens to your guests." Stephen vaguely waved a hand toward the building behind him. "You're not a… pack kinda guy. Ever since I met you, I thought you were an oddball. But I do know the one thing you care about the most." His gaze lazily slid toward me, then his voice rose, "Grab her!"

Several of his armed cronies advanced closer. I crouched, ready to attack.

Should I shift? Fleet?

None of those seemed like a good option. We were outnumbered. I might be able to save myself, but they would hurt Jake. Could I use my sensory powers to overwhelm them? No, not all of them at once. I shook my head.

Do something, Toni.

But what?

Stephen's men were almost upon me.

Jake spoke. "If you hurt her, you won't get the dagger either. Let everyone be, and I'll go with you. I'll take you to it."

"No, Jake. Don't," I protested, fear rippling over my skin.

I was on the verge of shifting and had to grind my teeth to keep my wolf at bay.

Jake peered at me, his expression calm and resigned. There was no doubt in his clear gaze. No fear or hesitation. He was doing what he thought was right, keeping these people safe, keeping *me* safe.

He didn't say a word, but I read the plea clearly on his features. It was intense and undeniable. *Let me go, Toni.*

I shook my head.

It's for the best. It's the only way to stop him from killing more people, I knew that was his train of thought.

But do you have the dagger? That was what I wanted to ask because if he didn't have it, what then? Bernadetta and Stephen would get angry, and they would surely kill him. And if he did have it…

Did that make any difference? No, it wouldn't. They would kill him anyway. Or worse, they would turn him into a hybrid. Either option was out of the question. I couldn't let Stephen take him. I might never see him again.

I snatched Jake's hand and squeezed it in mine. "I'll go with you," I whispered.

"NO!" His response was immediate and emphatic. He turned to Stephen. "She stays. The only way you'll get the dagger is if you let everyone else be."

Stephen's blue eyes flicked from Jake to me. He seemed to consider it carefully. In the end, he gave a single nod, no regret flashing across his expression, as if he liked the idea of leaving me in safety. Yes, I was right. He still hadn't given up on his idea of forcing me to be part of his pack. Would he ever? Would I have to watch my back until the day he died?

If so, all the more reason to kill him.

I let go of Jake, understanding, yet again, that this was the only way. I had to trust him. He was a strong alpha, and he knew what he was doing. Besides, I would not abandon him. I would find him. As soon as I was able, I would start tracking him. Stephen didn't know I had a new way now, a quicker way. I had spidey sense like Rosalina had called it. I'd used it on the amulet he wore around his neck and found out about his hybrid plans.

Jake nodded as if thanking me for going along. I wanted to tell him that I would come and help him, but I couldn't. If I sent him a message using my alpha skills, the others would hear it, too. It took a monumental effort, but I stepped back and schooled my features into a mask of indifference that matched his own.

"I will have your head, Stephen Erickson," I pushed the thought forward as loudly as I could.

To my delight, Stephen was startled by the piercing message. Those around us exchanged heavy glances and nervously shuffled their feet from side to side. What did they make out of a female alpha? From their reaction, it seemed they didn't like the idea very much.

Stephen scanned me from head to toe, surprise filling his gaze, a red eyebrow arching slightly. He hadn't known I was an alpha, and it seemed it only made him hungrier for me.

"You're full of surprises, Antonietta Sunder," he said. "Just another one of the reasons I like you."

"Fuck you," I growled.

Stephen cracked his neck, then signaled his hybrids. "Take him!"

The massive creatures took a step forward in unison, twin menaces, eager to serve.

Jake put a hand up. "No need." He turned his back on them and walked toward the SUV that had been driven onto the flowerbed. "I take it, this is your ride."

The circle of men and werewolves around us broke to let him pass. I stood with my hands clenched at my sides, trembling, doing my best to stay put as I watched him go. His gait was steady. His head was held high. He betrayed no fear despite the fact that he might be walking to his death.

Stephen's steps sounded behind me. He stopped next to me and also watched Jake walk toward the car.

"So noble of him," he said in a mocking tone that, no doubt, Jake heard. "I never understood the hold he has on you, and I understand it even less now that I know you're an alpha. I would let you lead by my side, you know? You would never have that with him. He's a creature of no ambition. He would be content with mere crumbs, and that's all he'll ever be able to offer you."

Jake reached the car and, without looking in our direction, got in the passenger seat and shut the door with loud finality. I clenched my teeth, peering at his darkened silhouette inside the tinted-window vehicle. He wasn't looking at me, but straight at the dashboard. I had the feeling that if he did, he wouldn't be able to play along. He would stay and fight, damn the consequences.

"Look at me, Jake. Look at me!"

This time my message was loud for everyone to hear.

Jake lowered his head further in response.

Next to me, Stephen snorted. "I never thought it would be this easy. I guess I underestimated his weakness."

What he called weakness was nothing but pure courage and honor. But of course, he wouldn't know those things if they grabbed him by the balls.

"Don't bother to track him, Toni," Stephen said. "By the time you're able, he'll be dead. And with him gone, you'll finally see clearly."

I didn't argue with him or try to explain that I would never see things the way he did. I would not waste my breath on him.

I would save my strength to track my mate.

CHAPTER 26

The SUV's tires spun for a bit, tearing the pretty landscaping and sending bits of grass into the air, and, with Stephen at the wheel, they drove away. Something wild stirred in me, wanting to take chase, to keep my eye on Jake, to protect him. But I managed to pull my attention away from the retreating vehicle and whirled on my heel.

Other cars followed, the armed men and werewolves inside them.

Heart pounding, I marched into the building. As I entered the larger room where the refreshments were served, I frantically searched for Rosalina. I spotted her in a matter of seconds and breathed a sigh of relief.

"Are they gone?" someone asked to my left.

I could do nothing but nod as I watched Rosalina approach, gratefully unharmed.

It wasn't until I wrapped her tightly in a hug and she did

likewise, that I noticed debris on the floor and bullet holes in the ceiling. But worse of all, a body, a man in a torn suit, blood spilling from his gut. Judging by the state of his clothes, it seemed he'd been mid-shift when Stephen shot him. A woman knelt by his side, sobbing and holding his hand, blood thick on their intertwined fingers.

I squeezed my eyes shut, hatred roiling inside of me, festering like a disease. I felt its effects, bashing me in waves, pushing me to the verge of madness.

"He'll pay for this," I said between clenched teeth.

Rosalina pulled away and held me at arm's length. I didn't know what I expected to see on her face, but it wasn't the grim determination that matched mine.

"He will," she said. "He will."

"He took Jake," I managed.

She gasped and squeezed my shoulders, understanding my raw pain better than anyone could. "You have to track him."

I knew what this could mean for our agency. We might lose our meager two clients if we didn't deliver in time. She must've seen the concern in my expression because she shook me slightly.

"Jake's life is in danger. Nothing is more important than that."

And of course, she was right, but I was still grateful for her generous soul which always seemed to know the right thing to do and never shied away from it.

Without any sort of hesitation, she took my hand and led me out of the room. Together we marched toward my Camaro. As we were about to get in, a familiar sedan pulled into a parking space and Eric Cross got out. He was fashionably late.

He glanced around, taking in the frazzled people spilling out of the building and the torn flower bed. When he spotted us, he trotted in our direction.

"What happened?!"

"Stephen was here. Apparently, he didn't get the dagger from

Walter," I said in a rush of breath, trying to explain as quickly as possible. We had no time to waste. "He showed up with weapons and werewolves and hybrids. He killed a man. Jake went with him, acting as if he'd give him the dagger, but I don't know if he has it. Or if he was only pretending to stop Stephen from hurting any more people."

Eric's blue eyes danced from side to side as he took everything in. At last, he said, "Shit!"

"I need to track him. Now! Can we go to your place?"

His house was closer than any other place where we could go—only ten minutes away. Besides, Jake had stashed a duffel bag there before we went to Wolfskeep.

Eric nodded and ran back to his car. We tore out of the parking lot, Eric leading the way. We broke every speed limit and disobeyed every traffic sign we possibly could and made it there in record time and, luckily, with no cops on our asses despite our reckless driving.

I drove my car into Eric's garage and was in the training room in a flash, my fleeting ability activating without even thinking. Before I knew it, I was kneeling in front of Jake's bag, digging out one of his T-shirts and clenching it between my fists.

Eric and Rosalina ran into the room a moment later, wearing matching expressions of surprise. I stared up at them, the T-shirt pressed to my chest as if it were some sort of lifeline.

"Can you sense him?" Eric asked as they cautiously walked closer.

I didn't know yet, so I closed my eyes. With his scent of rain and pine suffusing the fabric, I was immediately steeped in his presence. Quickly, I shut everything else away, focusing on Jake and only Jake.

I felt nothing.

Shit! This *had* to work. I couldn't go into a trance that would leave me useless to help him. My eyes sprang open and met

Rosalina's. I shook my head, feeling desperate.

"Try one more time," she said gently. "If it doesn't work, it's fine. You can still find him, and Eric will go help him. Right?"

Eric nodded without hesitation.

I pressed Jake's T-shirt to my face and inhaled deeply, squeezing my eyes shut, letting myself spiral, searching for that shimmering darkness that always welcomed me when I went into a trance.

Jake. Jake. Jake.

He was the only thought inside my head. His silver eyes, his strong shoulders and large hands, his scent, the feel of his hair between my fingers.

Where are you?

Rain and pine. Pine and rain.

And… something else, something that *wasn't* Jake.

I focused on the new scent and shuddered as I recognized it, immediately aware of where I'd sensed it before. I sprang to my feet, discarding the T-shirt on top of the duffle bag.

"I know where he is. Let's go get him."

"*Witchlights!*" Rosalina exclaimed.

"Holy fuck," Eric said at the same time.

I had no time for their amazement and ran out of the room, passing between them. I was in my Camaro, cranking the engine just seconds later.

"Hurry!" I screamed as Rosalina and Eric seemed to take forever to catch up with me. Though, they were only a few paces behind.

Eric squeezed himself in the back seat right away and used his phone to open the garage door.

Rosalina, on the other hand, veered to the back of the garage. "Give me a second," she called out, driving my impatience over the edge.

However, she was in the passenger seat just a few beats later, carrying her trench coat and a rifle, which, apparently, she'd also stashed here. It seemed Eric's house was quickly becoming our headquarters.

"I may need this," she said.

I stepped on the gas, tires squealing, the scent of burnt rubber heavy in the air. Taking a sharp turn, I veered north, begging the witchlights nothing would get in the way, so we could get there in time to help Jake.

"Where is he?" Eric asked.

"There's a cave," I said. "Jake took Blake there. I'm certain that's where they are."

Neither Rosalina nor Eric questioned my certainty. Maybe *I* should have wondered if I was leading us on a wild goose chase that would cost Jake his life, but I couldn't doubt myself. Jake *had* to be there. He *would* be there.

All the human gods must've been on my side as I drove my Camaro like The Road Runner on steroids. I broke more traffic laws during that twenty-minute drive than in my entire life but made it there unscathed.

By the time we approached the stretch of wooded highway, it was already dark. In the distance, I spotted two of the SUVs that had been at the funeral home, including Stephen's Escalade. They had pulled onto the shoulder, close to the slope that led to the forest. It seemed Stephen had dismissed some of his cronies, which probably meant he'd kept the hybrids with him.

I slowed down, approaching cautiously, unsure of whether anyone would be keeping guard inside one of the vehicles. I parked a few yards away from them, on the opposite side of the road. As soon as I threw the door open, I shifted, my dress tearing to bits and falling away.

All the scents and sounds tripled in intensity, flooding my senses. The smell of dogwood trees in bloom was the strongest and rode above all others. It was what had led me here.

Suddenly, there was a mechanical whir as a window lowered in one of the SUVs. A shot rang out, missing my head by a mere breath.

Wasting no time, I tore toward the tree line, sharp claws scraping against the blacktop at first, then digging into the dirt as I abandoned the road. A series of louder shots rang in response. I knew it was Rosalina, shooting back, offering me cover, but I had no time to glance back. All I could do was hope that she and Eric would be okay. I had to trust they could take care of themselves. It was the only way to get through the clusterfuck our lives had become.

Shots echoed through the forest, the sound bouncing off the thick tree trunks and boulders strewn in the area. They would alert Stephen and whoever else was with him, but I couldn't worry about that. I had to find Jake.

Nose twitching, I struggled to pinpoint his scent, but the many forest odors overwhelmed me.

At first, I ran in a straight line, bounding over fallen trees, paws kicking back dirt, as I tried to pick up Jake's trail. After several minutes of running without real direction, I cut left, then crisscrossed the area I'd just covered.

Still nothing. Had I got it wrong? There were flowering dogwoods all over the place. They were Missouri's state trees, after all. I was about to start howling in frustration, when I caught, not Jake's scent, but Stephen's. Strangely, his scent was marked by a heavy dose of something sharp.

Fear.

Why?

I slowed my full pelt down to a trot, and, when the sharp tang grew stronger, crouched, and stalked forward on silent paws. I veered toward a patch of thick brush, my keen wolf eyes piercing through the foliage.

About thirty yards away, surrounded by a circle of trees,

Stephen stood with his two hybrids and the man who had pointed his gun at me at the funeral home. I was upwind and hoped they wouldn't catch my scent as I watched them closely.

"Find him!" Stephen snapped, brandishing a handgun. "He couldn't have gone far."

The man shook his head, holding a weapon of his own. "I've looked everywhere. These woods are big, and he's familiar with them. Those shots are a bad sign. We should go."

The tension that had kept my lungs cinched ever since the Escalade had torn out of the funeral home released in an exhale of relief.

Jake had gotten away.

He was all right. Of course.

He was resourceful, always had been.

But where was he? The cave where he'd kept Blake? No, he wouldn't go into a cave. That would mean trapping himself.

"That's why we need to hurry, so I don't want to hear excuses, Marlowe," Stephen shouted, his eyes flashing with a blue glow as if he were about to shift.

Do it. Shift, and I'll fight you and tear you to pieces.

I waited for the change, but he remained in his human form. He wasn't going to abandon his hybrids and weapons to search for Jake. He was afraid of him.

"Send them!" Marlowe said, gesturing toward the hybrids that stood languidly, staring into the distance like soulless robots.

I shook my head, bearing my teeth. Hoping Stephen wouldn't send those beasts after Jake. To my relief, he didn't. I was puzzled by his reluctance, but when he spoke, I understood why he didn't want to risk it.

"They're killing machines, and I don't want him dead. Not yet, anyway."

"We shouldn't have come here without the others."

"Bernadetta needed them, and we should've been able to handle one fucking werewolf."

"She'll be mad," Marlowe said.

Stephen huffed. "I don't give a shit. She won't be a problem soon."

Marlowe frowned, clearly unsure of Stephen's meanings. Did he have a plan to get rid of Bernadetta? Of course, he did, the two-faced, back-stabbing bastard. He'd just betrayed us all and was getting ready to betray his new ally. It seemed he was bent on screwing everyone over.

"We need the dagger!" he spat. "Everything hinges on growing our army." His eyes flicked in the direction of the hybrids. "My plans won't work with only two of them."

Ahh, so that was it. They'd only been able to make two before I took the dagger.

It was a relief.

"If only there had been more blood left in the cup," he mumbled to himself.

My thoughts cartwheeled for a bit until I understood what he meant. He and Bernadetta hadn't created these hybrids before the coven temple. He had made them after he escaped, using the blood left in the cup.

At last, Stephen's frustration seemed to get the best of him. "Dammit! I'm gonna kill you, Knight." Then, turning to Marlowe, "Let's find him."

To my surprise, Stephen threw down his weapon, cracked his neck, and shifted.

In an instant, a russet-colored wolf stood in his place. At the sight of his animal, my fury roiled, and it took all of my willpower not to attack.

They will tear you to pieces, Red, my human instincts hissed, trying to prevail over Red's desire to make mincemeat out of that traitor. One paw moved forward involuntarily.

Red! I chided, cutting a glance in the hybrids' direction, a reminder that there was more than Stephen and Marlowe to deal with.

Marlowe shifted next, then the two wolves headed west, away from me.

I expected the hybrids to run after them, but they just stood there like statues, unmoving and expressionless. My thoughts reeled as I tried to decide what to do. Should I keep looking for Jake? It didn't seem like a good idea. For all I knew, he was already miles away from here. Leaving would've been the smart thing to do. Except, when I heard a rustling of bushes behind me and I whirled, my hackles standing on end, I discovered he was still here.

Jake's massive wolf blinked at me. Nearly jumping for joy, I walked to him, pressed the side of my face against his, and sighed in relief. The touch of his fur against mine was electrifying. A low purr rumbled in his chest, then he pulled away and gave me a critical glare with those silver eyes.

"What are you doing here?" He demanded, his alpha thoughts ramming into mine. I took two steps back and stretched to my full height, which was barely enough to get my eyes to the level of his thick neck. I let my own alpha power flow forward. I would not be intimidated by him.

"You're stupid if you thought I wouldn't come looking for you."

He huffed, blowing air through his nose, then moved his focus toward the stiff hybrids behind me. He scanned the area critically, his posture tensing by degrees as he evaluated the situation. Suddenly, he shook his big head as if angry at some realization, then an urgent thought sliced through me.

"Run!" He nudged me in the direction of the road. I hesitated for a moment, not understanding his panic, then, as a shape materialized from behind a thicket of brush to our right, I understood.

I had screwed up. I had, somehow, made my presence known to Stephen.

CHAPTER 27

The russet wolf slunk closer, his head low, his teeth bared. At a shake of his head, a second shape appeared to our left. Marlowe. He looked as menacing as Stephen did, and for a moment, I was almost intimidated by them, then realized…

They're no match for us.

Of course, that was Red talking, the human side of me wasn't so sure. Because, clearly, Red had forgotten about the hybrids.

I wanted to cut a glance in their direction to see if they'd moved, but I kept my eyes on Stephen and Marlowe, pretending that they'd forgotten about the monster helpers. As if.

A girl could hope.

"*The dagger!*" Stephen's voice ran inside my head.

I glanced sideways at Jake, waiting for his answer, except he didn't waste time with words. Instead, he attacked.

I barely had time to blink, then Jake was on Stephen, his huge clawed paws swiping at his face and barely missing as his target pulled back with a yelp of surprise. Jake pressed forward, a wall of muscle moving faster than it seemed physically possible. Stephen had barely recovered from the first attack, and Jake's sharp teeth were already snapping a mere breath from his neck. Stephen retreated once more.

I moved to join Jake, to get my revenge for Damien, but Marlowe came from the side, barreling toward me, his mouth opened wide, pointed teeth glimmering with saliva.

I halted and pivoted to one side, narrowly escaping.

Unrelenting, he pressed forward.

I had a mind to turn tail and run, but Red's instincts overpowered that desire. And good thing she was in charge because this was her territory, not mine.

Hackles raised, I let out a growl and pushed my alpha power forward. Instantly, Marlowe's ears leaned back, his tail curled down, and the light in his eyes dimmed. Yet, he prevailed over his instincts and kept coming.

Wild snarls came from behind me, but I couldn't turn to look. I just prayed Jake was all right.

As Marlowe came closer, I ducked my head and went for the scruff of his neck. My teeth snapped shut around him, cutting into thick sinew. Blood flowed into my mouth, driving my anger and instincts into a frenzy. I shook my head, teeth tearing chunks of fur and meat.

Pushing downward, I drove Marlowe to the ground, sunk my teeth deeper, and increased the pressure until I hit bone. I snarled and kept shaking my head, barely any human thought left in me. I was nothing but a savage creature overrun by instinct, fighting for her life. There was no pity, no remorse, nothing but the certainty that I would do anything it took to stay alive.

My rage remained even after my opponent stopped moving. It took me a long moment to pull away and blink at the mangled mess that lay at my feet. As reason returned, I backed away, unable to comprehend what I'd done. It wasn't the first time I'd killed, but it was the first time I'd killed one of my kind.

A *thud* brought me back to the moment. Jake and Stephen were still fighting, thrashing on the ground, rolling over each other in a flash of teeth and claws. It felt as if an eternity had passed, but I'd overpowered Marlowe in a matter of seconds. And during those few beats, Stephen had wasted no time in conjuring his monsters.

I didn't know how he'd called them, but I caught their movement out of the corner of my eye. My head snapped in their direction. They ran in a semi-crouched position, their hands lightly brushing the ground as they propelled themselves forward like twin ramrods ready to break us into a million splinters.

Shit!

Instinct taking over once more, I pushed my alpha power toward the hybrids, exerting my will and taking an intimidating stance as I growled, ordering them to stand down.

Nothing happened.

I tried again, showing more teeth, building a deeper rumble in my throat.

Still nothing.

Damn! Maybe they had been alphas before Stephen turned them into beasts. Maybe there wasn't enough *werewolf* left in them to be commanded. Whatever the case, we were screwed.

"Jake, they're coming!"

Jake's head snapped up and his silver eyes quickly assessed the danger. He had Stephen cornered against a tree and had injured him.

"We can't fight them. We have to get out of here," I thought at him.

Jake had only enough time to make up his mind. He could either stay to finish Stephen and then be killed himself, or he could run.

He ran.

Joining me, we leaped over an outcrop of jagged rocks. My ears swiveling backward, intent on any sounds from our pursuers. They snarled and panted, treading heavily over the undergrowth, letting me know exactly where they were.

"They're gaining on us."

"I know. Run faster."

"I can't."

I was going as fast as I could, but Jake had slowed down to stay by my side. He was a lot larger than me, each of his strides covering twice the distance of mine.

"C'mon, Toni! Faster. Faster!"

Trees blurred past. My paws slammed against jagged rocks. My legs pumped at capacity, but I couldn't go faster. As we reached a clearing, I knew the time to run had passed. I skidded to a stop, digging my claws in and whirling to confront my pursuers.

As if we'd agreed upon it, Jake did the same and stood tall and majestic, his back arched, his hair bristling, making him look bigger than he already was. He growled, and I felt the ground vibrate in my paws. He was half the size of one of the hybrids, and yet, they came to an abrupt stop at the sight of his impressive presence. But whatever thought had made them hesitate quickly vanished, and the larger one lunged for Jake.

Jake didn't shy away, not even for an instant. Instead, he pounced and met the beast in midair. Fast as lightning, the hybrid swatted a gargantuan claw at Jake and sent him crashing against a tree. He yelped, then collapsed to the floor.

The hybrid went for him again, but I lurched in his direction and bit into his calf. The beast howled and whirled, nearly missing my head as he threw a jab at me. Pissed off, he turned from Jake. I walked backward, drawing him away from Jake's fallen shape. The other hybrid advanced, joining him.

We're dead. Dead! Those were the only words ringing in my head, ricocheting like bullets, driving away all hope. I was almost resigned to that fate when Rosalina stepped from behind a clump of trees, her finger happy on the trigger of her rifle.

Shots rang out, sounding like atomic explosions to my sensitive ears. She was shooting high-caliber bullets, the kind that pierced armor. She'd gotten the rifle from Jake and had been like a little girl with a new toy, talking endlessly about the weapon's features. Now, she was finally getting to use it, and she wasn't being shy about it.

The bullets struck the hybrids right in the chest. They twitched with each impact, their bodies convulsing while, all along, Rosalina advanced in short steps, spraying them with a deadly shower of lead.

The smaller hybrid fell to the ground, but the biggest one stayed on his feet and single-mindedly jumped toward Rosalina. Her eyes widened as the hybrid reared up, claws shining with Jake's blood, ready to strike.

I went for the beast, but I was too late.

No!

Eric—a small but powerful tawny wolf—flew out of nowhere and slammed into the hybrid, sinking his sharp teeth into the monster's soft middle. The hybrid roared in pain and tried to grab Eric, but he'd already bounced out of the way, a chunk of meat in his muzzle.

Rosalina scrambled back, still pulling the trigger. A barrage of bullets hit the injured hybrid, weakening him further, and finally, he fell to his knees, blood gushing out of several holes in his stomach. But even as he bled, his wounds healed right before our eyes. And he wasn't the only one. The other one was also recovering, the holes in his naked chest spitting bullets out as if he was freaking Wolverine.

To make matters worse, Stephen had found us and was running toward us, wearing nothing but his Adam's suit and a handgun.

"We have to get out of here," Eric's voice broke through the chaotic mess that passed for my thoughts.

I started toward Jake who was struggling to his feet, legs trembling with the effort. But Eric was already there in his human form—fully dressed thanks to his shifter ring—helping Jake, hefting the huge wolf onto his back, and running toward the road.

"Run, Rosalina!" Eric commanded.

She wasted no time and did as she was told. I ran after her, bringing up the rear, zigzagging through the trees as Stephen shot at us. Bullets pinged on the trunks, sending splinters flying.

Rosalina quickly passed Eric, who despite his inhuman strength was starting to slow. There was no way a man his size should be able to carry a massive wolf like Jake, but he was not a regular man. He was a werewolf, a strong one. Despite his smaller size, his strength was formidable.

It took us an eternity to reach the gravelly slope that led up to the road, the hybrids getting closer all the while. I could hear them crashing through the brush, moving faster and faster as their injuries healed.

Eric reached the edge of the slope, tried to climb up with Jake on his back, but slid back down on the gravel.

I pushed my urgent thoughts at him. *"Hurry! They're getting closer!"*

Eric tried again with the same result.

"Put me down," Jake's weak thoughts whispered in my mind. *"I can climb. I've healed some."*

Eric deposited Jake on the ground. Jake's legs nearly gave out under him, but he started climbing. Eric grabbed him by the scruff of the neck and started pulling him up, helping. I started helping, too, pressing a shoulder to his backside and pushing. We started moving upward.

The hybrids broke through the tree line, snarling like possessed rabid dogs. We had pissed them off. Big time.

"We're not going to make it," the thought materialized in my mind just as Rosalina reached the top of the slope, whirled around, and started delivering bullets as if they were Christmas presents. From

her vantage point, she didn't miss a shot.

"Hurry, you can make it," she screamed over the deafening cracks of her weapon.

When we were halfway up the slope, she ran out of bullets, but quickly popped another magazine in, and it was Christmas time all over again.

I dared a quick glance over my shoulder and found that one of the hybrids was down on the ground, a bullet between the eyes. The other one, however, had just reached the bottom of the slope despite all his bleeding wounds.

Suddenly, the spray of bullets came to an abrupt stop. Rosalina struggled with a new magazine, baring her teeth as she tried to load it.

"Dammit, something's stuck." She threw the weapon to the ground and ran toward my Camaro.

Jake, Eric, and I redoubled our efforts and finally reached the top of the hill.

Rosalina jumped into the driver's seat. The engine roared to life and tires screeched on the asphalt as she backed up in our direction, turned the car around in one smooth maneuver, and came to a stop next to us. Reaching across, she threw the passenger door open.

"Get in! Get in!"

Eric and I helped Jake into the back seat. I jumped in after him—we were packed like sardines—then Eric pushed the seat back, got in, and slammed the door shut.

"Step on it!" he said.

Rubber melted against the blacktop as the tires spun. The big hybrid had reached the top of the slope. Limping and slick with blood, he ran toward us in his unrelenting pursuit and obedience to his master's orders.

But we were off, Rosalina flooring the gas pedal, the beast growing smaller and smaller in the back window, and my heart quieting down for the first time since Jake was taken.

I laid my head on top of his as his irregular breaths slowed and his wounds healed.

CHAPTER 28

We rode in silence, not a word passing between us. Rosalina stared straight ahead, her hands firmly on the wheel at ten and two o'clock. By the time we got to Eric's house, Jake had healed and was sitting up, still in his wolf form, looking out the window.

As soon as we slipped into the garage, Eric hopped out of the car saying, "We can't stay here. We have to go. Grab whatever you need and let's get out of here."

"Where are we going to go?" Rosalina asked, meeting him outside the car.

"I have a hideout that no one knows about. This house is pretty safe, but everyone knows where I live. Whatever truce was between us, it's over. We need to hide."

I knew he was right, but I hated the idea. I exchanged a heavy glance with Rosalina. Fugitives didn't keep businesses afloat, did they? Still, when this was all over and if we survived, we would need our jobs.

I hopped out of the car. *"Can we swing by the agency?"* I asked through my alpha mind. *"There's something I need to pick up."*

Eric made a face, and I was afraid he would say no, but he nodded. "Whatever it is, just make it quick."

"It'll be quick."

Jake followed. His coat was matted with blood, but he'd completely healed. We walked together back to the training room, shifted, retrieved our duffel bags, and dressed without looking at each other. When I was done, I turned to face him. He was standing, unmoving, staring at his reflection in the mirror. Dry blood stained his abdomen. A black T-shirt was gripped in his hand.

"Are you all right?" I asked.

His silver gaze traveled slowly to meet mine. He nodded once. "I'm fine."

"Are you sure? You look, I don't know…"

"I almost had him." The latent anger in his voice stripped me raw, and right away, I knew exactly how he felt.

Stephen should've been dead tonight, but once more, he had escaped.

I approached, letting my eyes travel over the expanse of his muscular chest and stomach, making sure he was all right. A dusting of brown hair traveled between his large pecs, stopped short, then began again below his navel. The sight of the blood made me shudder. Angrily, I pushed away the negative thoughts that tried to take over my mind. So much could have gone wrong tonight, but we'd escaped with our lives.

Gently, I laid a hand on his heart. "I'm glad you're all right."

He captured my fingers in his and pressed them tightly to his chest. I felt his heartbeat, pounding strongly, and I could be nothing but grateful for his strength, for his healing abilities.

"You shouldn't have come," he said reproachfully.

I opened my mouth to protest, then realized that he'd only gotten injured because I *had* come.

"I'm sorry," I said, tears pricked in the back of my eyes.

He shook his head and pressed a finger to my lips. "*Shh.* You don't need to apologize. Of course, you came. I would've come after you, too. No matter what." Wearing a sad but understanding smile, he leaned forward and kissed me on the forehead with immense tenderness. "Nothing could ever keep me away from you. I would fight a thousand hybrids to be with you."

A tear slid down my cheek. I swallowed the lump in my throat to hold back the onslaught, then wrapped my arms around his waist and laid my cheek on his bare chest.

"I'm glad we understand each other," I joked.

He blew air through his nose, amused.

"You two ready?" Eric called from the door.

Reluctantly, we broke apart and followed him. On the way, I called my mom and sisters and explained what had happened. Blake had attacked Mom, and I wasn't taking any chances this time. Reluctantly, they had agreed to stay in a hotel for a few days and to keep a low profile. For once, I was glad that my brother wasn't around.

When we reached the garage, Eric pointed towards his dark sedan. "I've thrown a few things in there, stuff that might come in handy. Here." He pressed a piece of paper into my hand.

"What is this?" I asked, unfolding it.

"It's a map and an address."

"Everyone, leave your phones there," he pointed toward a shelf on the wall. "We can't take any risks. They could use them to track us."

I hated to part with my phone, but I did as he said.

"I'll pick up some burner ones on my way. You go by your agency and we'll meet you at that address. Sounds good?"

I nodded.

We got in the Camaro, with me back at the wheel. We tore out of there, the heavy silence returning as we headed toward The Hill. Jake, sitting next to me, looked over the map Eric had given us and marked it with a pen, tracing a route.

"I don't know how people used to get around without GPS. I already miss my phone," Rosalina said behind us, trying to make light conversation.

"Me too," I said. "I don't think I could get us there with that thing. Glad you're good for something, Jake."

He threw a sidelong glance my way. "Oh, I'm good for more than that."

"Maybe you too can wait to get hot and heavy until we get there." Rosalina glared at me through the rearview mirror, wrinkling her nose.

At the agency, I parked right in front of the door. We peered inside through the glass door at the darkened interior, weary of what might lurk inside.

"It seems safe," Jake said. "Give me the key. I'll go."

I didn't argue. I knew there was no point. I held my breath as he keyed the lock and rushed inside. My heart knocked like crazy inside my chest as I waited, biting my thumbnail.

Rosalina groaned behind me. I glanced back and found her pressing a hand to her mouth.

"I swear," she mumbled through her fingers, "this suspense," she gestured between us and the office, "is harder than shooting at those fucking hybrids."

I knew just what she meant. The not knowing was like waiting for an enema to take effect.

When Jake came out of the office, Rosalina and I both released pent-up breaths of relief. He locked the door behind him, rushed back into the car, and handed me one of the padded boxes we used to store our potions.

"Is this what you needed? I scooped a bit from each slow

cooker."

I'd started brewing two potions this morning, one for each of our clients. I'd asked Jake to get a bit of both.

I opened the box and peered inside. "Yes, this is it."

"How do they look?" Rosalina asked.

"They're both shimmering. I think they're fine."

"Good, let's get going toward I-44." Jake stabbed a finger into the map.

I shifted into first and got us on the way. I'd barely made it a few streets away from the agency when I slammed on the brakes. Everyone's neck whiplashed.

"What the hell?!" Rosalina exclaimed.

"Fuck!" Jake said in more colorful tones. "Is something wrong?" He glanced all around, peering into the empty street. It was late and there wasn't much traffic.

"I got to get Blaze."

"Blaze?"

"Her cat," Rosalina said. "You met him that day at the office the day she found it."

Jake had come into the office that day while I was at the pet shop. Apparently, they hadn't gotten along.

He pulled a face. "That awful pest?"

"Just because he doesn't like you, it doesn't mean he's awful. He's smart like that."

Jake narrowed his eyes. "Whatever you say, Toni. I don't think we need to get your cat. He'll be fine."

"No! That's the same thing Eric said about Cupid, and now he's dead."

"He had lived a long life for fish."

"Um, he really had, Toni," Rosalina piped in. "You need to stop blaming yourself for that."

"No!" I shook my head. "I don't care what you two say. Cats need more care than fish. I have no idea how long we'll be gone, and he's locked in my condo."

I wound the wheel all the way to the left to make a U-turn.

"You can't be serious." Jake slumped in his seat. "If we get killed because of a cat, of all things, I'll make sure little Blaze goes down with us."

"See, you're the one who's awful. He's just a defenseless cat and you're a mean wolf with no heart."

Rosalina snorted.

Jake raised an eyebrow at her.

"What?" Rosalina asked. "I kinda agree with her."

"Of course you do."

"We girls have to stick together." I stepped on the gas and hurried toward Compton Heights. A few minutes later, I started to pull into the underground parking lot of my building.

"No, don't go in there. Not safe," Jake said.

I wanted to argue, but he was right. There was only one way out of the parking lot. Going in there was like asking for it.

"I'll tell you what… you take the wheel and drop me by the front entrance and I'll go get him."

"Uh-uh, you're not going in there by yourself."

"Okay, Rosalina takes the wheel and you and I both go together."

She waved a hand in the air. "Don't mind little old me. It's fine if I stay all by myself, unprotected by a gallant and fierce werewolf."

I glanced at her through the rearview mirror, fresh out of ideas.

Rosalina rolled her eyes. "Just go. I'll be fine." She pulled out a huge handgun from her trench coat and blew into its muzzle. I had to admit she looked badass. Though, that didn't mean we shouldn't worry about her.

I shook my head and gave Jake a pointed stare. "You stay with her, and I'll get Blaze."

Jake opened his mouth to argue. I narrowed my gaze further,

brooking no argument. I could feel his *alphaness* trying to exert itself over mine.

"Don't do that, Jake," I warned, letting my own alpha mojo flow.

Something like an electric jolt ran through me as our wills clashed.

"This is new," I thought as Red seemed to gear herself up for a fight. Except, we didn't have time for this shit. So I undid my seatbelt, got out of the car, and marched toward the front entrance. Jake's muffled curses reached me as I walked away. I flipped him the bird for good measure.

At the front door, I used the access code to get in. One of the night workers was using a polishing machine to freshen up the floor. He inclined his head in greeting as I walked toward the elevators. I punched the up button and waited. The bell dinged. The metal doors slid open. I took a step forward, then jumped back with a yelp.

"What the hell?"

"Everything all right, ma'am," the worker called.

"Um, yeah, it's fine."

My jaw hanging open, I stared down at Blaze. He was sitting right in the middle of the elevator, blinking his intense orange eyes at me. He meowed, stood, and strolled out of the elevator. Passing me by, he made his way toward the front door as if he owned the place.

The worker paused his polishing to stare at the newcomer. "Hello there, little fellow," he said, looking amused. Blaze ignored him and kept going.

As I watched him, perplexed, he stopped, glanced over his shoulder, and gave me an *are you coming or what?* annoyed look.

"Is he yours?" the worker asked.

"Yep." I smiled apologetically and tried to pick the cat up, but he hurried forward, making me look like a fool. "He's got a mind of his own, that one. Have a good night," I called as I opened the door for my very strange new pet.

When we stepped onto the landing, I placed my hands on my hips and demanded, "How did you get out, young sir?"

I scratched my head, aware that I was wasting my breath. Questioning a cat wasn't going to lead anywhere.

Jake pulled up to the curb, and Blaze sauntered down the steps and hopped in as Jake threw the passenger door open. They stared at each other, Jake frowning. I got in after Blaze, picking him up and setting him on my lap.

"That was fast," Rosalina said.

"Yeah, he… um… actually came down in the elevator," I said.

"He what?" Jake's eyebrows furrowed, and he gave Blaze another distrustful stare.

I nodded, avoiding eye contact.

Jake's nose twitched as he took in the cat's scent. "Is this thing trustworthy?"

"I think so," I blurted out.

"Where did you find him again?"

"By the dumpster, behind our building."

A muscle twitched in Jake's jaw as he silently considered. The Camaro's engine idled.

"I vote you throw it to the curb," Jake said after a moment.

"What?! No! I'm not going to do that." I protested.

Blaze hissed his disagreement.

Jake bared his teeth and growled back at the cat. Any sensible creature would have been terrified of a werewolf like Jake, but Blaze just stood on my lap and, nonchalantly, started licking his paw.

"Let's vote," Jake said. "All of those in favor of getting rid of this mongrel raise their hand." His large hand shot up in the air. We both peered back at Rosalina, who sat in the middle of the backseat, her eyes flicking from Jake to me, looking very much like someone who didn't want to get involved.

To my surprise, she slowly raised a hand. She shrugged. "Sorry, Toni, but Jake's right. We're going into hiding, and the cat is a liability."

"You can't be serious."

"I mean," she added, "if it was Cupid, I'd be all for it. He was a nice fishy."

"Blaze is a nice kitty," I retorted.

"This is stupid." Jake's hands twisted on the wheel, making the leather creak. "We're sitting in the open, arguing about a stupid cat. Just throw it out, Toni."

"I'm not going to," I spat, my anger flaring, surprising me and the others.

Logically, I knew Blaze would, most likely, be all right by himself, either on the streets or back inside, but I couldn't leave him. He'd only been with me for a few days, but I felt a connection with him. I couldn't abandon him. I just couldn't.

Jake put his hands up in the air. "O-kay, if you feel that strongly about it, he can come. But if he does something suspicious, I—"

"Whatever it is you're about to say, don't."

He squared his shoulders and stared pointedly at the street ahead. After a few deep breaths, he shifted into first, and we were on our way. Once we got on the interstate, Blaze curled up on my lap, purred for a bit, then fell asleep.

As I watched his whiskers twitch with his kitty cat dreams, I petted his head, baffled at how silly we'd been, arguing over a defenseless cat.

It wasn't long before his warmth on my lap, and the rhythm of traffic lured me into my own dreams.

CHAPTER 29

I awoke to a loud bang as the driver-side door shut. Blaze wasn't on my lap anymore, and I glanced around in a panic, looking for him.

"He's back here," Rosalina said.

He was asleep on my friend's lap.

"You traitor," I said, then stretched and squinted at our dark surroundings. "Are we there yet?"

"Yeah, Jake's checking to see if it's safe."

I peered through the front window as Jake cautiously went up a set of wooden steps of what appeared to be a log cabin. Trees surrounded us, and there were no electric lights. The only illumination was a waxing moon.

Eric's car was parked on the other side of a dirt driveway.

"It's so dark," Rosalina complained, squinting out the window. "Can you see anything?"

With her Stale eyes, I had no idea how much she could actually see. "Um, yes, there's a log cabin, but the windows are dark."

She made a noncommittal sound in the back of her throat. Just then, Blaze woke up, hopped off Rosalina's lap, and arched his back, stretching. Suddenly, he leaped into the driver seat, then onto the dashboard, where he took a watchful position.

"That's an odd cat," Rosalina said. "My abuelita says cats can't be trusted. She prefers dogs."

Blaze blew air through his nose as if to scoff at Abuela Esperanza's preference in domestic animals. He didn't glance back, though. He just continued staring toward the cabin, the tip of his tail twitching. He stirred as soon as Jake reappeared, accompanied by Eric.

"It's all good," I said to Rosalina, then got out of the car.

Blaze was out in a flash, bounding from the dashboard to the seat I'd just vacated, then onto the ground. I pulled the lever to scoot the seat forward and let Rosalina out. She took my offered hand and stretched out to her full height. Groaning, she pressed a hand to the small of her back and jutted her hips forward.

"Gah, I'm so stiff," she said.

"How long did it take us to get here?" I asked, wondering for the first time.

"A bit over an hour," she said.

Not too long at all. For an instant, I'd worried it had taken much longer than that, but it'd just been the right amount of time for a nap. Since I was little, I'd been able to snooze away during car rides. But my siblings? Not so much. They always preferred arguing over stupid stuff.

"All good?" Eric asked, coming to a stop a few feet away from the Camaro.

I nodded.

Blaze chose that moment to step away from the shadows of a nearby tree, where he'd disappeared for a bit to, most likely, do his business. He leaped onto the hood of the car. I cringed, afraid he would scratch the paint job, but he landed smoothly. He sat and stared haughtily at Eric, who made eye contact and scanned him carefully, assessing him as if he were a person.

"See," Jake said. "I told you he's weird."

Slowly, Eric bent at the waist, leaning forward until he was eye to eye with Blaze. He stayed like that for a long moment, nose twitching, hands clasped at his back. Finally, he straightened, making a sound of agreement in the back of his throat.

"What?" I said.

Eric shrugged. "Nothing. He's a fine cat. C'mon, let's go inside."

"A fine cat?" Jake murmured under his breath, looking annoyed with Eric's assessment.

I stuck my tongue out at him. He pulled a face in response. Huffing, he pointed two fingers at his eyes then at Blaze.

"I'm watching you."

The cat seemed to roll his eyes, but cats didn't do that, did they?

As I got going, Blaze padded at my side and entered the cabin. The place was a decent size with a kitchenette, a table for four, and an adjacent sitting area with a sofa, coffee table, armchair, rocker, and a weaved rug to define the space. A stone fireplace sat in one corner, its entrails dark and in need of the warm glow of a fire. It would've made the place look far cozier, more than the lamps that illuminated the space.

Beyond this area, there were three doors which I assumed led to the bedrooms.

Blaze immediately hopped on one of the armchairs and made himself comfortable, curling up into a tight donut shape. As promised, Jake watched his every move.

"Get a grip. You're scared of a cat," I said.

"I'm not scared. I just don't trust him."

"I grabbed a few things from a convenience store on the way here," Eric said from the small kitchen, taking items out of large paper bags.

A few cans of chili, a large packet of hot dogs, mustard, ketchup, chips, soft drinks, and bread. So very thoughtful. Who would've thought? Jake seemed surprised too, judging by the raised eyebrow he gave him.

"Chili dogs!" Rosalina exclaimed, clapping her hands. "I'm so hungry."

Together, Eric and Rosalina pulled out plates and utensils from the cabinets and got a small microwave going, heating the hot dogs and chili.

"What about your cat, Toni? Do you think he'll eat hot dogs?"

I shrugged. "I've no idea. I'll cut one up and see."

Blaze didn't only eat the hot dog, he also ate a couple of potato chips that Rosalina set on his plate. We all watched him with interest as we devoured our own food.

"I worry he might get sick," I said. "But he never ate any of his cat food so eagerly."

"Maybe he's possessed," Jake suggested. "You know that can happen. To cats, especially."

"He's not possessed," I protested. "Your ass is possessed."

Jake wiggled on his chair as if to test the feel of his backside. "Hmm, no. My ass feels normal."

"Is it always like this?" Eric addressed his question toward Rosalina.

"Most of the time," she said.

Eric grunted. "Then we'd better come up with a plan quickly, so we can get out of here. Otherwise, I doubt we'll survive within such close quarters."

I ignored his jab and chose to discuss said plan. "Okay, before we leave, I'll need to do a tracking trance for at least one of our clients. We picked up what we needed on the way here."

Eric frowned. "Is that necessary?"

"Yes!" Rosalina and I said in unison.

I hardened my expression and glowered at the men. *I swear if either of you offers us money…*

Jake examined the rafters.

Eric nodded. "So… how long will it take?"

"It depends." I shrugged and wiped my mouth with a rough paper towel, which was all Eric had for napkins. "The trance doesn't take long, but the recovery can, depending on how quickly I can track my mark."

"Can't it wait?" Eric asked, looking annoyed.

"No, it can't."

Well, in reality, it could. It wasn't as if Mr. Taylor or Mekare would die without a mate, but things with the agency were already hanging by a thread. We *had* to survive this rough patch.

Jake polished off his fifth hot dog and patted his belly. "Can't you call your customers and explain that something came up? Just say it'll take a few extra days."

"We made one of them wait already since I was otherwise occupied fighting hybrids, and the new customer is too high profile to mess around. No, it's not an option."

I glanced over at Rosalina to judge her thoughts on the matter. She wore a neutral expression, which was probably her way of making me feel less pressured.

"I don't mean to sound insensitive," Jake said, "but there are more important things going on right now."

I knew he was right, but still, his comment rubbed me the wrong way. "That's easy for you to say, *Mr. I've just inherited the Knight fortune*. Some of us aren't that lucky."

Jake heaved a sigh and leaned forward, pressing a hand flat on the table and letting his eyes dance between Rosalina and me. "Look, I know you're worried about losing the agency, but you don't have to be. I can help you. Like you just said, I have the *Knight fortune* at my disposal."

Again, I knew he meant well, but his offer just pissed me off. I opened my mouth to tell him off, but Rosalina beat me to it, speaking with tones and words that were far kinder than I would've used.

"We appreciate the offer, Jake. It's very generous of you, but I'm afraid we cannot accept it. The agency means more to Toni and me than you know, and its success *or* failure will depend entirely on us."

I met my friend's sharp green gaze and gave her an almost imperceptible nod of agreement. For her sake, I might've been tempted to accept Jake's help, but I was glad to see we were on the same page. We would both go down with the ship if it came to it.

We would have no one else to blame but ourselves. But if, on the other hand, we succeeded, the victory would be that much sweeter.

"Well," Eric said, "it seems it's decided. Can you do the trance tomorrow? Or do you require preparation?"

"We have everything we need," I said. "I can do it first thing tomorrow after I get a good night's sleep."

Eric rose from his chair, picking up his plate and walking to the small metal sink to wash it. "A good night of sleep is something we all could use. There are two bedrooms. One is, of course, mine." He pointed toward the door on the far left. "You all can flip a coin for the other. Whoever loses can take the pullout sofa."

"I'll take the sofa," Jake offered. "If the extra bed is big enough for two people."

"It is." Eric put his now-clean plate on the drying rack and picked up one of the shopping bags he'd gotten at the convenience store. "This is the bathroom," he said, standing in front of the door next to his room. "There are enough towels for everyone." He lifted the paper bag and shook it. "I also got some toiletries."

With that, he walked into the bathroom and locked himself in.

He'd been thoughtful to get food and toiletries for everyone, but he was far from a perfect host. He had no trouble letting us know he was in charge and would get first pick on everything. That was Eric, all right.

"I'll go get settled." Rosalina washed her plate, then disappeared into the second bedroom, leaving Jake and me alone.

CHAPTER 30

We sat in silence for several minutes. So much had happened, and I had no idea what to say. Without a word, he stood, picked up both our plates and washed them. I stared at his wide back and followed it down as it tapered into a narrow waist. Inevitably, my eyes fell to his butt and his tight, worn blue jeans. I liked a man who wasn't shy about doing a few chores around the house. When we lived together, forever ago, he'd always helped around the apartment. I found it sexy as hell, especially when he went about it in nothing but his boxer briefs.

I tore my gaze away from him just in time to avoid being caught checking him out. I would've never heard the end of that one. Instead, he found me peering at my intertwined fingers.

"What are you thinking about?" he asked.

I shrugged. I couldn't tell him I'd been thinking about his fine butt.

He made a sound in the back of his throat at my lack of answer, then walked to the living room area and proceeded to take the cushions off the sofa. Cautiously, he pulled the bed out. I jumped to my feet and moved a few pieces of furniture out of the way to make room for it.

"Thanks."

The shower began running in the bathroom, which made me realize the oddness of the situation. If a few months ago someone had told me I would be in a log cabin with two alphas and my best friend, I wouldn't have believed them.

"The sheets look pretty clean, don't you think?" Jake asked, his head cocked to one side as he appraised his accommodations.

"I guess."

They were badly creased and crumpled since the bed had been folded in place without removing them, but other than a bit dusty, they seemed fine.

"Oh, well." Jake sat at the edge of the bed. "I've slept in worse places." He rubbed his forehead and stared straight ahead.

I sat next to him, leaving several inches between us. "Are you doing all right? I mean, you never got to see your grandfather buried." I frowned. "Do you think they… did it?"

"I've no idea. I should call tomorrow."

I nodded uncertainly. *What a clustermess.*

"I can't stop wondering about the dagger. Where did he put it?" He shook his head in frustration. "Why did he have to be so fucking ambitious?"

So Jake didn't know where the dagger was. He *had* been bluffing in order to protect everyone at the funeral home.

"I'm sorry, Jake." I reached for his hand and squeezed it.

We were quiet for a few beats, then he glanced in my direction, and caressed my cheek. "Thanks for being here."

I smiled as if to say *that was nothing.*

He leaned forward, his lips parting. As he was about to kiss me,

Blaze squeezed himself in the narrow space between us. Jake pulled back and glowered at the cat.

"What?! Now, you're going too far, bud," Jake told him. "It's like he's jealous or something."

I snickered and petted the top of Blaze's head. "Maybe he is."

"Not that I'd blame him." Jake's clear eyes met mine again, a wealth of emotion inside them. "It's ironic, isn't it?"

I cocked my head to one side, unsure what he meant.

"Allison… she's also in love with someone else. Four people's lives will be ruined if we can't figure out a way to break the pact. I've gone through all those books, and I've found nothing."

"All of them?!"

He nodded.

How?! He must've gotten absolutely no sleep in order to do that. I'd barely perused a few, and he'd had his grandfather's funeral to worry about.

"I think I would rather die than marry her," he said in a barely audible whisper.

I shook my head. "Don't say that. We'll find a way."

He lowered his head, a muscle jumping in his jaw as he clenched his teeth. Anger radiated off of him like heat.

"What's the matter?" I asked.

"It's Allison's father. He wants to move up the wedding."

"What?! Why?!"

"He says the unrest doesn't bode well for any packs that are considered weak. He's not wrong."

"Gah!" I clenched my head between my hands as if I could somehow eject all the bad things that, lately, seemed to plague my every waking hour, my dreams, and certainly my nightmares.

"I'm sorry, Toni. I've been such a fool for so long. So misguided in my attempts to do what's right. I thought I should honor my father, my family, and didn't realize that by accepting this pact, I was doing exactly the opposite. My father never meant for me to be unhappy. Yes, he wanted me to continue the legacy, but I'm sure he never meant for any of this. I could blame Walter. He lived through the prime of the Knight pack. It was on top when he was a young alpha, and he enjoyed a lot of power and prestige. He and his father are responsible for amassing the large Knight fortune. When my father showed no interest in upholding the legacy and chose to marry for love and not pack, Walter was very disappointed. They didn't see eye to eye until my brother showed signs of great leadership. He had all the qualities my father didn't. He was Walter's perfect candidate to take his place."

Jake's shoulders sank a couple of inches as if weighed down by sadness. "Then Neil disappeared and everything came crumbling down. My father, my mother, the entire Knight legacy. After that, I don't know, I just… lost sight of what really mattered."

"You don't have to explain yourself anymore, Jake. I understand."

And I did. I'd made my own share of mistakes—not least of all moving in with him right after high school. It didn't matter that we'd been crazy about each other. It didn't matter that I hadn't been able to picture a future without him. What had mattered was that we'd been too young to make those types of decisions.

If I'd listened to my mother, if I'd gone to college instead of playing house with him, he might have stayed. He might've never left to go to New Orleans. Moving in together made him feel pressured, torn between his responsibilities and his feelings. We had rushed into things when what we'd needed was time to grow up, to get to know ourselves as individuals. Not as "us", but as a separate Toni and separate Jake.

The almost two years we'd spent apart had given us some of that. Even if Jake had still needed a little extra time to find his path, a path that led to *his* happiness, not Walter's or anyone else's. Only his.

"Whatever happens," he said, turning to me with the most

serious expression I'd ever seen on his face, "you should know that it is you I want. It is you who has my heart. It's always been you. Since the day I saw you at that party, I never wanted anyone else. Even then, I knew deep in my bones that you were the one for me. I love you, Toni."

He pressed his forehead to mine and caressed my cheek, running his thumb back and forth. His gaze dove deep into mine as if he meant to fall straight into my very soul. Slowly, he leaned closer to kiss me.

His chest rumbled, making me shiver. "My love. My reason for being. My m—"

Blaze made his presence known again.

"Damn cat," Jake growled.

I, myself, was on the verge of agreeing with Jake when I noticed that the cat was sitting on top of something.

I frowned. "What is that?"

Jake blinked and looked down. "It's… a book."

"Where did it come from?"

"One of Eric's books," Jake added as he took a closer look.

We glanced around the cabin, scanning the walls for bookshelves. There were none. We returned our attention to the cat.

Purring, Blaze pressed a paw to Jake's thigh, then, with a satisfied look in his amber eyes, turned on a dime, walked to one corner of the sofa bed, and curled himself to sleep.

"Did he just… approve of me?" Jake asked.

It sure looked that way.

With a strange, anxious feeling in my chest, I picked up the book, turned it, and read the title. "*Blood Treaties: My life in France,*" I said under my breath. "This book…" I started, unsure of whether or not I should keep talking.

"What?"

"It was in my condo. It's one of the ones I took with me."

Jake's eyes darted from side to side. "And you… brought it?"

I shook my head. "I didn't." I looked at Blaze who seemed lost in his pleasant sleep.

"So… the cat brought it?" Jake said tentatively.

I scrubbed at my face, feeling at a loss. "I think he did, which means…" I hated to eat crow.

"Which means I'm right," Jake finished for me. "That cat is weird."

I nodded reluctantly. I couldn't deny it anymore. There was definitely something up with Blaze, but what? And did it mean I needed to get rid of him? Or that I should have him evaluated by a Witch Vet? Maybe they would be able to tell me if he was possessed like Jake had said. Or maybe he was just… special, like from Elf-hame or some other realm where cats were super smart and, on top of that, magical.

"Why this book?" Jake asked.

I was afraid to even say the words out loud, to even hope, so I started very slowly. "I think… I think there's something here that may help us break the pact. He tried to bring the book to my attention before, but I got distracted and then forgot."

He snatched the book from my hands, threw the cover open, and ran a finger down the index, his eyes moving back and forth across the page. Nothing caught his eye in the first section, so he turned the page and continued searching. There was such a desperate quality to his movements that I immediately understood how he'd managed to read all those books so quickly. I watched him curiously as he devoured the words, page after page, his attitude far more desperate than mine had been when I'd methodically gone through my pile of research.

Nervous agitation sizzled around him, and I found myself feeling embarrassed and terribly flattered at the same time. Embarrassed because I should've been as invested as he was in finding the answer, and flattered because he was doing this for me, because he loved me enough to risk his life by breaking the pact.

Without thinking, I lifted a hand to his hair and ran my fingers through it. Reluctantly, he peeled his eyes away from the book and glanced in my direction. As he noticed my expression, the intense quality that shaped his features slowly changed.

"What?" he asked, appearing confused by whatever emotion he saw in my face.

"Nothing," I said. "I just love you so much."

He let out a short exhale as if I'd punched him in the gut. Recovering quickly, he set the book aside and slid closer. "I love you too, Toni."

His lips parted, and he glanced down at my mouth. Unable to resist the temptation of his delicious mouth, I threw a leg over his lap and straddled him. He blinked in surprise but recovered quickly. Smiling, he placed his large hands on my hips, then slid them upward, deftly pulling my shirt out of my waistband. His fingers trailed over the bare skin of my abdomen and back.

I lowered my lips to his and kissed him. A jolt of electricity passed between us, and he tightened his hands around my waist, pulling me to him.

"I've been wasting my time," he said as he nibbled on my lower lip. "I've been dying to make love to you. It was stupid of me to hold back. I want you." His chest rumbled as his tongue caressed my lower lip, sending a pang of desire straight to my middle.

I deepened my kiss, one hand intertwined in his soft hair and the other one exploring his hard chest. Suddenly, he rolled to one side, laid me on the bed, and covered my body with his, fitting snugly between my hips. His erection bulged against me, sending my desire from the *lets-make-out* category in the *rip-my-clothes-off-now* one.

"I dream about this every single night." He trailed kisses down my neck as his hand slowly made its way toward my left breast.

I arched my back, wrapping my legs around him to feel him

better.

"I wake up sweating and… aching for you." His tongue made swirling patterns near my collarbone while his hand finally covered my breast and gently squeezed it, his thumb and forefinger pinching my nipple over my silken bra.

"I love you and want you so damn much," I hissed.

Suddenly, he stopped. Just stopped.

I blinked up at him in confusion, then finally became aware of two things: the shower had stopped, and Blaze was standing right above our heads, staring at us in a disapproving way.

Cursing inwardly, I unwrapped my legs from around Jake's waist and threw my hands to the sides, feeling hopelessly defeated.

"I guess our timing wasn't the best," Jake said, hovering over me, still devouring me with his beautiful eyes.

"That's an understatement," I replied breathlessly.

"I gotta get you alone, Toni. Soon, or I'll go crazy. I haven't had sex for so long and just watching you *walk* around makes me want to fuck you senseless."

His tone was savage and made my belly tighten in response. Curbing my own desire, I scanned his features in awe. I still couldn't believe that, like me, he hadn't slept with anyone since the last time we'd been together.

"When I take you, it's going to be perfect. Like our first time, remember?"

How could I ever forget when he'd set out to make that night unforgettable. Starting with a perfect dinner and ending with a luxury suite where he schooled me in all the ways a man can pleasure a woman. A shiver ran through me at the memory of his hooded eyes as he'd trailed kisses down to my very core. It had been my first time, and he'd shown me so much.

"I remember," I whispered. "But right now, I don't care if it's perfect. We can go outside. My Camaro would do. It wouldn't be the first time."

His eyes grew distant for a second as if he were remembering that time I pulled him into the back seat of my car and licked him until he shuddered in pleasure.

"Hmm, tempting. Very tempting, but I'm not sure even the Camaro will be private enough." He threw a dirty glance in Blaze's direction, who was still sitting in the same spot, watching us with his perfectly round eyes. "But I promise, first chance we get to ourselves, I'll make sweet love to you."

"That's a promise I'm gonna hold you to," I said, giving him a crooked grin.

"Fair enough."

Wincing with regret, he rolled off me and got to his feet. As if on cue, Eric came out of the bathroom, dressed in a fresh T-shirt and a pair of baggy sweats. He veered toward his bedroom but came to a sudden stop. His nostrils flared, then he glowered at us. He seemed on the verge of saying something but thought better of it and disappeared through the door.

"You'd better go in with Rosalina," Jake said, then picked the book back up. "I'll be up for a while looking through this."

I didn't want to leave. I wanted to stay and sleep with him on the pullout couch, but I didn't think I would be able to keep off him unless I put a wall between us. Besides, I needed to rest for tomorrow's trance.

Dragging my feet, I walked away. Jake watched me go, biting his lower lip and scanning me from head to toe, his gaze lingering on my ass for a long time. But, by the time I reached the door and turned the handle, he had focused his entire attention on the book, regaining the same feverish air as he read.

CHAPTER 31

When I woke up the next morning to the sound of chirping birds and wind rustling through the treetops, I stretched lazily, giving Rosalina a sideways glance. She was still asleep, her tanned face relaxed, her black hair spread over the pillow. She looked peaceful and innocent, nothing like the rifle-toting badass she'd turned into.

I snuck out of bed, careful not to make a sound. Out in the main living area, things were pretty much the same with Jake, asleep on his back, the book resting on his chest as if he'd fallen asleep in the middle of reading. To my surprise, I found Blaze curled up next to him. They looked like best buddies.

Yep, weird is the word.

On my way to the bathroom, I grabbed my duffel bag, ready for a hot shower. I'd been worried the plumbing in the cabin might not be up to standard, but the water was perfect and helped ease yesterday's tension and prepare me for the day ahead. As usual, I wasn't looking forward to the trance and its side effects. All I could hope for was that it would go fast, and I wouldn't lose my senses for very long.

When I was done showering and went out dressed in a comfortable pair of shorts and a T-shirt, the others were already up. Rosalina and Jake were busy at the stove, frying eggs.

"Good morning," they said in unison.

Rosalina kept her focus on the food, but Jake paused and checked me out, his thick eyebrows arching as he admired my legs.

"You look… comfortable," he said.

"I feel… comfortable," I replied with a wicked grin.

"Spare me," Eric huffed from the small kitchen table, his nose buried in *Blood Treaties: My life in France*. "I'm afraid this cabin won't be a safe place to hide for much longer."

"Huh?" I frowned at him.

He set the book on the table. "I mean that I'll lose it with all this syrupy romance, and I'll kill everyone in sight."

I might've laughed at the joke, except for the fact that Eric had already lost it once in his lifetime, and it had resulted in the annihilation of an entire pack.

Jake seemed about to say something but sagely returned his attention to scraping burnt spots from overly brown pieces of toast. He could be an impulsive idiot, but sometimes he actually thought about the consequences of his actions. He had a couple of promises to keep, and it was just smart not to poke the vengeful wolf.

I padded into the kitchen area and procured plates from the shelves and silverware from a rickety drawer. Once we were seated on the table with enough scrambled eggs for twenty Stales, Eric set the book aside.

"I think it could work," he said.

My ears perked up. "What could work?"

Jake stepped closer, a frown line on his forehead. "I think… I might have found a way to break the pact."

"Really?!"

He nodded. "It won't be easy, but I'm willing to do what it takes."

Why had his gaze darkened?

Eric sighed tiredly. "This is not the priority. Same as your trance."

Witchlights! He wouldn't know sympathy if it chomped on his werewolf tail. I hated to get derailed from Jake's important news, but I went on the defense, opting to get the details from Jake later. This topic concerned only us, anyhow. Jake might have asked Eric's opinion on whether or not what the book said would work, but ultimately, this didn't involve Eric's grumpy ass.

"*These things* are still important to us and need to be done," I bit back.

Sticking a fork-full of eggs into his mouth, he rolled his eyes and mumbled, "Sure, but one thing at a time and in order of priority. I very much miss my old life, and I would like to get back to normal as soon as possible."

"Life? What life? You mean the one where you're a cynical hermit?" I said.

Rosalina sucked in a breath and exchanged a panic glance with Jake. Clearly, they didn't think that talking to the murdering werewolf in that tone was such a good idea, but honestly, I was tired of Eric and his crotchety ways. Just when I thought he'd made progress, he would take two steps back!

"That very same one," he replied with an expression that seemed to suggest he was very proud of that life, which kind of took the wind of my sails. "I didn't get rid of everyone so I could get stuck with the likes of you."

"What's crawled up your butt?"

He narrowed his eyes and, without a word, continued eating his eggs. Maybe he was just irritable in the mornings. Sometimes I wondered why I tried so hard with him.

Eric refocused his attention on Jake. "While Toni does her tracking trance, how about you and I do some reconnaissance? Make sure everything is safe. Also, we'll need more provisions, and there's a small town a few miles north."

"Sounds good," Jake said, looking glad to have something to do.

"Yeah," Rosalina said in a chipper tone. "It sounds like a great idea."

I snorted. She sounded about as ready as Eric to get rid of them. Just then, Blaze meowed and jumped on Rosalina's lap, surprising her.

"Oh, hey there!" she exclaimed, scratching his head. He purred and threw his head back, reaching his little nose toward her chin.

"He wants a kiss, Rosalina," Jake teased.

"Aw!" She continued petting him until he settled on her lap and let her eat her food.

After breakfast, I followed Jake outside the cabin as he took a backpack to Eric's car. They'd pack bullets for one of Rosalina's guns, but mostly, the bag was full of snacks. *Wolves!*

"Hey," I said, catching up with him. "What did the book say about breaking the pact?"

Jake grew serious again, his pupils dilating even in the morning sun, which seeped through the thick branches above.

"It's complicated and dangerous." He set the backpack on the ground and turned toward the woods, his jaw setting.

"Yes?"

"We'll have to figure out how to make it work and—"

"Jake, tell me!"

He sighed and faced me, a resigned expression on his handsome features. "Well, since the pact is a blood covenant, and it burns in my veins, we need to root its magic out."

"And… how do you do that?" I asked cautiously.

Jake swallowed. "We… let a… blood demon eat it out of me."

"What?!"

With a frustrated grunt, he picked up the backpack and walked toward the Mercedes.

I followed in his heels. "How does that work? Where do you get a blood demon? And isn't that like possession?"

"I have as many questions as you, Toni, and just as few answers." He opened the sedan's back door, threw the bag in, then faced me. "We'll have to look further into it."

I shook my head, at a loss. My throat grew tight, making it hard to breathe.

"Oh, Toni." He gathered me in his arms and rested his chin on top of my head. "Let's not worry about it right now, okay? At least I've found a way out of this."

I nodded, then pulled away from him and stared him in the eye. "Promise me you won't do anything stupid, that you won't try anything without discussing it with me."

A smile quirked his lips. "Don't worry. I learned my lesson. It's you and I together from now on."

"Good."

He kissed me gently on the lips, and we held each other, surrounded by the sounds of nature. A moment later, Eric stomped out of the cabin and climbed into the car without a word.

"Maybe he'll lighten up once he has a bowel movement," Jake whispered in my ear.

I snickered.

"I heard that!" Eric's muffled voice called from the car.

Jake got in the passenger seat and they were off.

Once on our own, Rosalina and I got the bedroom ready, setting up the potion in a shallow bowl we found in the kitchen, and propping up a few pillows so I could be at ease while I got lost in the overwhelming din of my senses.

"I wish we could do this at my place," Rosalina said.

"It's all right. I'll be all right."

"I know. It's just hard when you come out of a trance, and I think it helps for you to feel as comfortable as possible."

She always made my recovery bearable. She prepared different kinds of tea to calm my nerves, had books in hand to read and pass the time, burned candles so I could smell something pretty when my sense of smell returned, and more…

"It sure helps," I admitted. "But I promise you, it'll be all right. I'll just try to sleep it off."

She nodded with a sad smile. "Ready then?"

I removed Damien's token, and the arrow bracelet Jake had given me, then turned to the shimmering potion. We had opted to track Mekare's mate first since it made the most financial sense. Gently, I dipped my hands into the thick liquid. As it stirred, the smell of pancakes and syrup rose from it. When my hands were coated, I held them in front of me and climbed into bed, careful not to touch anything. Rosalina pulled the covers up to my chest as I made myself comfortable on the pillows.

"You'd better take Blaze." I gestured toward the cat, who had hopped atop a rustic chest of drawers and was watching us from his high vantage point.

When she reached for him, he shied away and tried to resist her.

"Come on buddy," she said sweetly. "Toni needs privacy. We could throw things off for her if we stay."

As if he understood, he allowed her to pick him up and carry him out of the room in the crook of her arm. She closed the door.

I stared at my glimmering hands, which appeared covered in sequin gloves. Dreading the always unpleasant trance, I gradually brought my hands towards my face and touched my eyelids, ears, nose, and mouth, tasting the sweet potion.

After a few beats, the potion vanished, leaving my skin clean, and I was transported to that familiar, glittery blackness. Immediately setting to work, I activated my sense of smell, allowing in a myriad of scents. One, in particular, was extremely prevalent and triggered my memory banks.

Honeysuckle blossoms. The last time I'd smelled them this strongly, it was in Elf-hame when we'd run into Prince Kalyll. Was Mekare's mate a fae? Could it be the Prince? No, no way. That just didn't feel right. Besides the honeysuckle, I also sensed an overly sweet smell of roses, which was also familiar. I'd perceived it before, but where?

I needed to know more. Quickly, I release my sense of hearing. A cacophony of sounds overwhelmed me. Loud music, the whirring of machines, an incessant pounding, and more. I rifled through the sounds as fast as I could until there was a particular one that seemed familiar. It was an engine backfiring. It ran unsteadily, making a peculiar clank.

It sounded just like Em's Vespa.

What the hell?

Em? Was Liliana's petite neighbor Mekare's mate?

That also felt wrong.

What was happening? Were my tracking skills broken?

Despairing, I released my sense of sight. My most powerful. If I couldn't find Mekare's mate this way, there was no hope for our agency.

At once, flashes of Kalyll's face tattoos and Em's green hair filled my mind. I fought to catch a glimpse of something else, but that was all I could see. Inked lines and lime-colored strands of straight hair.

The images bludgeoned me with insistence, blocking all else. Worst of all, they felt flawed without that sense of rightness I'd experienced before. This had never happened.

Oh, God! I'd only done one trance since discovering I was a werewolf. Maybe my tracking skills had also changed—everything else had, so why not? Maybe they were entirely broken, and I would never be able to track someone's mate again.

Whatever the case, it was time for me to break the trance. I'd been under long enough, and I had used all my senses. I would be deaf and blind for hours.

I shut my senses off, expecting to return to my shimmering void, except I continued to smell, hear, and see the same sights.

Panic raised its head, but I fought it, envisioning the cabin, willing myself to wake up.

Nothing happened.

My heart sped up, knocking against my ribcage and filling my ears with its loud thuds. The pounding combined with the other sounds. I pressed my hands over my ears, whirling in the emptiness, searching for a way out. The gentle shimmering lights that always surrounded me slowly receded, the already-tiny dots swallowed by the backdrop. I reached out as if I could stop them, but the pinpricks disappeared, completely blinking out of existence and leaving me in utter darkness.

Tears sliding down my cheeks, I fell to my knees and wrapped my hands over my head, rocking back and forth.

Please let me out. Please, please, please, I recited inside my mind, but no one listened.

I was stuck.

CHAPTER 32

It had always been easy to snap out of the tracking trance. As soon as the wish materialized to go back, I always resurfaced—without my senses—but I resurfaced.

Now, here I was, curled up, cloaked in darkness, tears sliding down my face.

At first, there had been smells, and sounds, and sights, but they were gone now, and all that was left was a vast nothingness I couldn't push away.

I had screamed without a voice. I had fought in the oblivion in which I floated, all to no avail. It felt like punching at the air, like clawing at the vacuum of space as I tumbled and tumbled through a bottomless abyss.

Rosalina, help me! Help me!

But my friend, my savior, couldn't hear me. She wasn't here. I was alone.

Jake, Jake, Jake.

He wasn't here either. Did they know I was lost? How long had it been since I took Mekare's potion and I closed my eyes? Minutes? Hours? Days?

If I woke up, I might never be able to smell, hear, or see anything again.

Oh, God! Please, help me!

Somebody.

Anybody.

Help me!

But no one came. No one heard me.

And even though I tried and tried to get myself back into the real world, I remained lost.

ꙮ

Silence and darkness were all I had left around me, and yet my mind roared with desperation, constantly screaming for help that wouldn't come.

I dug my claws into my scalp, trying to feel something, relishing even the pain over the emptiness that had swallowed me.

Suddenly, I felt something wet on my fingertips. It was the first thing I'd been able to perceive, something other than the void. I pulled my hands away, tried to peer at the wetness.

Was it blood?

It had to be.

Desperate for something, anything, I dug my claws into my palms. I clenched my teeth and moaned in pain.

A tiny whisper registered in my mind. I sat bolt upright, my head swiveling on my neck, and my eyes roving in their sockets.

Darkness.

Only darkness.

The whisper grew louder. I strained to understand, to catch the meaning of the sound. Where was it coming from? Was it a voice?

Yes! Yes! It *was* a voice.

I pushed my fists against my eyes, throwing my entire focus onto that small breath of sound.

"Toni."

"Toni."

"TONI!"

My name. Someone was calling me.

Jake! It was Jake. *I'm right here. Please, help me. Please!*

"Toni?"

Yes, yes, yes!

"Oh, thank the witchlights! Open your eyes."

I can't. I can't.

"You have to. You have to wake up. We have to get out of here. Now!" He was desperate, urgent.

What was happening? I didn't know, but I tried again, with all my might, I tried to break out of the trance, but I couldn't. I was stuck. Maybe even for good.

"C'mon, Toni. You can do it."

I shook my head. *I can't. It's not working. Nothing is working.*

Jake's voice changed, becoming a fierce alpha command. "*Do it now!*"

Red bristled at this. Her first instinct was to refuse, to fight back. No one told her what to do. No one. Except, she couldn't be any more wrong. Today, she had to submit.

Do as he commands, I pleaded, hoping she would see reason.

She didn't. Instead, she hunkered down like an idiot.

"You've been out for an hour," Jake said. "*You have to snap out of it. DO IT NOW,"* he repeated even more forcefully than before.

An hour?! Fucking witchlights! That meant my senses would be out for almost three days, and what if they didn't return? I'd never remained in my trance for more than ten minutes.

I know it goes against every fiber in you, Red, but you have to listen, I pleaded. *Just this once. I'll never, ever, ask you to submit again. I swear.*

Her resistance died by degrees as she saw the sense in my request. Slowly, her will and strength melded with mine, and suddenly, I knew I had the strength to break free.

I woke up with a jolt, confusion washing over me as I tried to get my bearings. My body was upside down. My stomach was pressed against something hard, and a tight grip kept my ankles in place. My arms dangled from side to side as my entire body jostled up and down, each jolt pounding against my gut.

It took several beats for my brain to grasp what was happening. I was moving, being carried on someone's shoulder as they ran.

"Jake!" I exclaimed desperately. "What's happening?"

But if he replied I didn't know because I couldn't hear anything and, now, instead of nothingness, I felt only the battering of what felt like a desperate escape attempt.

Witchlights! They had found us.

༄༅

The next thing I knew, I was flipped over and thrown down, none too gently, in what felt like a bed or couch. My head hit something hard, and I groaned and rubbed it, wincing. Someone grabbed my legs and moved them aside. They sat next to me. Awkwardly, I struggled to a sitting position.

A slight rumble started under me. I pressed a hand to the surface where I'd been deposited. It felt smooth, like leather. We lurched forward, then I slammed back into what must be the seat of a car.

The rumbling underneath me grew more intense, and I realized we were driving. Fast. Over a very bumpy road.

A hand twined with mine. I recognized it immediately. Rosalina.

After a brief squeeze, she released me and spelled the letters C-

A-R in my palm. I nodded my understanding.

"Did they find us?" I asked.

She tapped my hand once.

"Shit!" I tried to calm my breathing, which was ragged.

My mind raced as I tried to process our situation. Jake had said that I'd been under for an hour, which meant he and Eric had been gone at least that long. Had they been spotted? Or had they fled before being noticed?

"Are they chasing us now?" I asked.

Two taps on the back of my hand. No.

I exhaled in relief, then something else occurred to me. "Where's Blaze?"

No response from Rosalina. It was the stupidest thing to worry about, my cat, but I couldn't help it.

"We left him?" I asked.

I felt Rosalina's fist on my chest as she moved it in a circular motion.

Sorry.

She was apologizing.

No one had thought of Blaze as we ran out of the cabin.

I pulled away from her and grabbed my head. I felt awful, disoriented, panicked, lost. Why was this happening? Why, no matter how hard I tried, did my life not settle into a semblance of normalcy? I hadn't asked for any of this. I just wanted to be left alone and live my life like everybody else. Instead, a deranged werewolf, an ancient vampire, and a Midnight Witch were after me.

And I couldn't even keep my cat safe.

I let out a groan that morphed into a sob. A heavy hand fell on my knee. I knew instinctively it must be Jake's. It offered little comfort.

Closing off, I pulled away from him, drew my knees to my chest, and pressed my body tightly to the side of the car, hiding my face and doing my best to cry in silence.

The car jostled for several long minutes, then eventually pulled up onto a smooth road where we started going much faster. Knowing that there was nothing I could do but feel sorry for myself, I squeezed my eyes and willed myself to sleep.

The next time I awoke, I wasn't in the car. There were covers on top of me and a soft pillow under my head. I was in a bed.

Where?

I could only try to imagine because none of my senses had returned yet. Another hideout? A motel? And what if they found us again? The Midnight Witch was powerful and, somehow, she'd been able to find us in that remote cabin. Or maybe, they'd hired a tracker, someone like me. Stephen and Bernadetta certainly had the funds to hire the best of the best.

I sat up. Rosalina took my hand in hers as soon as I pushed to the edge of the bed and settled my feet on the floor.

"You're here," I said.

One tap on my hand followed by the letter "H". She was asking if I was hungry. It was part of the simple hand gestures we'd come up with to be able to communicate.

I shook my head.

A "T" followed.

Thirsty?

"Yes," I said, realizing that my tongue was practically stuck to the roof of my mouth, and my throat felt like sandpaper.

She was gone for a moment, then back, pressing a plastic cup into my hands. The water was cool, and ice swam in it. I drank every drop. Rosalina took the cup back.

I sat at the edge of the bed, trembling. "Are Jake and Eric here?"

She tapped my hand once.

"Where is here anyway? A motel?"

Two taps in my hand.

"Another hideout?"

Another two taps.

"Eric's house?" I didn't think we would've gone back there but maybe.

Rosalina tapped twice again then traced the letter "S" on my palm.

Sleep.

I shook my head. I didn't want to sleep anymore, but just as the thought materialized, a groggy feeling descended on me, and my eyelids became heavy. I blinked slowly, fighting to keep my eyes open even though I couldn't see a thing. I swallowed thickly, tasting something bitter in my mouth.

"There was something in the water," I said. A half question, half statement.

Rosalina patted my hand, then, pushing on my shoulders, guided my head into the pillow and lifted my legs, depositing them on the bed.

Like a curtain falling, I immediately went to sleep.

CHAPTER 33

I awoke by degrees. There was a *whoosh* in my ears, and the inside of my nose stung as if with the cold air of winter. An orange glow pressed against my eyelids.

My eyes sprang open, then squeezed shut as light pierced through them like needles. I sat up, a hand pressed to my brow to shield me from the glow. Slowly, I peered between my fingers, letting my vision adjust to what appeared to be the warm glow of many candles.

Oh, thank God my senses are back!

Slowly, I took stock of my surroundings. I was lying on a large four-poster bed, covered with several thick blankets. The rest of the furniture was as imposing, and the walls were made of bare stone. There was a window on the far right and, from what I could see through the sheer curtains, it was nighttime. The place was entirely foreign, somewhere I'd never been.

I was alone, no one in sight. Not Rosalina, Jake, or Eric.

Throwing the covers off, I scooted to the edge of the bed. My feet dangled several inches from the floor. There was a plate with sliced fruit and a glass of water on the night table. I licked my dry lips, reached for the water, and was about to drink it when I remembered what had happened the last time.

Rosalina had given me something to make me sleep, surely to spare me from the anguish of not having my senses. It was always easier when I dozed off, but I really must've been in rough shape if she decided that was necessary. She'd never done that before.

Whatever the case, I didn't need to sleep anymore.

I set the glass back down, and though the fruit was tempting, I didn't touch it either. Maybe there was a bathroom where I could drink water from the tap. I glanced around. There was only one door, so I figured it must lead out of the room and not to any type of restroom.

On bare feet, I padded toward the door, then stopped when it abruptly opened, and Rosalina walked in. She wore a pair of jeans and a blouse I'd never seen before.

"Oh, good, you're awake." Her green eyes met mine. "I'm glad to see you all better."

"I don't know about better. I've got my senses back, but I feel weird."

"It's understandable after what you went through."

I nodded as my gaze roved around the room. "Where are we?"

"In a safe place. No one will be able to follow us here. It's protected by magic… Or so they tell me." She smiled sheepishly.

"Where are Jake and Eric?"

"In the study, arguing."

I rolled my eyes.

"What happened exactly?"

She opened her mouth to answer, but instead, rushed in my direction as my legs gave way under me. She caught me just in time and practically dragged me toward an armchair where she deposited me with a grunt.

"Witchlights!" she exclaimed. "I thought you were going to faint. You sure you're all right?"

I pressed a hand to my forehead, feeling like I was in the heavy-duty cycle of a washing machine. My stomach tightened, seized by nausea. "I don't know what's happening."

She backed away and sat at the edge of the chair opposite mine, attentive as if she expected me to topple face-first into the rug. She fiddled with her hair, wrapping it around a finger.

"Just rest until you feel better. There's no hurry. It's really safe here. It's already been two days and no one has found us."

Two days?! Witchlights!

What of our clients?

The jumbled mess of my trance rushed into my mind, reminding me what a failure it had been. I hadn't the faintest idea about the whereabouts of Mekare's mate. How could I tell Rosalina? I peered at her concerned expression. She hadn't asked me about the trance. Her thoughtfulness knew no bounds.

I closed my eyes and reclined my head, taking deep breaths. We were silent for several minutes, and slowly, the dizziness passed.

When I opened my eyes Rosalina glanced away, pretending she hadn't been watching me like a mother hen. Absently, she pulled out a cell phone from her back pocket, crossed her leg, and started scrolling.

I frowned. That didn't look like one of the burner phones Eric had gotten us.

Making a disgusted sound in the back of her throat, she put the phone away. "The news is awful."

"What happened?"

She waved her hand, acting as if she didn't want to worry me with something so mundane.

"What, Rosalina?"

She heaved a heavy sigh. "There's been a lot of unrest

everywhere, but especially in Skew zones. The mayor has established a curfew, and a bunch of people were arrested. Last night, more than twenty Skews died at a dance club when a battle broke out between vamps and shifters. Apparently, rhabo has flooded the streets in the last few days. They've started an official death count, and they say more than five thousand vampires have died since rhabo hit the market."

Five thousand vampires!

The drug had only been introduced about three months ago. That number was staggering, and there was no telling how many more had already tried the drug and would inevitably perish.

"If only Damien had found a way to make enough elixir for everyone," Rosalina said, her green eyes clouding with sadness as she recalled the mage. "And we only have one more dose. I wish someone could use it to make more."

I clenched my fists, my hatred toward Stephen and Bernadetta smoldering inside my chest.

"Maybe…" Rosalina started tentatively, her voice growing quiet. "Maybe we should give it to someone who can analyze it and figure out how it's made. Maybe… maybe we should retrieve it."

A hitch in her voice made me look up from the floor. There was something in her expression that seemed a little desperate. She cracked her fingers—something she never did.

I glanced around the room. My eyes paused on the glass of water on the night table. "Hmm, I… don't think retrieving the elixir is a good idea."

She rose to her feet. "We have to do something! We can't let more people die. Those damn vamps are dropping like flies. It's horrible."

Damn vamps?! Rosalina had never referred to vampires with such contempt. Besides, wasn't she talking about saving their lives?

Something was wrong. This person… she wasn't… Rosalina.

"Yes," I said, my hands trembling slightly. "You're right. We'll find someone to examine it. Maybe my sister, Daniella, knows a healer who specializes in that sort of thing. She knows…" I slowed my words and blinked lazily, "…a lot of people in the field."

"Yes, that's a great idea." She smiled coldly.

I nodded, stood, and trudged to the bed. "I think I might lay down for a bit. I'm feeling dizzy again, and I can hardly think straight."

She inclined her head in understanding and smiled, though it didn't reach her eyes. "We should go as soon as you feel better."

"We will, but the elixir is secure at the safe deposit box for now."

"Yes, of course."

I almost choked but managed to keep a straight face as I climbed back onto the huge bed. I let my head collapse on the pillow and sighed, closing my eyes and pulling the covers tightly under my chin. I was tempted to peek through my lashes, but I kept my eyes shut, listening intently.

Feet shuffled quietly over the floor, but the door didn't open. After a couple of minutes, I measured my breaths, keeping them at a steady rhythm. After a few more beats, I deepened them, doing my best to simulate sleep.

Finally, after what felt like two eternities, the door opened and closed. Even then, I didn't dare move for several minutes—not even my eyelashes fluttered. When I was certain I was alone, I turned on my side as if restless in my sleep, and took a peek.

She was gone.

Throwing the covers aside, I hopped out of bed and ran toward the window. Frantically, I pulled the curtains aside and looked out. I was on the ground level of what looked like a house in the middle of the woods—not much different from Eric's cabin. A thick, moonlit forest started about twenty yards away. There was no sign of a road or anything civilized.

No matter. As soon as I was out of here, all I had to do was shift and lose myself between the trees. There, I would fleet the hell away from whoever was pretending to be my friend.

Please don't be stuck. Don't be stuck, I chanted inside my head as I flipped the window latch. Tentatively, I pushed up. There was a loud creak as the wood rose from its casing. I winced and went utterly still, my ears focused on any sounds coming from the door.

Nothing.

I let out a pent-up breath and started to push on the window again.

Someone other than Rosalina spoke behind me, though the tone was still familiar.

"Going somewhere?"

I stopped dead, my heart pounding against my chest. Slowly, I turned to find Mekare Graves, all six-foot-two of her, standing by the threshold.

CHAPTER 34

Aside from her impressive height, Mekare Graves barely resembled the woman I had met in my office. The bangs of her previously plain blond hair were two-toned—one half green and the other jet black. Braids cascaded behind her, their strands a mixture of yellow, black, and green. She wore a leather mini skirt, torn pantyhose, and tall Doc Martens boots with dangling chains. Her top was tight and studded with so many spikes that she looked like a porcupine.

My thoughts raced, tripping over each other, fighting for attention. One, however, was louder than the rest.

"Where are my friends?!" I demanded. "What did you do to them? Where is Rosalina?" I peered over Mekare's shoulder, looking for my friend.

Was she even here? Was *I* even here? What if I was still stuck in the trance?

"I can almost hear the wheels turning inside your head," Mekare said in a quiet voice very unlike the peppy one she'd used before, the one that had made her seem outgoing and nice. Instead, her entire demeanor was cold and calculated.

"Who the hell are you?!"

"I bet what's really going to mess with your noodle is wondering whether or not you're really here. And more importantly, whether you're still in your trance," she added with a tiny smile that barely stretched her thin lips.

I felt dizzy all of a sudden.

Shit!

What if everything I'd experienced since I closed my eyes in Eric's cabin had been some elaborate illusion? But how? I racked my brain, then a realization hit me like a blow to the chest.

The tears for her potion!

Oh, God!

My heart hammered out of control as my eyes desperately darted around the room.

"What did you do to me?!" I demanded.

She shrugged. "But you already know, don't you?"

"The tears," I whispered.

My stomach convulsed, and I swallowed hard to stop myself from retching. Suddenly, I felt dirty inside as if I'd been contaminated with the worst type of imaginable cooties.

Witch cooties!

Because she had to be a witch. She had used a glamour to pose as Rosalina. That or she was implanting all of this in my head. Either way, I couldn't believe I hadn't seen through it right away. Looking back now, I could see all the signs. Rosalina didn't fiddle with her hair.

I shook my head. *Toni, snap out of it!*

If I was still in the trance, I needed to wake up. I bit the inside of my cheek until the taste of blood filled my mouth.

Ow, that feels real.

But if I was in a strange place, how had Mekare taken me from the cabin and brought me here? Rosalina, Jake, and Eric would've never let her take me, would've fought for me. Though, Jake and Eric hadn't been there. Or had they returned? Jake had helped me break out of the trance, hadn't he? Or maybe it had been Mekare all along?

The fucking witch!

How had she known where to find me? The answer was the same: the tears. She'd used some spells to track me through them. I gasped as another realization hit me and as anger and my desire for revenge swelled like a tidal wave inside me. "*You* killed Damien."

She daintily blew air through her nose and put on a demure expression. "I did." She sounded proud as if she were the kid who'd won the science fair in school and not the monster who killed my friend.

"You'll pay for it."

In an instant, my fangs grew, and my claws unsheathed. Filled with rage, I lunged in her direction, ready to rip her head off, but I smacked against an invisible barrier, my mouth smashing against what felt like the stone walls around us. I shook my head to get rid of the pain and stared at Mekare with undiluted hatred, the kind that clogs the arteries.

The witch stood with her hands clasped at her back, looking blasé. "I expected him to be a worthy opponent, but he disappointed me."

"You ambushed him, you bitch!"

"A mage should always keep his guard up. It seemed he had grown careless. You can't blame me for taking advantage of that.

Everything is fair in war and love. Still, I couldn't get what I wanted from him. So I guess he still had a few tricks up his sleeve."

What she wanted from him. The same thing she'd been trying to get from me. The cure! Damien had concealed it with magic.

I stood in place, my chest heaving. "Remove this," I demanded, placing a hand on the invisible barrier, "and I'll show you what's fair."

She rolled her eyes and took a step closer. "A safe deposit box, you said. Where exactly?"

"Screw you! I don't know why you want that elixir, but you'll never get your hands on it."

Mekare chuckled. "I always get what I want, dear. Like, for instance, the Unholy Vessel, cup and dagger."

What? No! It wasn't possible.

"It's nearly sacrilegious that the old and once-powerful alpha of the legendary Knight pack was never properly buried, don't you think?"

I shook my head. "What did you do?

"You didn't think we would let him take the secret of the dagger's location to the grave?"

As she said the word *we*, Stephen Erickson walked into the room, wearing a smile that stretched from ear to ear.

Stephen is here?!

Real. This is real.

The more time passed, the more certain I became. This was no trance, no magic-induced hallucination.

"Even the dead talk when one asks the right question," Mekare finished, giving Stephen a sidelong glance.

"And talk he did." Stephen held up the silver dagger with its jade handle. "Jake thought he was so smart pretending he had the dagger, but we knew the old man had hidden it. That greedy bastard, so out of his league."

They both laughed. God, they'd caused that chaos at the funeral home in order to prevent Walter's burial. It had all been a diversion.

A choking sensation took hold of me at the sight of the dagger in Stephen's hand.

No, it can't be.

"Now," Mekare laid a hand on Stephen's arm, "if she could just take us to Damien's elixir, we would have everything we need, right, love?"

"Right," Stephen said, giving her a smile that spoke of bedroom secrets between them.

I threw up a little inside my own mouth just at the thought of the two together. They were both despicable, and people like them had no business doing the ugly together. They should have enough sense not to risk bringing offspring into the world. Nothing short of abominable could result from their union. Gremlins would be nothing compared to the kids these two would produce.

The witch took the dagger from Stephen and, giving it a dexterous twirl, made it disappear. "So…" she came closer, "exactly where do you bank?"

I retreated a step, trying to reach the window, but I ran into another barrier.

Mekare waved a finger in my direction, then twirled it around. "*Tsk, tsk,* the force field goes all around, silly. Otherwise, what would be the point?"

"Why do you want it?" I asked, struggling to understand.

Were they really afraid that Damien's single leftover cure could be used to make more? That would surely mess up their rhabo distribution, killing the goose with the golden eggs.

"We just do," Mekare said. "So now, tell us where to find it, or we'll get the location out of you."

I clamped my mouth shut and just stared at them, letting my hatred show in full force.

Stephen let out a tired sigh. "I wish the trick with the tears had worked."

I frowned. What was he talking about?

"Me too," Mekare said. "But all I saw while she was in her trance was… chaos. I couldn't root out one useful piece of information out of her head, except for general details about her friend and beau. That little communication method of taps and signs you two have is pathetic. In fact, the entire way your tracking skills work is pathetic."

Oh, the bitch! She'd invaded my mind.

That dirty feeling from earlier returned, a nasty sensation that I didn't think a hundred showers and ten lobotomies could get rid of. At least her attempt had failed. She hadn't counted on the messed-up way my powers work. Even *I* had trouble deciphering all the smells, sounds, and sights sometimes. No way anyone but me could make sense out of that turmoil.

I thought back to all the things I'd sensed and realized that the reason I'd seen Prince Kalyll was that Mekare had been looking for the elixir's hiding place. But what about Em? Why had she come up? It would take me forever to figure out exactly what had happened though some things were starting to make sense. She had used the tears to search my mind and to track us to the cabin. I was sure she got there before Jake and Eric got back and played the charade of running away and helping me out of the trance in hopes of learning the cure's hidden place. But what of Rosalina and Blaze? Where were they?

My train of thought was interrupted by a sudden irritated exclamation from the witch.

"Well, we're waiting. Tell us where the elixir is!" Suddenly, the whites of her eyes went totally black as she glared at me, like ink filling an empty well.

Blasted Midnight Witch!

Once more, I said nothing.

"What now?!" she demanded, turning toward Stephen. "Will you continue to ask me not to hurt her? I could've gotten the truth out of her ages ago, but you continue to hold on to the stupid little idea that she'll come to you."

Stephen lowered his blue gaze to the floor as my eyes flicked in his direction. He looked ashamed for a moment, then his head snapped back up, his expression harsh.

Uh-oh! Not good.

"You can do whatever you want with her," he said, though there was a hint of disappointment in his voice. "Don't say I didn't give you a chance, Toni. I didn't want things to end this way. I would have given you everything, but it seems you prefer to scrape by at your mediocre agency and to beg Jake to look your way."

"Fuck you," I said. "When you have something other than scum to offer me, get back with me."

"Thank the witchlights you've seen reason!" Mekare told Stephen, then raised her hands, weaving them in an intricate pattern.

My ears rang as panic took hold. I rammed my shoulder into the invisible barrier and bounced back, pain flaring down the length of my arm. I felt my way all around, fists pounding against the magical cage that surrounded me like a glass cylinder, but there was no way out. I was at the witch's mercy. I thought of shifting, but what good would that do?

Pain exploded inside my head. My hands flew to my temples as I fell to my knees, screaming in agony. Mekare's chilled voice rose above the pain, ringing inside my head.

This is nothing compared to the well of pain I can make you feel. But you can spare yourself the entire experience if you just tell me where to find the elixir.

I clenched my teeth, growling, lowering my head to the floor as if to find a position that would relieve the torture, but there was none. There was only pure, unadulterated agony.

I can make it all go away. She snapped her fingers, and the pain stopped immediately. *See.*

"I can even make you feel better." Her fingers snapped once more, and a wave of well-being washed over me.

I exhaled, sinking to the floor in relief.

"Now," she cocked her head to one side, looking at me with near motherly concern, "are you ready to speak?"

Breathing rapidly, I pushed up to my knees and nodded.

Her eyebrows went up, and she turned in Stephen's direction. "I thought you said she had a strong will?"

He narrowed his eyes. "She's probably thinking of lying."

Bastard! I hated him, though I had to give him some credit for knowing me well.

"A lie won't do, dear," Mekare said. "I will know if you're not telling us the truth."

Would she? Was that something Midnight Witches could do? Sniff out a lie? I had no idea. I'd never met any, and I didn't think I ever wanted to meet any others—not if they all had the power to turn my brain into a smoothie.

But all I could do was try because I couldn't let them get hold of Damien's elixir.

"It's in Eric Cross's house," I said in a halting voice as if it pained me to reveal it.

Pain exploded inside my head once more. I threw my head

back, an anguished cry tearing out of my throat. Then my entire body went limp, and I collapsed to the floor with a *thud.* My limbs convulsed. My back arched to a breaking point.

The pain stopped as abruptly as it had begun.

Tears slid out of the corner of my eyes and splattered onto the floor. A string of saliva ran out of my mouth, and my tongue lolled like a limp flag.

White flashes disturbed my vision as I tried to look at my torturer. One of my eyes seemed to wander in the wrong direction. I blinked, feeling disoriented and unable to process a complete thought.

"She won't be able to tell us anything if you kill her," Stephen complained.

"Come closer and I'll kill you, *you asshole,"* I pushed the thought forward with my alpha skills.

He chose to ignore me.

"Oh, she's fine." Mekare waved a hand in the air. "Maybe now she's ready to tell us the truth."

My breaths came in short spasms now. In through my mouth, out through my mouth. More drool leaked out and hung like a string to the floor.

"No?" Mekare bent her knees, lowering herself to look at me better. "Not ready yet? Perhaps," she wriggled her fingers, "we do it again?"

The thought of that awful pain returning almost made me wet myself.

Tell her. Just tell her.

She wouldn't be able to get the elixir from Prince Kalyll anyway. He said he would keep it safe, and he wouldn't let anyone learn of its existence. If she went to Elyndell, she would have to fight the Prince and his guard to get what she wanted.

I opened my mouth, the first syllable forming on my lips. Mekare widened her eyes expectantly, waiting, savoring the fact that she had broken me. But just as I was about to tell her, a wave of strength and utter foolishness came over me, and I clamped my mouth shut.

I couldn't repay the Prince's favor like this. If I told them who had the elixir, they would bring trouble to Kalyll and his realm, and I couldn't allow that.

Tiredly, Mekare blew air through her nose and stretched to her full height. "Dead or alive, she's of no use to us, so I guess I'll give it another go." She raised her hands to weave her torturing spell once more, but just as she was about to shoot it in my direction, the stone wall behind the bed exploded inwardly, sending debris flying in every direction.

CHAPTER 35

Large pieces of stone and splintered wood soared through the air. Turning on a dime, Mekare directed her twirling hands toward the explosion. The debris that had been about to hit her struck a force field and thudded to the floor, instead. Stephen hurried and hid behind the witch, narrowly avoiding a flying chunk of stone.

I curled tightly on the floor, wrapping my arms over my head. A piece of something hit my side. I grunted, but the pain was nothing compared to what Mekare had put me through. Apparently, as she'd turned her attention from me, my invisible prison had gone by the wayside.

Through a gap in my arms, I watched the dust settle around a wide, ragged hole. Jake and Eric materialized in the space as the air cleared. They were in their wolf forms and immediately lunged forward, murder written in their glowing eyes.

"No! Stop!" I croaked in a barely audible squeak.

There was nothing they could do against a Midnight Witch. They thought they were saving me, but they were only running toward their deaths.

But of course, they didn't listen to me, and Mekare was already twirling her hands, readying a spell that would surely kill them. She had bested Damien. She could easily beat two werewolves.

Shaking, I pushed to my hands and knees.

Red, c'mon!

If I could shift, it would trigger the healing abilities, and I would be able to help them. I felt the change coming over me, but it was slow, too slow. Dark light shot out of Mekare's fingertips, sailing straight toward Jake who was in the lead.

No!

I watched helplessly as the witch's magic hit him straight on. I expected him to yelp in pain and fall to the floor, but instead, he leaped in the air, unscathed, sharp claws aimed at the witch's chest.

Mekare's mouth opened in an "O" of surprise that exactly matched mine. Her spell had washed over the gray wolf as if it were nothing more than a harmless breeze. And now, Jake was upon her, and he would rip her to pieces. Or at least that was what should've happened except he sailed right through the witch as she turned to smoke for just an instant. *What the…?*

Jake crashed into Stephen instead, who was still hiding behind the witch. His claws tore at Stephen's back as the coward tried to turn away and run.

Mekare solidified again. She seemed intent on blasting Jake into the next century, but as she aimed her next attack Eric clamped his jaw around her calf. She cried out in pain.

In the next instant, there were three wolves instead of two. Stephen had shifted in the blink of an eye and was now snarling at Jake, circling. Mekare re-aimed her crackling hands toward Eric's head.

Please no!

Again, I tried to shift. This time Red rose to the task, and my body rippled with transforming energy. Muscles and bones grew. Sharp teeth sprang into place and claws ripped my skin ready to exert revenge. My clothes tore and fell away. My head cleared, all lingering effects of Mekare's torture washing away.

My attention snapped back to the fight. Jake and Stephen were rolling on the floor, guttural growls reverberating in their chests as they did their best to tear each other apart. Eric was nowhere to be found while Mekare stood where I'd last seen her, shooting healing energy into her leg.

"No, Eric! Where are you?" My alpha thoughts projected forward.

What had the witch done to him?

"I'm right here, Sunder." There was a flick of movement by the hole they'd carved in the wall, and Eric stood there, unharmed.

Huh? How had he gotten there? Last I'd seen, Mekare had been about to turn him into a fried egg.

A shadow lingered behind Eric. I strained to see past the darkness outside, but all I managed to make out was the outline of a person. Was it Rosalina? No, that didn't make sense. They wouldn't bring her with them into this dangerous situation. Besides, she would have been shooting her rifle if she were here. But if she wasn't here, where was she? Was she all right? And who could the shadow be? I shook my head and focused on Jake. I had to help him, especially since Mekare had finished healing herself.

With an upturned lip, she flicked a hand in Jake's direction. A blast of magic hit him and sent him soaring through the air. He crashed against the wall.

Seething with rage, I pounced, intent on repaying the damn witch for the pain she'd caused me. Just as I was about to reach her, though, Stephen threw a pointed look in my direction, warning her. In a flash, her hands twisted in an elaborate spell, and a gossamer of crackling energy materialized in front of me. Unable to stop, I got trapped on the web. My legs windmilled under me.

I fought, clenching my teeth, and instinctively, released a blast of sensory energy, using my tracking powers the way I'd used them at the coven temples against the hybrid. A sensory overload fizzed through my entire body reacting against Mekare's magic.

I took two steps forward, my eyes locked with the witch's. She was staring at me as if I were an alien with three heads. She'd never met the likes of me, a werewolf with magic.

She leaned forward, thrusting her hands toward my head and intensifying her attack. I redoubled my own defenses and took another step forward. My entire body trembled with the effort, but I managed to advance.

Mekare's face tightened with panic. The shiny pool of her all-black eyes trembled. I took another step, my every muscle latent with tension, so much that if she stopped her attack, I would fly off like a missile from a launcher. Good, maybe I'd go right through her, carving a huge hole in her middle.

Changing tactics, she raised one hand and wriggled her fingers, making a fireball. Viciously, she shoved it in my face. I reared back, the heat singing my lashes and blinding me for a second.

I shook my head to clear my vision, and when I glanced back I noticed Jake was back on his paws and Eric was closing in on the witch again. Behind Mekare, Stephen was hunkered down, his head low to the ground, his glowing blue eyes furtive as they flicked toward the door.

The coward was already planning his escape, just like last time. But today, he would pay for everything he'd done. For Damien, for all the vampires rhabo had killed, and all of those who still suffered its effects and had no hope left.

It was three of us against two of them. No, four, I realized, as the other person I'd noticed outside chose that moment to reveal their presence.

For a moment, I was hopeful, thinking that whoever Jake and Eric had brought with them would even the scales, but I was wrong. Very wrong. Because the person who stepped into the room was none other than Bernadetta Fiore.

The Dark Donna was here, and she was definitely *not* on our side.

CHAPTER 36

The air froze inside my lungs, and breathing became impossible. Whatever hope I'd harbored died an ugly death. The scales had tipped the wrong way, so much that I felt as if the room was off its axis.

I glanced in Jake's direction in a panic. He was intent on Mekare and Stephen, ignoring the vampiress's presence. Had he not noticed the vicious vamp come in? That was impossible. His sharp werewolf senses wouldn't miss a thing, though there was still a ton of dust and magic tang floating in the air, which were making it hard to catch scents.

Eric was also oblivious to her presence, advancing toward the Midnight Witch, teeth bared and hackles standing on end.

Were they both blind? Or had Mekare zapped my brain so thoroughly that I was hallucinating? *Ayep*. That was it. My brain was nothing but a fried chicken wing. There was nothing else that could explain what I saw next.

Blaze strolled in and stood at Bernadetta's side.

What in the holy witchlights?!

What was my cat doing here? And why were his eyes glowing like embers?

I blinked and shook my head to clear it, then took another look. Blaze was still there, and everyone was acting as if nothing weird was going on.

Well, not really.

Mekare and Stephen had gone utterly still, and their eyes were fixed on the vamp with the smoky-gray cat at her side.

"At last, I find you," Bernadetta said in her deep voice. "You have proved quite elusive."

Mekare took a step sideways as if to show that Stephen was also there, hiding behind her. Revealed, Stephen looked ready to pee his pants, or more precisely the floor since he wasn't wearing any. But he wasn't the only one who looked scared. Mekare also seemed in need of an adult diaper.

Now, I was really confused.

Mekare's gaze lowered to Blaze. She shook herself and visibly straightened, making an effort to appear less intimidated. "Is that all you've got? A cat?"

"This is no ordinary cat. He's a Copper Mage who's incredibly pissed at you for many reasons," the Dark Donna said, her petite figure appearing intimidating even amid the big pieces of debris that lay around her.

What?!

The cogwheels in my brain started turning. A Copper Mage? My heart skipped.

Damien?

No. That was impossible. I'd seen him die. But if not Damien, who?

Oh, witchlights! Blaze wasn't a cat at all. No wonder he'd never behaved like a proper pet. Panicked, I tried to remember all our interactions. I'd always been nice to him, right? Did he hate me for treating him like an animal?

"You might feel you have an advantage..." Mekare's eyes roved around in a circle as he assessed every one of us. Three werewolves, an ancient vampire, and a Copper Mage… the tables had really turned.

"And maybe you do," the witch admitted. "But you won't catch me alive. You're weak *Dark Donna*." She pronounced the moniker with a heavy dose of sarcasm. "You're a shadow of your old self, and you'll be dead soon."

Bernadetta's face twitched, registering an edge of fear. I watched her closely, trying to read between the lines. There was an undertone to the witch's words, a truth that couldn't be denied. And that was when it hit me, the Dark Donna was sick, which could only mean one thing.

She had consumed rhabo.

Holy shit!

Mekare laughed, a deep, throaty sound that came out forced. Even if she thought the vamp's health was compromised, the witch was still afraid of her.

"You'll pay for your betrayal. Both of you," Bernadetta said, her fierce voice ringing with promise. "Hand over the Unholy Vessel, and I may consider dispatching you quickly."

Practically shaking, Stephen took several steps back, his ass scooting right up against the wall. Then, he leaped and dashed toward the door, but before he made it past the threshold, Eric fleeted there and blocked his path. Stephen backed away, inching his way back toward Mekare. She whirled on him and kicked at his ribs.

"Get away from me, you coward," she spat. "I've wasted my time with you. You've outlived your usefulness."

He yelped, legs thrashing. He frantically scanned the room, his attention stopping on me. Suddenly, his ears drew back, and his tail curled inwardly. Moving as if he had a cork stuck up his butt, he headed it in my direction.

"Toni, don't let them kill me. Please, help me."

I let out a short bark that sounded like a laugh. "*Help you? Help YOU?! After all, you've done? Damien is dead because of you.*"

Stephen shook his head. "*No. It was Mekare. Not me.*"

He inched closer, so much that I could practically taste his fear, his cowardice. A killing instinct washed over me. He needed to die, to pay for what he'd done. I bared my teeth, ready to rip his throat out.

"Please, Toni. She... Mekare, she has the Unholy Vessel, not me. It's always been her."

Before I could move a muscle to attack Stephen and exert my revenge, the Midnight Witch moved in a fluid attack, the jade dagger tight in her hand, and stabbed her weapon right through Stephen's shoulder blade, accompanying the attack with a burst of magic.

Stephen growled in pain, throwing his head back and twisting. Mekare pulled the blade out, a sparkle of glee in her dark eyes. Stephen collapsed to the floor, his legs becoming useless under him. He lay there, blinking a few times, then his gaze drifted toward mine. There was a plea in his expression that was impossible to miss.

A twinge of pity rose in my chest, and I hated myself for it. He didn't deserve it.

"I've n-never even killed anyone," he projected the sad thought, and I couldn't tell if it was regret or repentance.

Either way, it didn't matter. He might not have killed anyone directly, but he sure was responsible for the deaths of many. That he'd never wielded the weapon in his own hands meant nothing.

I took several steps away from him, neither relishing his slow death nor allowing my pity to take over. Instead, I turned my attention to the witch and the scene in front of me. A tiny smile twisted her lips, and when I glanced at Bernadetta, I found that she, too, wore a similar expression.

"I must thank you for doing that," the Dark Donna said. "I believe everyone here held a grudge against him for one reason or another. Even you." She glanced down at Blaze, who still stood at her feet, sitting in that placid way cats have, heavy on his haunches, front paws aligned perfectly, and tail wrapped around his bottom.

Increasingly labored breaths came from Stephen. The metallic scent of blood saturated the air, and I still refused to look at him again.

"Now, it's your turn," Bernadetta said. She gestured toward Jake and Eric.

And the wolves began advancing toward the witch.

CHAPTER 37

Mekare, still holding the jade dagger, lifted her free hand and shot a stream of dark magic toward Jake. Acting on instinct, I leaped over Stephen's body and went for the witch. She jumped out of the way and released a second stream of magic in my direction. I flinched, my body tense as it foretold the pain, except, it never came.

I was unharmed, and so was Jake.

The witch cursed, and this time, she sent an attack toward Eric. Amber-colored energy fired out of Blaze's eyes and met Mekare's, effectively blocking it. She sent a hateful glower toward the cat.

"I regret not killing you," she spat and flung a jolt of dark energy at him, which missed as Blaze gracefully leaped out of the way.

Crap!

From the looks of it, those two had a history.

Changing tactics, Mekare twirled her free hand in the air, and the jade cup—the second piece that completed the Unholy Vessel—appeared there.

"Why don't you give me a bit of your blood, *Dark Donna*?" the witch said mockingly. "Perhaps, I'll feed it to Stephen so he can become a loyal servant. I think he's still alive." She threw a sidelong glance toward the fallen wolf, whose chest was now barely moving.

Bernadetta glowered at the witch.

"No?" Mekare said, returning her attention to the vamp. "Shame. Though, I guess it doesn't matter since I already have a couple of those."

A couple of those?

Did she mean the hybrids we'd fought in the forest?

Oh, God!

Were they here?

Mekare inhaled deeply, her eyelids fluttering as she threw her head back. "Come to mama," she called, a wide smile spreading across her lips.

From somewhere in the house came a series of crashes that sounded as if a clumsy giant were tearing through the place in their haste to get here.

Jake and Eric's ears swiveled in that direction and so did mine.

Without warning, the Dark Donna charged forward, blurring as she went for the witch. It all happened too fast for my eyes to follow, but the next thing I knew, Bernadetta had crashed against the wall behind where Mekare had been standing.

In place of the witch, a cloud of black smoke remained.

Blaze growled, his back arching and tail standing high in the air. A stream of amber magic shot from his eyes headed straight for the wavering smoke. Before it could hit it, the hazy cloud shrank down as if the floor were sucking it down like a spaghetti noodle, then it traveled sideways and regained its original size a few feet away.

I went for it, snapping my teeth around the smoke, biting into nothing. Jake and Eric moved closer to help but had to spin around as the hybrids appeared at the door. The beasts knocked into each other, baring their huge teeth and snapping at one another as each tried to enter first.

As the hybrids figured out the mechanics of the door, Blaze hunkered down and sent another attack toward the witch. Again, the smoke shrank out of the way, scuttled along the floor, and reformed a distance away from where it had been.

She was headed for the hole in the wall, I realized.

"We can't let her escape!"

Not with the Unholy Vessel. Not with her life.

I went after her as she kept scurrying away using the same trick, moving quicker and quicker by the second. In a few beats, she was out of the house, her shadowy, insubstantial body blending into the night.

We had to do something, at this rate, she would be miles away from here in a matter of minutes. If she left with that vessel, the city would be doomed.

I ran outside, followed by Blaze, while behind us, Jake and Eric contended with the hybrids. I didn't want to leave them, but they could take care of themselves. Putting them out of my mind, I peered into the darkness, doing my best not to lose track of the witch.

A white light shot out of Blaze's tail and exploded overhead, illuminating the area. We were in a weed-sprinkled yard surrounded by tall trees. For a second, I thought I'd lost track of her, but I spotted a wisp of smoke snaking around a bush and ran at full pelt after her.

Blaze kept pace, trotting beside me. I glanced at him sideways, confused to have such an unlikely partner in this chase. As the light from his previous spell died out, he shot another ball of energy ahead of us. My wolf eyes would've been enough to track normal prey even in the darkened woods, but a curl of smoke was a different story.

In the renewed light, I realized that Mekare had doubled the distance between us, leaving me no doubt that she was gaining momentum with every second that ticked by. If I was going to catch her, I needed to move faster.

Recalling the anger that triggered my speed, an electric tingle zipped down my spine, shooting into my limbs. My legs began pumping at a prodigious speed, and I was off. Trees blurred at either side of me. Blaze choked on my dust, and before I knew it, I'd caught up with Mekare. I ran at her, but, like Bernadetta, all I managed to do was to go through her.

Putting on the brakes, I skidded to a halt and whirled around. The plume of darkness stopped and hovered in midair, undulating in a threatening way.

Oh, shit! Now what?

I'd been so intent on catching her that I hadn't stopped to think what I would do if I managed it. Now, here we were, facing each other, and I was clueless and doomed.

She solidified.

"So you have the fleeting skill, I see." One of her eyebrows went up, and she appeared mildly surprised at the discovery. "I bet you think you're brave, but you're just stupid. Who do you think is going to help you now? I've wanted to kill you for a while now, but Stephen was so blind. And now, you've come to find me." Smiling sardonically, she twirled a hand in the air, magic crackling in her palm.

I searched for the Unholy Vessel on her person but could only guess where she'd put it, not in the folds of her tight outfit for sure.

My heart hammered out of control as she drew her hand back, ready to unleash her dark magic on me. I focused on anger, on my fleeting ability. If I moved fast enough, she wouldn't be able to hit me.

Please, don't fail me now.

Abruptly, she flicked her wrist and shot out a spider web of energy. To my relief, I managed to tap into my speed and leaped out of the way just in time. Mekare's attack hit the ground and sizzled the dirt out of existence, leaving a hole behind.

She made an assessing sound in the back of her throat. Her eyes narrowed, giving her the look of someone who was calculating a very hard math problem. Her mouth tipping in a cool smile, she prepared another spell. A new ball of energy formed on her palm, growing bigger than the last.

"See if you can dodge this." She drew her hand back.

I watched closely and when she flicked her wrist to the right, I fleeted to the left. Except she twirled her hand in the opposite direction and released her spell straight into my path.

Searing energy hit me square in the chest.

The heat of a thousand suns enveloped me. I flew back and struck the ground, my fur going up in smoke and my skin sizzling like meat on a griddle. I howled in pain, twisting as if that would make the agony go away, but it just made it worse, as the hard ground peeled away my blistering skin, exposing raw flesh.

At the fringes of my consciousness, I sensed Mekare hovering over me. I clenched my teeth, fighting the pain, and tried to focus on her. My vision was blurry. My eyelids were nothing but thin veneers of exposed tissue. I could barely keep my eyes open as I blinked up at her, my desperate movements finally coming to an end as my strength waned.

"New pups can be so arrogant," Mekare said. "You actually thought you could fight me? You may have a few skills not all alphas possess, but I've been around the block quite a few more times than you have." She blew air through her nose in a display of amusement at the sight of my mangled body. "I'd love to leave you here to suffer, but I prefer not leaving anything to chance if I can help it, especially the death of my enemies. Bad things tend to happen, like that damn cat."

As every cell in my body screamed in anguish, I watched as the witch prepared a killing spell with the flex of a few fingers. I thought I should move, try to do something to save myself, but why? She was about to put a stop to the pain.

"Goodbye, Toni Sunder." She lowered her hand to deliver the killing blow, then screamed instead. Her hands flew to her head. A snarling, savage creature had jumped on top of her and was doing its best to claw her eyes out.

Blaze!

His little feline shape clung to the witch's head like a vicious, murdering hat. He hissed and made a series of throaty sounds as he repeatedly batted a little paw at Mekare's left eye, claws raking across her eyelid, drawing blood.

For a confused moment, Mekare stumbled about, trying to dislodge the feral creature, her magic forgotten in her instinctual panic. As clarity returned, she weaved a spell and, hands crackling, grabbed Blaze by the scruff of the neck. A bolt of power zapped through his body, and he went stiff. With a disgusted bark, the witch threw him to the ground where he crashed with a *thud*, his body giving off sparks as if he were his own little thunderstorm.

I watched him through hazy eyes.

No, Blaze!

I wanted to reach out for him and caress his soft fur, but all I could do was look on as Mekare's spell ravaged his tiny body.

"Infernal mage," the witch spat, pressing a hand to her torn eyelid and muttering a spell that immediately healed her injury.

Who are you, Blaze?

As if in answer, his body flickered, and his gray fur fell away, leaving him looking like a naked, wrinkled newborn. Then his spine elongated, and his feline features morphed into something different… something human.

A shock of gray hair grew on top of his head even as he kept growing. His pointed ears disappeared and repositioned themselves on the sides of his head. His front toes lengthened into fingers. His tail vanished, and the joints of his back legs changed direction.

Fighting my pain, I stared intently as his round eyes became ovals and thick eyebrows sprang into place, and a very familiar face took shape.

Damien, Damien, Damien!

Blaze was Damien. Damien was Blaze!

How?! He lay unmoving next to me.

No.

No.

NO!

My eyes roved over his body, desperately searching for signs of life.

Damieeeeeeen!

His name was alive inside my head.

Please, please, please, be alive.

I stared at his chest and his abdomen.

Are you breathing? Please breathe.

I thought I perceived a slight movement, but I wasn't sure. My eyes were injured, and I couldn't see clearly.

Mekare's mouth twisted as she scanned Damien's wasted shape. "How the hell? Did no one ever teach you to stay dead?" She shook her head. "You are all a pain in the ass." Coming closer, she prepared two killing spells, one in each hand. "Two birds with one stone."

No.

I had a power that no other alpha had and she could never suspect its magnitude, its capacity to kill, and if it had worked on vampires and hybrids, it would work on fucking Midnight Witches, too.

Before she had time to point her hands in our direction, I drew strength from the depths of my soul and sprang to my feet. Then, opening my mouth wide in a scream of agonizing pain, I locked my jaws around her thigh.

Releasing all my anguish and desperation for Damien, I pushed an onslaught of sensory signals into the witch. My body glowed as I did a perfect Christmas tree impersonation.

Scents, sounds, sights, and even the pain that I felt like a million tiny flames scorching every cell of my body, everything, I poured it into her.

I hate you more than I've ever hated anyone.

With every ounce of who I was, I wished for her death, wished to obliterate her from the face of the earth so she could never harm anyone else again.

When a raw cry tore from her throat, I relished the sound, and, using it as fuel for my loathing, I clung to the edge of consciousness, mustering an extra ounce of energy to continue my attack.

A metallic tang overwhelmed me as Mekare's blood flooded my mouth. Judging by the powerful spray, it seemed I'd pierced a vital artery.

Viciously, I shook my head, my sharp fangs tearing skin and sinew at the same time that my tracker magic emptied into her. My eyes rolled into the back of my head, and my legs trembled under me.

C'mon, Red. Just a little bit longer, and you'll kill her.

But I was too weak, and my sensory attack was diminishing.

Vaguely, I sensed as Mekare recovered her self-control and cast a spell. That same cloud of smoke I had chased moments ago materialized before me. My jaw went slack around the witch's insubstantial form.

With nothing else to hold onto, I collapsed to the ground, legs twitching, my vision and life fading away. As I lay there, feeling utterly spent, I watched as the wisp of smoke haltingly slithered away. It hadn't needed to move with that much care before.

I almost had you, bitch!

Though I was at the edge of death, I imagined I could still catch her and make sure she never drew another breath, but it was only a hazy thought inside my dwindling mind.

As my life slipped away, I peered at Damien.

I'm sorry. I should've known. I'm sorry.

CHAPTER 38

"Hang on, Toni," a hoarse voice registered at the edge of my consciousness. "Don't… don't let go."

It took a monumental effort to raise one eyelid and look at the blurry figure that lay next to me, one of his trembling hands reaching for my paw.

Damien was crawling in my direction one painfully excruciating inch at a time. My eyes drifted closed.

"T-toni," he rasped.

I blinked and caught a glimpse of his finger brushing mine. A barely perceivable pang of magic crawled up my leg, and for an instant, I thought he might have enough energy to save me, to save himself, but he didn't. He'd tried, but he spent what little he had left then fell on his face with a final exhale. An instant later, I also drew my final breath.

ஐஐ

I sat up with a jolt.

Mom was at my side in an instant, gathering my hands in hers. "Toni!"

"No, Mom. What are you doing?! Get away from here."

"*Shh*, *shh*, it's all right, sweetheart. You're safe."

My heart pounded. My lungs pumped as fast as a mouse's. Desperately, I glanced around and found that I was in a sterile hospital room. Lucia and Daniella stood behind Mom, looking pale and worried under the fluorescent lights.

"W-where… where…"

Mom's mouth opened and closed, but nothing came out. Daniella gently nudged her out of the way and took her place. She smiled and eased me back onto the pillow, her healer bedside manner on like a badge.

"I'm sure you have a thousand questions," she said. "Let me anticipate a few while you take a deep breath."

Her brown eyes, so much like mine, were full of reassuring energy, which redirected my attention to my agitated state. Part of me felt like lashing out, demanding to know everything, but my sister's way had always had a calming effect on me.

I took a few deep breaths and nodded.

"Good," Dani said. "Let's see… you've been in the hospital for a few days. You were in bad shape, but you're all right now. Damien was also in bad shape, but he has also recovered." A smile stretched her lips, but her eyes were untouched by it.

That meant there was bad news, and I braced myself for it, holding my breath.

"Your friends are outside," she added. "They want to see you. Let me get them."

I exhaled, and the fist of dread that had been squeezing my heart let go.

Lucia stepped closer. "Hey, sis. Gave us quite the scare. First Mom then you. I wonder who's next?"

"*Shoosh*, girl," Mom said. "No one else will be next. C'mon, let's go get you something to eat. We'll be back, sweetheart. Lucia hasn't left your side since yesterday."

That surprised me. Lucia smiled sheepishly, avoiding eye contact at all cost. Tears welled up in my eyes. As the youngest, she always seemed to expect all the attention and acted like she didn't need any of us. It was nice to know she cared.

They followed Dani out of the room, and a moment later Jake walked in. He took three huge strides across the room and wrapped me in a tight hug.

"Toni!"

"Jake." The tears that had pooled in my eyes spilled as his warmth enveloped me. "You're all right. Thank God."

Through the haze of my tears, I saw Eric as he approached the foot of the bed. He nodded once, his gaze appearing as flat as Dani's had.

Jake freed me from his embrace and, his eyes roving over my face, caressed my cheek.

"She got away," I said. "With the vessel."

"It's okay," he said. "It's not your fault."

"Damien, he's alive." A hysterical bark of laughter escaped me.

Eric's blue eyes came alive for a second. "That bastard is harder to kill than a cockroach."

I was about to say something, then paused, glancing toward the door. "Where's Rosalina?"

Jake and Eric exchanged loaded glances.

My heart started drumming out of control. "Where the hell is Rosalina?" I demanded.

"When… when we got back to the cabin, you were both gone.

Blaze, Damien, led us to you. We fought the hybrids and killed them. After we found you and Damien, we searched that entire place, but we couldn't find her. Toni, I'm sorry," his clear eyes lowered to the floor, "we don't know where she is."

Pain like hot fire tore through my heart, and I screamed and screamed and screamed, batting Jake's arm away as he tried to restrain me. I clawed at the sheets, threw them to the floor, and staggered out of the bed as Jake uselessly tried to stop me.

"Rosalina," I called.

Jake grabbed my shoulder. "Toni, we'll find her. Please calm down."

"Let's go now. Now!"

Both Jake and Eric looked helplessly at me.

"NOW!"

A couple of male nurses rushed into the room.

"We've got a shifter," one of them said. "Call a code violet on a Skew."

The other nurse pulled out a device from his belt and punched a few numbers. An alarm sounded over the PA system followed by a female voice saying *Code Violet, Skew status. Trained personnel are called to the 5th floor.*

"Toni, calm down," Jake pleaded, glancing down at my clawed hands.

I shook my head and turned to the nurses blocking my path. "Get out of my way! I have to find her."

A third nurse showed up, holding something in his hand. A syringe filled with a white liquid. He walked between the other two and gave me an amused smile. He was short and stocky.

If he thought he would be able to stop me from finding my friend, he was—

There was a pin prick in my arm, then pressure. I rubbed my arm and glanced back at the nurse, his syringe was empty.

His amused smile grew, revealing a pointed fang. He was a

fucking vampire and had stuck me before I had any time to blink.

My thoughts grew hazy, and I swayed on my feet. Jake caught me, picked me up, and deposited me back on the bed.

"We can't abandon her," I slurred. "We have to go back and get her."

Jake pulled the sheets over me. "I know."

"She's my best friend. She… she might be scared."

Jake nodded. Eric turned away, and I could've sworn his eyes had wavered.

"She needs us."

My eyelids closed heavily and no matter how hard I tried, I couldn't open them again, and I drifted away into a restless nightmare.

ꕥ

The silence was like an anvil on my chest.

I stood just inside the agency's door, staring at Rosalina's empty desk, a knot clogging my throat. My eyes burned with the need to cry, but my tears were spent. My knees wobbled, and I collapsed on the couch and stared blankly at the floor. This past week had been an endless nightmare, relentlessly clawing at my sanity, threatening to undo me. As time ticked by, I felt the last of my control slipping away, my hope drowning in a sea of futility.

I was a damn tracker and couldn't find my best friend.

As soon as I'd awakened after the hospital staff sedated me, I walked out of there, intent on using my skills to find her. Jake and Eric had protested at first, saying I needed to rest, but they soon relented. They knew me well and understood there was no way I would wait another second to track my best friend.

"I paid a good tracker to try to find her," Jake had said as he drove from the hospital to my place. "They had no luck."

"*I'll* find her," I said between clenched teeth.

"You're the best," Eric put in from the back seat. "I'm sure you will."

Except I had failed. Miserably.

At first, I tried to track her the way I'd tracked Jake. I used a jacket she'd left at my condo but got nothing from it. I didn't let that discourage me, so next, I tried to track her in a trance. Except that didn't work either. I used all my senses and was met by a whole lot of emptiness.

I had snapped out of the trance and sat up screaming hysterically.

"She's dead. She's dead!"

Jake wrapped his arms around me and rocked me back and forth. He didn't know how to communicate with a deaf and blind person, but he took care of me until my senses returned hours later.

"She's not dead," I'd said later, sitting up in my bed, arms tightly circling my legs. "I won't accept it."

Jake and Eric said nothing to that, but when Damien got out of the hospital the next day, he agreed with me.

"Magic could be concealing Rosalina's location from Toni's powers," he'd said, then we'd gone on to look for her in every other way we knew. His magic also yielded no answer.

For several days, we searched Eric's cabin, Rosalina's apartment, and anywhere else we could think of and found nothing that magic or enhanced wolf senses could trace. I called her family, and we filed a missing person's report with Tom's help. That also brought us zero leads.

Jake put people in his pack on the alert, and Damien asked mage and witch friends to help.

Still nothing.

My hope sank a little more every day and was now kicking desperately, searching for the tiniest lifeline.

I sank my face between my hands, trying to work out where she could be.

The door opened with a chime, and Jake, Eric, and Damien walked into the agency.

"Ready?" Jake asked.

I nodded but didn't rise from the couch. We were all going back to Eric's cabin to search again. Maybe we'd missed something before. They stood awkwardly for a second before also taking a seat.

Damien sat across from me, looking much more like himself. His hair was completely white again, not gray like when he'd regained his human form. He smiled sadly, his blotchy pupils filling most of his copper irises. He wore a suit, but no cloak or top hat. He had seemed less of a diva lately and spent a lot of time lost in reflection.

I matched his sad smile. "I don't think I've said this—it's obvious and all—but I'm glad you're here."

"Yeah, I have to agree," Jake said as he settled next to me on the couch.

All eyes turned to Eric.

He crossed his arms and, eyes roving around the room, said, "Me, too. I guess."

We knew he wasn't big on expressing his feelings, but the sentiment in his gaze was true enough.

Poor Damien. The news about his daughter's death had hit him hard. Worst of all, he'd learned of what had happened while in his cat shape. It turned out all that time he was in my condo, he'd been able to come in and out, and he hadn't been idle. Instead, he'd been catching up on what he'd missed, eavesdropping and scampering about the city, learning what he could.

I had apologized for not getting to Liliana in time, but he reassured me he didn't blame me. "Mekare is the only culprit," he'd said to me, hate flashing in his copper eyes.

The details of how Damien had managed to remain among us after Mekare's attack were short of a miracle. As a Copper Mage who very much liked being alive, many years ago, he'd taken care to craft a spell to protect his life essence.

"I admit it's not a very elegant spell, and I wasn't sure it would work, but alas…" he'd told us as he explained how he'd achieved resurrection.

He said that the spell took care of preserving his life force, keeping it safe inside his dead body along with a tiny spark of magic.

"Once I was buried, I was able to use that bit of magical energy to transfer my life force into another body."

"A cat?" Eric had asked.

"Well, not at first." The mage was reluctant to elaborate, but he owed it to us, so he explained. "In the beginning, I was an… earthworm."

Eric laughed uproariously at that, earning a disdainful glare from Damien.

"It was a painstakingly long process," Damien continued. "Half the time I forgot what I was supposed to be and went on being a miserable worm. When I remembered my true identity, I endeavored to gather enough magic for another spell. Soon, I graduated to a mouse and then to a cat."

"Sounds risky being a worm," Eric said. "What if you got swallowed by a bird? Could you have risen from its shit?"

Damien's jaw twitched. "No. And I wouldn't have wanted to either. Anyway, once I had enough human sense in me, I found my way to Toni. You know the rest."

In the end, we had Blaze/Damien to thank for so much. The book that gave us the answer to breaking Jake's blood covenant with the Blackridges, saving my life by lending me a bit of his energy as I lay dying after Mekare's attack, and, most importantly, finding me in her clutches.

In his cat brain, he had figured out that Mekare and Stephen were after the cure and not the dagger. And not only that, he'd also guessed the reason. It turned out, the geniuses had poisoned the Dark Donna, surreptitiously slipping her rhabo when her guard was down. It had taken one dose, and the vamp was hooked. Doomed. They had betrayed her, sentenced her to a painful death to be rid of her.

In the beginning, the vamp had been the mastermind of the entire plot. Their initial deal had been to cause unrest by selling rhabo. This was meant to anger vampire leaders and create a rift between them and werewolves. Bernadetta's scheme was to destroy her competition and, in the void left after the conflict, position herself as the most powerful Skew in St. Louis.

Stephen had been in charge of the drug operation while Mekare's job had been to free the Unholy Vessel using her magic. As I'd been told, Bernadetta Fiore had uncovered the dreadful item after decades of searching for it, but it had been locked under a powerful spell and had needed strong magic to liberate it.

However, the Donna's plot had backfired. Big time. Her allies had poisoned her and then pursued me, determined to destroy the only cure and all possibility of the vamp ever surviving their backstabbing assault. They had royally pissed her off, and Bernadetta Fiore was too powerful an enemy to disregard and let live, even in the throes of a ravishing disease.

If we had only listened to Bertram in Liliana's house, this disaster might've been avoided.

"We need to talk," he'd said, but we hadn't listened. We'd assumed he'd been there with the hybrid, and we ran.

At length, to Mekare, both Bernadetta and Stephen had been a couple of pawns to her ultimate plan, whatever that was. I imagined she wanted power, but who knew for certain.

What we knew was that Blaze/Damien had led Jake and Eric to Bernadetta and, with her help, they had figured out our enemies' hiding place. Bernadetta had been searching for the traitors and, discovering that they'd kidnapped me, gave her what she needed to find them. She had a tracker at her services who could tell her the whereabouts of anyone the vampiress had ever desired.

It was a shock to learn that the Donna had a thing for me—or maybe it was for my blood, I wasn't sure—but I figured that was a good thing, or they would've never found me.

All the revelations made my head spin. All week, I'd been in a state of constant stress, and there was still so much more weighing on my mind.

It wasn't enough that we'd delivered the news of Stephen's death to Ulfen. That Walter's body had been desecrated and never found. That I'd been summoned to Wolfskeep for another Pack Rule meeting. That I still needed to track Gonira for Prince Kalyll. That Damien had promised to give Bernadetta the cure in exchange for helping them find me, and I was yet to tell him where it was hidden. That Mekare Graves had been a false client, her check had bounced, and the agency was in shambles. That Craig Blackridge wanted to move the wedding date, and Jake and I had a blood covenant to break. Or that there was a crazy Midnight Witch with a hybrid-making relic in her possession.

No. None of that was enough.

Or in fact, none of that really mattered. Because what was really more than enough was that Rosalina was missing, and I could not deal with anything else until I found her.

Because I would find her. I would not rest until she was back, safe and sound, until I made it up to her for dragging her into a world of danger.

WWW.INGRIDSEYMOUR.COM

www.ingramcontent.com/pod-product-compliance
Lightning Source LLC
Chambersburg PA
CBHW020336310726
48979CB00015B/2399/J

* 9 7 8 1 7 3 6 0 6 1 2 3 7 *